ONE LEFT INSIDE THE WELL

One Left Inside
The Well

A novel
by

SKYLER NIELSEN

Adelaide Books
New York/Lisbon
2018

ONE LEFT INSIDE THE WELL
A novel
By Skyler Nielsen

Published by Adelaide Books, New York / Lisbon
adelaidebooks.org

Editor-in-Chief
Stevan V. Nikolic

For any information, please address Adelaide Books
at info@adelaidebooks.org

or write to:

Adelaide Books
244 Fifth Ave. Suite D27
New York, NY, 10001

ISBN-10: 1-949180-86-7
ISBN-13: 978-1-949180-86-2

Printed in the United States of America

For Pops, Thanks.

Content

Chapter I

Tijuana, Mexico

Diego Velarde finds himself thinking of Suerte, the family dog, beaten for soiling a mother's rug. Suerte would never be happy again; his world would never be right. The man on the sidewalk is like this; devoid of anything save sorrow and pain. That thing in a gaze that reveals life, what's it called? Papa Velarde called it *el Corazon* or *la sangre*; it always goes back to heart and blood for the old ones. Diego Velarde doesn't call it anything, but he knows when it isn't there. There's no life. No pride. No regret or anger. There is no sense of injustice. Nothing.

Everything else is there; several layers of tattered clothes, an unshaved face caressed by dirty hands, white string holding together wingtip shoes. His cheeks and ears are cracked by years of cutting wind. The man's face remains veiled in shadow, even as passing cars illuminate the street; the shine of headlights recoiling from his touch. His lower lip has split several times from constant exposure to the elements. An abscess festers on the side of his neck. This wound will never heal.

"Get out of the street you bastard!" Diego cries.

The man sits, unmoved, only a slight nod betraying the astonishment at being addressed.

"Fuck off then."

Diego turns away, wanting nothing more than to get lost in revelry fueled by alcohol and driven by loose women. He wants it all. All those stories about the world across the border, he wants to live them. He wants to taste the smells and feel the sounds. He doesn't need the image of this old man sacrificed to the street. He doesn't need memories of a dog dead ten years; a dog whose last remaining testament is a stain on a rug.

A violent shake of the head and Diego returns to the alien rhythm of the Mexican night. The street is lined with bars, nightclubs and strip joints. They resemble those found in any American city, with bright neon signs, bouncers and lines of anxious people waiting to throw it all off. He closes his eyes absorbing vibrations that play off the walls. *El Rincon* and *Corazon de Aztecan, the cool kids on the block,* compete from across the street while trouble making strip joints are smeared with pictures of half-naked women and flashing beacons offering SEX SEX SEX! The atmosphere is strangely familiar, like looking at something through a funhouse mirror. The buildings all stand two stories tall and are made of either red brick or concrete covered by white plaster. They lean toward the middle of the street, especially those few that have large spotlights shining skyward. The leaning structures and the towering shafts of light give Revolucion Avenue the feel of a cathedral; a great cathedral dedicated to corrupting the flesh.

The street lamps do nothing but hang overhead like morbidly obese fireflies, with most of the illumination coming from the glowing signage decorating the thoroughfare. A layer of smoke spews from cigarettes dangling on the lips of tourist and local alike. Between slow moving cars, Diego catches glimpses of the pavement with its large cracks intersecting the terrain like an intricate network of rivers flowing to and from potholes peppering the asphalt. The lines on the road are faded and, in places, have completely vanished.

A simple Saturday night traffic jam, like those happening all over the world at that moment, but lacking any agreement on the unwritten rules of conduct. American drivers try to interpret backhanded waves and quick honks of the car horn. The Mexicans who call the city home watch these trespassers stubbornly refuse the entry of any car not using a blinker and wait impatiently as pedestrians pour from the sidewalks onto the road.

The din of skirmishing vehicles to his right joins with the music seeping from the walls and doorways to his left. It sounds like chaos at first but the more Diego listens, the more it comes together to form a kind of rhythm. The smell of car exhaust blends with tobacco smoke and bacon covered hotdogs cooked by street venders, creating a unique texture that only exists here. This street never sleeps; he knows this even though he's only stood there for a short time. Every smell, sound and sight ensures its survival as an entity. Like any ecosystem in the natural world, if one thing changes, the street as a whole dies.

Anticipation grows with each small step toward the entrance of the Rockadile. Only the image of the homeless man, whose presence Diego still suffers, interrupts his happiness. Would anyone care were he to drag the vagrant down the nearest alleyway?

"What's the matter Diego, you need a written invitation?" Mauricio calls out before passing through the stainless steel doors of the Rockadile.

One step and Diego stands beside Jon Heffron. "You know if Marty had come we wouldn't be here with that fucking asshole."

"You're right 'bout Diego. Then we'd be dealing with a more familiar specie of asshole." Jonathan has two smiles. His common, dry smile used for ordinary greetings, his girlfriend and family gatherings. Diego turns to see that toothy ear to ear grin Jon uses every time he makes a witty comment. Whether others agree that the comment is amusing means nothing, Jonathan's the only judge on such matters.

Using the first two fingers of his right hand Jon salutes Diego and goes in. Once inside, the cool air of the Tijuana night is replaced by thick heat radiating off gyrating bodies. The natural rhythm of the street is replaced by the artificial bump of dance music and of the scents outside, only the tobacco lingers. The strange balance of bacon fat and car exhaust recedes as the odor of cheap perfume and cologne becomes dominant. Neon lights that flame along the walls and over the bar are overshadowed by strobe lights, green lasers and spinning balls of mirrors that disorient more than entertain. Mechanically, Diego digs at the black linoleum floor with the tip of his shoe.

Diego nods to Jon who answers with another, quicker salute. Navigating the pulsating crowd Diego takes the only empty seat; conveniently stationed next to a gorgeous solitary woman. It's a typical bar, though much longer than those found in the Valley. Sadly the size does little to improve the selection behind it. Diego searches the stock for strange exotic drinks not found in the States. He settles on Cuervo and Coke, then asks one of the three bartenders to fill the glass of the woman next to him.

Using the corner of his eyes Diego scans her from top to bottom. He does this quickly but slows enough to ensure she notices. He takes in her long legs accentuated by a pair of painted on blue jeans. She's just petite enough to get away with going braless under her black tank top. Shiny, brown and hanging down to the middle of her back, Diego imagines running his fingers gently through her hair until they brush her skin. He sees her walking down a street as a gust of wind lifts her hair, causing it to float gently behind her. Focusing on the perfection of that hair, he compares it with the matted mange of the homeless man. Hers personifying perfection, his that of hopelessness.

Experience makes the routine second nature. Start with something attention grabbing. It can be shocking, funny or sad. With the right girl it can even be a little insulting, but this is always risky. Once the comment is out, he examines the reaction. Adjust the meaning with entertaining elaboration. "No what I meant was…" or "Ha! I'm sorry that's not what I was trying to say." Some playful banter mixed with questions about the girl's life. Never ask anything too intimate of course, just enough to suggest genuine interest.

The ruckus of the nightclub should make it too loud for Diego to take notice, but he does. He swivels his seat and, through the crowd, sees the cause of the disturbance. Standing face to face, no more than a few inches apart, are a young college student and a middle aged Mexican businessman. The student wears a gray hooded sweater with USC written on the chest and a pair of oversized jeans. His brown shoes look too dressy relative to the rest of his garb.

Facing him, the businessman equals USC's height, but complements it with a thickness earned over a lifetime. He's draped in an expensive blue suit and Diego wonders whether his shoes are real alligator skin or a good imitation. Hanging on the businessman's shoulder is a long, black trench coat that must be suffocating in the sweltering club. Strangest of all, he holds a pearl handled walking cane, gripped lightly in his right hand.

Shouts pouring from USC's mouth rise over the music. He keeps glancing behind him at a young woman and in an instant Diego understands everything. It could be as much about impressing the group of friends backing him. No, look how he's sticking his chest out with that exaggerated bravado. Playing the peacock to impress the girl. The dancing and chatter stop, leaving only the music and the hum of the neon lights to fill the silence. The clatter of glasses and bottles slows at first before disappearing completely. Even the man walking around pouring tequila into people's mouths for twenty pesos a shot, scurries away toward the rear of the club. Looking at USC run his mouth, Diego braces for the impending fight. Everyone in the club has taken notice, and the crowd fidgets with anticipation.

Sliding his gaze six inches to the right, the feeling of excitement vanishes. Diego doesn't even notice his longhaired companion pulling at his arm. The dapper businessman shows no sign of understanding the verbal bombardment directed at him. They were insults and curses so violent they make Diego blush; still the businessman does not move. He simply stares back, saying nothing, with a posture like his portrait is being drawn. His sense of foreboding aside, Diego pulls away from his pretty companion, needing closeness with the pair.

His initial read of the crowd was wrong, as only the American half watches while the Mexicans in the room intentionally turn away from the altercation. They move not in fear or disgust, but shame, the way one might turn from a crime being committed because they're too afraid to stop it.

"You fucking Mexican piece of shit. You think you can wink at my girl and nothing's going to happen?" USC tenses, preparing to defend himself.

Only Diego detects the businessman's quick tapping of the pearl handle, like a nervous twitch. The insults continue and with each passing word the finger moves quicker, taking inventory of each offense. Diego has seen Martin Dougherty hospitalize people for less. Even Jon would have done something by now. The twisting knot in Diego's stomach grows with the increasing tick of the businessman's finger. Now standing only a few feet from the pair, he can see deep black rings underneath the businessman's bloodshot eyes.

"So, you just going to stand there bitch?"

USC takes a quick glance over his shoulder to make sure his three friends are still behind him. They all laugh at the apparently awestruck businessman standing motionless save, for his tapping finger. Turning back, USC starts to enjoy the encounter. His muscles relax, the tension replaced by a joyful bounce.

"Yeah, yeah you're just going to stand there staring. Maybe you weren't looking at my girl. Maybe you were looking at me. Hey, you wanna give me a kiss *hombre*?" USC looks back at his friends who all doubled over with laughter. Even the girl grins through her thin lips.

The businessman still doesn't move, but something has changed in his eyes. Previously devoid of emotion, the eyes turn wild, suddenly waking to realize what was happening. Diego notices this, but he doubts anyone else does. Those in the Rockadile who might have detected the subtle change are too busy ignoring the confrontation. USC shouldn't have made the gay reference.

The cane flashes as it lifts above the businessman's head. It holds, almost for dramatic effect, before cracking like a whip behind USC's left ear. The force of the blow makes every bone in his spine pop and he folds like an accordion against the vinyl floor. Quickly, the dapper businessman falls on top of the unconscious man. Then he sinks his large white teeth into the side of his foes face.

The three friends stand helpless while the thin-lipped girl-friend cries hysterically behind them. All in all the attack lasts a half a minute, but once the businessman climbs off, Diego can see a long, deep gash over the victim's ear from where the cane landed. The fallen American's nose and upper lip are gone; chewed away and spit onto the floor. Promptly covering his own mouth a rush of faintness almost overcomes Diego. The few locals that have not fled the club keep their eyes turned away. They stare at their drinks, at the floor, at anything other than the fat businessman standing over the student like a mountain lion defending a kill.

A sudden jerk to Diego's left shoulder causes him to drop his drink. Bouncing off sweaty bodies, it feels like his arm might be torn from its socket. Still feeling queasy, he swallows the tequila, coke and bile as the pressure on his arm subsides. The spinning stops and he once again stands on the sidewalk of Revolucion. The rich night air, though not exactly fresh, fills his lungs and slowly the vertigo subsides. It's comforting to be back in the natural rhythm of the street after experiencing the manufactured bedlam of the club. Turning to discover that Jonathan had been dragging him through the club. Mauricio is there too, eating a hotdog wrapped in bacon, and the grease dripping from Mauricio's lips makes the bile rise again.

"Where the fuck have you two been!" Diego shouts without opening his mouth.

"The other side of the dance floor near the back of the club." Mauricio answers through oily smile.

"So why the fuck didn't you come and get me!"

Before Mauricio can say anything Jonathan answers, "What are we, cock blockers? You gave me the nod so we left you alone." Suddenly Jon frowns intensively at Diego. "Did you and Marty assign a new definition to the nod?"

Diego feels a tug on his still tender arm. Aiming his gaze downward he finds a small child, no more than six years old, smiling up with crooked teeth and crossed eyes.

"Usted quieres chicle, senior?", asks the barefooted street urchin.

He throws a dollar at the boy, taking nothing in return, and looking away only to see the homeless man limping around a corner, disappearing down a dark alley. This image meshes with the hopeless child's but unlike the enticing mélange of hotdogs and cigar smoke, this blend feels polluted. Papa Velarde often spoke of the suffering that existed in places like Tijuana, but surely it was a lie. Only stories meant to keep his beloved grandson away from the dangers of Mexico. The sudden death of his denial shouldn't anger Diego, but it does.

"Let's get the fuck out of here." Diego rubs his head, hoping it'll banish any memory of this night before it takes root.

"Yeah we'll go to another place. That one over there!" shouts Jon. He would have walked into the sluggish traffic had Mauricio not stopped him.

"No!" Diego groans, "I mean let's go back to San Diego or even L.A. If you still want to go places, we can do it there."

A cab stops on the curb in front of them, and Diego jumps through the door, freeing himself from the overwhelming sense of vulnerability. Once packed into the cab Mauricio speaks first. "Senior, take us to get a haircut. You understand what I mean."

The cab driver affirms with an understated nod.

"What the fuck are you talking about?"

"There's this whorehouse not far from here. On the outside it looks like a barbershop, but it's really the best place to get women in all of TJ." Mauricio fidgets in his seat as he pushes the cab driver. "Come on my good man, we're in a hurry."

"You want to go to a fucking whorehouse after what we just saw!" Diego can smell the contents of his stomach churning, aching for an opportunity to emerge.

"How often are you down in Mexico? Regardless of all that stuff between the natives, we should take advantage. Besides, you don't have to do anything, just sit back and relax. I've been to this place, this guy who works at the bank told me about it, and these girl's will do things you won't believe."

Jon laughs. "I haven't seen enough unbelievable things tonight."

Diego leans forward enough to make sure Mauricio and the taxi driver are engrossed in conversation before whispering to Jonathan, "Have you become so jaded that it doesn't bother you that we're about to go into a whorehouse. Shit Jon you're six months away from being a grammar school teacher, and you're basically married."

"Well seeing as there's a good chance we'll all be enjoying our first herpes outbreak by next week I'll be able to teach using the example of my own misdeeds. When the time comes for sex education I'll just wave my rotting unit at the kids at eight o'clock in the morning and scream 'Look what sex did to me children! It happened to me and it will happen to you!' I promise you none of them will have sex until their thirties." Another ear-to-ear grin crosses Jon Heffron's face. "You see! A good teacher can find valuable lesson in the darkest of out-comes."

"You could end up with HIV."

"I had a great aunt who died from an STD. I think it was syphilis. Whatever it was, I should be safe from the more lethal diseases."

"Even in joke, that comment should get you fucking thrown out of the credential program."

"If you keep your mouth shut I'll pay for your blowjob." Now Jon bends forward to get a look at his friends face. "Man I'm not gonna to do anything here Diego so don't worry. I mean I haven't had sex in a while since Laura hasn't 'been in the mood', but I'm not so desperate that I'd copulate with a Tijuana prostitute." He leans back and looks out at the passing landscape of the Tijuana night. "A Las Vegas prostitute maybe, but not Tijuana."

Ten minutes pass and the three stand in front of the finest purveyor of sin Tijuana has to offer. Mauricio shakes with anticipation, Jonathan sways with drunkenness, and Diego focuses his attention on a gentle pulse beating somewhere in the distance. Looking over his shoulder, rays of light tower above the Cathedral of Debauchery only a few blocks to the north.

"That son of fucking whore! He just drove us around for fifteen minutes too charge us more. Look we're only a few blocks away from the Rockadile! He charged us eighteen dollars for that."

In a haughty tone Maurcio snarls, "You don't want to go walking around the streets of Tijuana in the middle of the night if you don't know what you're doing. Believe me, it was worth the money."

Jon whispers "Besides, if that driver is really the son of a whore, his sister might work here, so keep your voice down."

Following Mauricio into the whorehouse Diego says in a murmur, "Jon if we're not going to do anything can't we wait outside. I don't want to go into this filthy place."

Entering the front parlor Jon calls back, "I don't know. This place looks cleaner than most real hair salons I've been in."

Large black and white photographs displaying men and women with elaborate hairstyles cover the white walls. Six barber stations, three on each side, equipped with the necessary tools of the trade. The white linoleum floor looks new, except for a worn pathway leading from the front door to the back. Along the rear wall next to the hallway, a simple manicure station covered with hundreds of bottles of nail polish. Resting his hands on the counter, waiting for the fat madam to waddle her way to the front, Diego is impressed by the attention to detail. There's a clipboard and pen with ten generic sounding names in the right column, all written by the same hand. On the right side of the counter stands a set of shelves lined with dust covered hair care products for sale.

The madam, a fat woman with drawn on eyebrows, wears a floral skirt that hangs to the tip of bare feet and under the woven maroon shawl is a white blouse that's two sizes too big. She wears a collection of necklaces and loop earrings, making Diego wonder at the history of this Mexican gypsy.

After some awkward greetings Mauricio begins negotiating time, money and acts while Diego continues to scan the salon. It should smell like bleach, shampoo and fruit scented conditioners. The snapping of scissors and buzzing of electric shavers should fill the air. Instead Diego inhales the scent of cheap body oil, scented candles and hints of old sweat.

Mauricio and the madam come to an agreement and all three are led into the functional part of the building. As the congregation passes through the hallway, which feels more like a portal to another realm, the available women wait patiently in a line against unfinished plywood walls. Diego remembers his father saying to always treat women with respect, never like a piece of meat. Diego thought of every butcher shop he'd been to, and they always had finished walls.

Jon jabs Diego in his ribs with an elbow. "I'll take that one."

"What the fuck are you talking about Jon! You said…"

"Diego please, I have to take advantage of this." Putting his hand on Diego's shoulder, he gives it a friendly squeeze. "Don't worry man, Laura will understand."

With this Jonathan walks toward a beautiful little Mexican girl, put his arm around her and together they stride toward one of the eight doors lining the southern wall. As Jon is led through the door Diego leans to see a cell wide enough to accommodate one thin military cot and Diego is reminded of those padded rooms used by mental institutions in the fifties.

Turning back to the meat rack Diego watches as Mauricio strolls calmly up and down the row of prostitutes. He's adopted the role of a dilettante in a vast wine cellar, trying to pick out the perfect vintage. Beside him walks the madam, who takes two steps for each of Mauricio's. Out of breath and clearly aching in the joints she tells (in broken English) each girls name along with her specialty.

"Mauricio, pick already!" Diego shouts while turning away.

"Aren't you going to take one?"

"Just hurry the fuck up!"

Papa Velarde used to joke with him, 'You're too soft Diego. You've been in the United States too long. You would never make it in Mexico. Not even for a week.' The old man was wrong in the end; Diego couldn't even last a night.

Finally selecting his girl, Mauricio is led to the holding cell adjacent to Jon's. The madam ambles over to the seven remaining hookers who glance over as the madam issues orders on how to get money from the third American. She has to try; it's her job to make sure the business turns a profit. He's an American after all, and Americans always have money.

The older generations remind Diego where he was born, but still consider him a Mexican. When filling out a census he's a Chicano American/Latino. Among his friends, he's affectionately known as "The Mexican", while his enemies think of him as "A Mexican." He hoped to find some modicum of acceptance south of the border, another person enjoying an evening on Revolucion, not falling into any category. As it is, in Mexico he's "*Un Americano*" and every time he fights off another desperate prostitute rubbing against him, another strip of illusion is stripped away. Each woman would walk away, leaving him unbothered for a moment, but once the smell of body spray dissipates, another arrives. It's like their telling him, 'Come on *senior*. We know you want to. After all you're an American.'

As the fourth woman rises from the couch, head hung in failure, laughter mixed with angry shouts erupts behind Jon's door. A sharp bang against the wall and the madam shuffles across the room, reaching the door as it bursts open. It swings around; slamming into the wall and Jonathan stumbles out, almost falling into the advancing madam, and he has to side-step to avoid being slapped across the face. The hooker follows, immediately relating her tale to the surprised madam.

"Jon, what the fuck is going on?" Diego says springing to his feet.

Jonathan Heffron looks up and takes a moment to soak in the bewildered expression of his friend. Straining to bring the laughing fit under control he says, "All I wanted was a haircut." There's that damn smile again.

"You crazy white fuck!" Diego laughs.

"Well I wanted to make your first trip to the homeland memorable for something other than cannibalism and the purchasing of sex."

Returning his attention to the group of hookers watching from the far corner of the room, Jonathan asks, "Will any of you give me a haircut?"

A quick jab to the shoulder jolts Diego back to reality. The stout little madam snarls and barks at him. He's a Mexican again, being asked to gain control of his Gringo companion. If anyone should be yelled at it's Jon, but she chose Diego?

Another thud followed by a shaking wall and Mauricio rejoins the group.

"Forty dollars for a hand job! I can give myself one for free and I'd probably do a better job. You said out there that it's only twenty. Do you think I'm some ignorant prick who forgets the value of money in the presence of sex?"

The madam storms toward her small desk in the far corner and Mauricio follows even as Diego grabs at him.

"Mauricio, let's get out of here." With a yank of his arm Mauricio pulls away.

"Yeah if you still want a cheap handjob we'll stop at a truck stop in Bakersfield." Jon says, having grown tired of harassing the poor women of the salon.

Nudging up next to Diego, Jonathan whispers, "If he can see to himself better, why would he be willing to pay any price for a handjob."

"You're a goddamn philosopher Jon."

Mauricio suddenly freezes before backing from the madams' desk. Slowly raising his hands he says in an undertone voice, "Guys do something." Stepping out from behind the desk the little woman demeanor transforms into that of colorful boulder bearing a sawed off shotgun.

"Americans go!" she shouts.

No sense of fear overtakes Diego. His hands do not tremble and sweet isn't running down his cheeks. There's shame though, and it runs deep, preventing him from looking at the madam. Instead he looks to the line women shivering against the unfinished wall.

"Jon, Mauricio, we're fucking leaving." Down the hall and out the front door, Diego is already waving down a cab as the other two come running from the building.

"If either one of you fuck heads have plans other than going back to San Diego and getting a room for the night, then you'll have to get your own cab."

A cab pulls up to the curb and its headlights brighten Mauricio's face. In that moment Jonathan sees the banker's son trying to hide his tears. Jon doesn't need to see Diego's face, he can tell from the way his old friend stands that his nerves are fried.

"Is it possible to fall lower than getting thrown out of a whorehouse in TJ?" Jon casually asks.

In the distance, the white light of the American border station cuts through the darkness, and Diego watches merchants hawk cheap ponchos and second rate souvenirs to drunk tourists rolling steadily toward the border.

Chapter II

About Laundry Rooms and Valley Oaks

It's symbiotic; like those rare days when light pierces thunderclouds formed against the western side of the Sierra Nevada's. The roses need the breeze to carry their fragrance, like the light needs the clouds for contrast. Martin Dougherty shuts his eyes, the clouds close, and as the breeze dies down the roses vanish.

After four hours and seventeen minutes not one person has left. Does nobody in the backyard of Leo Radmonavic's country home have children to look after, or an early morning appointment the following day? None question whether they left the stove on after making their morning coffee.

Hope is a powerful thing, but it has limits. Now Martin knows his hope has a limit of four hours and seventeen minutes. It's time to move. One last beer, muster some courage, then a quick escape. With any luck, Leo will be too drunk to notice. More hope, that's all it is, because the boss decides when the party's over at Bodie Trucking Company. The ultimate micromanager, Leo would rather people exhibit fake enjoyment to his face than experience genuine fun behind his back.

Two Valley Oaks (*Quercus lobata*), already old when Father Garces led his expedition into the San Joaquin, reach sixty feet into the sky. At one time the giant hardwoods littered the Valley floor, back when herds of Tule Elk roamed the land. Agriculture transformed the Valley, and the trees disappeared along with the herds. Peering through the canopy to find the apex of the most southerly tree, Martin follows the line of the outer branches until they stop above the Eastern horizon. He lifts his thumb and closes an eye. It's the exact width of the sliver of blue sky between the bottom of the lowest branches and the top of the Sierra Nevada's rising to the east. On a day like this, just after the last shower, the ancient mountain range can be seen like a sentinel of granite and ice, lording over everything for hundreds of miles. In a few days the smog will return and the snowcapped ridges will be invisible until the fall storms. The thick oak trunks, wrapped with dark green ivy and surrounded by a thick carpet of lawn are easily five feet across but they still can't hide those mountains.

Along the rear wall of the bleached house stand overflowing beds of flowers and bushes, still blooming in the early summer. The voice of his long dead grandfather, a former biology teacher at Bodie High, tells him the scientific name of each plant. It's always the scientific name. Martin asks why knowing the common name isn't enough, but is always answered by disappointed silence. Raised three feet, the gardens are held in place by short brick retaining walls. The plants are perfectly placed with the colors and foliage blending in complete harmony. California Poppies (*Eschsaholzae californica*), various types of Sage (*Salvia*) and Birds of Paradise (*Strelitaea reginae*) all grow to their greatest magnificence here. The gardens follow the line of the house and continue around the newly built redwood deck that Leo and the office staff use as their pedestal. The deck crowd surrounds the man and behind them a brand new stereo system plays generic music. There must be a flaw somewhere. Maybe it's the rose bush fence that borders the backyard. A yard should have a real fence. He follows the blooming line of the roses until... those mountains again.

Gathering himself, Martin walks toward the deck, turning his back on the Range of Light. He'll thank Leo for the invitation before making a quiet and hasty exit. It's shameful, even after a year he feels nervous talking to the man. Not nervous in the sense of fear, but from knowing that every conversation with Leo is an interview. Every word is judged. Every statement analyzed.

"Marty I need to talk to you for a minute." One of the truck mechanics, Jose Velasquez, grabs his sleeve hard enough to stop his movement.

"What's up Jose?" Martin asks. Pure naivety to think his six-foot five 250 pound frame could sneak away. His curly red hair contrasts so perfectly with his pale skin that Martin might be a giant, lit cigarette gliding across the oval lawn. There must be a color out there, or maybe some pattern, that will make him invisible. Of course there's nothing to do about the tattoo. All the years of trying to make himself inconspicuous and in one impulsive moment he paints his arms with a coiling rattlesnakes moving through a meadow of bright orange *Eschsaholzae californica*. Martin pulls on his beer, looks around the party and turns to Jose. "You having as much fun as me?"

"This thing has ruined my Saturday. I'd be drinking a bottle of wine and swimming with my family down at Dead Man's River, God forbid." Jose sips his beer and sucks at his mustache; not because there's any foam but after twenty years of the same mustache, habits form. "Did you talk to the idiots in the office about giving us a heads up before dispatching a truck?" Jose whispers.

"I haven't had a chance, but I will."

"They schedule a run, they don't tell us, and the drivers show up angry because nothing's ready. After you left yesterday, a driver came in wanting his truck and I'd just started replacing the head gaskets. He won't drive any other truck. So he waits two hours, the whole time he sits in the shed yelling at me. Those guys in the office need to get their heads out of their asses, Marty. You've gotta to talk to them."

Martin scratches the side of his cheek violently. "You can go tell them as easy as I can Jose. There's no law saying the mechanics can't speak to the dispatchers!"

"They won't listen to me, and you know it. They only listen to you." Jose releases Marty's arm and waits patiently for a response. "The drivers listen to you too. You should tell them they don't need to come and piss in my ear when the office messes up. I'm not going to be talked to like that again. And that's not a threat, I'm just sayin."

"I'll talk to them about it Monday Jose, I promise. I'll, tell the drivers to back off too." His memory wanders back to the staff meeting where Leo announced Martin raised efficiency twelve percent, which meant little to him, but everyone in the office understood. Twelve percent sounded so trivial, but apparently, it meant a great deal. How'd he do it? Graduating from Bodie High stood as a hurdle almost too high to clear. He didn't know anything about shipping, or the conventions of the business world. Nothing more than coincidence as far he could tell, like a farmer who makes a fortune because every crop but his is devoured by locust. Martin remembers the proud look on Leo's face when he made the announcement. To a man like Leo business is science, and in science there are no coincidences.

Climbing up the redwood steps to the top of the podium, he might as well be stepping into a different world. Below on the lawn everyone wears comfortable jeans with reasonable shoes. Their hands are calloused, their bodies bear the weight of manual labor. They talk about sports, fishing and their families. On the deck, there is the smell of aftershave and perfume. Everyone is soft and fresh as they maneuver through conversations that are really extensions of interoffice politics, topic notwithstanding.

Martin hears the conviction in his voice as he speaks, but looks nobody in the eye. "Hey Leo, I gotta take off so..."

"Hey Marty-boy!"

Martin can feel his body temperature rising; an uncontrollable reaction at being addressed as Marty-boy.

"I gotta get over to my aunt and uncles house Leo. I promised to have dinner with them."

"First you gotta listen to the big news out of Bodie." Leo takes a rather large sip of wine and uses his tongue to lap up the dribble running down his narrow chin. "I got a call; the High School hired Oscar Rocha to be the new varsity baseball coach."

Martin wrinkles his brow, trying to understand the importance. "Oh yeah, he coaches little league right. I think he coached the Angels; at least he did when I played. Did old man Lewis finally retire?"

"Hell no! He'd have coached until he died if they'd let him."

"They fired him? He's been the coach for more than forty years. He won fourteen valley championships for this town."

"So that get's him a free pass? He hasn't won in eleven years! He hasn't even won a league title in the last three. They should have fired him a long time ago. The game passed him by. It's the sentimental element in this town kept him around. If they had fired him five years ago we'd have sixteen valley titles instead of fourteen. You know if Selma wins one more, and they might next year, they'll tie us for the most in the San Joaquin." The other four people with Leo all agree that this would be a calamity, and eye Martin, wanting to see what the golden boy has to say.

"Well Marty-boy, are you one of those whiners?"

Martin wants to say, "I don't care about how many state championships Selma has. It means nothing to me if Bodie never wins acclaim in anything from now until the end of time. I'm done with that school, and it was waste of my time when I was there. Now never remind me, in any fashion, of that lost period of my life." That's how he wants to answer, but that wouldn't get him home any sooner.

"I don't know, I think we should respect what he's done for this town" Martin says. "But I guess we have to move on at some point. I know he was one of the few good coaches I've ever known. He loved his players, and he was always fair with them. The rest of the coaches I've met were useless egomaniacs."

"Were you even listening, Marty-boy? You talk about fairness. Are we, being fair to these kids by giving them a skipper that can't handle the game? If we're going to talk about fair, let's give them the best chance to win. In fact, I've always said he was an overrated manager. I think the only reason he won those titles was because he had an unprecedented run of talent. Once that went away and the talent pool went back to a normal level, it became about his ability as a manager and he couldn't cut it. The people in this town have to grow up and realize it's about what's best, not what makes us feel better."

Martin tries to care about the new coach of the high school baseball team. For a good thirty seconds, he tries really hard, but in the end all that matters is leaving the party. "You're right, I just didn't know about any of this so I didn't have time to process." The urge to punch himself in the face is overwhelming. The crowd flanking Leo repeats variations of what the great man said. Each toady makes sure to take a quick shot at Martin's outdated, overly sympathetic philosophies.

Maybe all of Leo's admirers will miss doctor appointments; appointments that will prevent them from suffering through long drawn out infirmities. During their recovery, they'll become dependent on prescription drugs, and miss extended periods of work, resulting in termination. They'll be unemployed for months; which will only add to their drug use. Finally, their wives or husbands will leave them, taking the children and maybe even the dog. Right there, gun in hand, they'll realize that somehow their fall was connected to making fun of Martin Dougherty.

"Hey, I gotta go Leo. Thanks again for the invitation."

"When I was your age Marty-boy, I'd drink till two in the morning, and still be up for work at the crack of dawn. Damn kids these days are all a bunch of weaklings."

Out of the corner of his eye Martin spots Estelle standing at the edge of the deck talking to Paul Connolly.

"I gotta go see my aunt and uncle, Leo."

"Hell, you're how old and you still worry about your aunt and uncle? Fuck um both. Besides, it ain't like what your Dad thinks matters." Leo says, his glass of wine now empty.

Without responding, Martin gives a half-hearted nod in the direction of the toadies before descending from the redwood deck. Nobody else at the party notices him leave. They're all too busy enjoying their last celebration before the onset of the busy season. The workload increases as the Valley harvest cranks up, but it won't reach full production for another week. It's an ominous truth for everyone accustomed to California agriculture, one that dwarfs any drama unfolding atop the red-wood deck.

They don't notice the hulking figure of Martin Dougherty storm across the lawn toward the gate at the side of Leo's House. They're all oblivious to the wink he shoots toward Estelle and they don't notice her return his wink with the slightest of smiles. However, the crowd does hear the rustling emanating from the canopy, and in unison they turn to watch Martin absorb the blow from a falling finger of Oak.

Martin sees black as his body warps, then with a flick of his forearms, he grabs the branch, and sends it skipping across the lawn where it gets tangled in the rose bushes.

The truck drivers have inferiority complexes which they project toward everyone. The secretaries and mechanics are enemies, each department blaming the other for the ills of the company. The secretaries are convinced the mechanics don't turn in any receipts on purpse. In return, the mechanics loath that the secretaries yell at them every time they spend money to fix a equipment the company need to function. The dispatchers hate everyone, but that's only because everyone hates them, yet for one brief, inspiring moment Bodie Trucking Company unites to laugh at the Golden Boy.

"Estelle, take Marty-boy inside and see to him. I don't want his aunt and uncle calling me up asking why he's late."

The calls of past Dougherty's chastise Martin, like they always do at such moments. If he were considered a real Dougherty nobody would dare laugh. They would have snickered into their sleeves and turned away. They would have followed their hysterics with apologies and confessions that that they were wrong to show amusement. Those that showed the most delight would have followed by criticizing the homeowner for his unsafe garden. Instead, they all laugh outwardly, without shame, as though it happened to anyone but a true Dougherty. Martin hears the voices and it makes him feel a little better knowing he's failed again.

"It's alright Leo, just a few scratches."

"No, no, no, you go inside with Estelle. After all, I don't want a lawsuit down the road."

Martin feels her touch his wrist, and like that it's over. She caresses the palm of his hand with her middle finger while leading him into the house. He wants to leave, but he can't pull away; he never can. Once in the small laundry room she releases her grip but he holds on until she surrenders a smile. He watches her pull out the first aid kit that Leo and her used before they stopped camping together.

Estelle lays the First Aid kit on top of the dryer, and begins rifling through its contents. The washer and dryer, like every appliance in the house, are top of the line. Above these machines are shelves, crammed with detergents, house care products, and a wealth of worthless junk. A half dozen wicker baskets storing keys that open nothing, old wallets and thousands of spare pennies.

At last, Estelle turns with a small square of cotton treated with antibiotics. She steps close enough so he can smell her perfume. Grey streaks accent her thick brunette hair that hangs below her shoulders. Her brown eyes are dark and penetrating, though she rarely looks at people directly anymore. Everyone marvels at the way she blushes when she laughs, and it can cause excitement when she wears her hair up to reveal the small leaf-shaped birthmark on the back of her neck. She's gained a few pounds since turning thirty, but she carries it so well that those who said she was perfect before now argue she had always been too skinny. Over the years her attire has become conservative, but the tight fitting dresses that never fall shorter than the knees still bother some.

Estelle stands on her toes, but still has to reach to wipe the scratches along Martins cheek.

"I'm sorry about that Martin."

"It's not your fault the branch fell." He pauses and takes a breath. "It's also not your fault Leo's a prick."

"I know. I'm sorry for asking you here. You should have gone to Tijuana with your friends."

Marty watches her drop her head before snapping it back up. He's said how much he hates seeing her head hang, but old habits die hard.

"I wanted to see you."

Estelle reaches behind Martin's head to clean the cuts on the back of his neck. "I wanted to come over and talk, but I couldn't get away from Connolly." She feels comforted that even after four months her flinty laugh still gives him goose bumps, and tries to remember the last time Leo reacted to anything she did. "Every time Leo has one of these parties, no matter how I try, Connolly corners me. Then I have to spend the whole evening listening to him drone on about the wrongs he's suffered."

"That's because you're the only one who still pretends to be interested. You're too nice Estelle."

"I doubt it would matter if I wasn't. It took you getting smacked in the face with a branch to get me away. Anything less, and I'd be with him right now while he explained how his high school football coach ruined his senior year."

"Glad to help. Maybe next time I'll get burned with some barbeque coals or something."

"You're such a romantic Martin."

At any moment some company clown could stumble in searching for the bathroom and witness everything. Her arms around his neck, bodies pressed together for five blissful seconds. It's the only way the woman knows how to kiss.

Estelle pulls back and keeps wiping the cuts. "I want to give you some money to get your own place."

He pulls her hands down and places them at her side without letting go. "I told you it's not like that."

"I'm not trying to make you feel like…I don't know. I'd like to have a place where we can meet other than that motel. Plus you can quit this job. I know how much you hate it here."

Forgetting everything else, Martin runs fingers up and down the seam of her dress, imagining having a place to themselves. He sees himself cooking for her, and lying together on an old couch watching TV. Nothing exciting, or vulgar. Nothing that you could write about, or would make a good scene in a movie. Just a bunch of normal, unmemorable moments.

"Even if I did get a place I don't know that I'd quit. It's kind of nice to be doing well at a job for once. I'll leave eventually, but maybe I'll try and hang around a little longer, until I find something better."

She leans in, kissing him again only this time Martin doesn't feel nervous. He pulls her tighter so he can feel the seams and buttons of her summer dress. As her underwear drop to the ground she hops atop the dryer, not releasing her lock on his lips.

The music outside mixes with sudden bursts of laughter that might have distracted anyone else, but as Estelle wraps her legs around him, holding her kisses until he can barely breath, nothing matters. If someone walked in at that moment and shouted Martin wouldn't stop. Somehow he knows she wouldn't want him to. It would have been different twenty years ago, but neglect is like thirst and Estelle's needs to quench the urge.

Martin slides his right foot to the side, and as he slips on a dirty sock he can hear Ian Heffron. "It's always the little things that bring down the empire boys." In this case it's one of Leo's sweat socks, still moist from his morning jog. To keep himself from doing the splits Martin reaches out and grabs the dryer. It keeps him from falling, but not from slamming himself, hips first and with full force into the side of the machine.

Martin Dougherty turns white as he doubles over with the shock of the pain, collapsing to the floor.

"What happened baby." Estelle asks cradling his head between her knees.

Martin summons all his powers to focus on this question. What would a proper Dougherty say? "It's a gentleman's matter."

As Martin rolls to his back Estelle jumps down and readjusts her clothes. She thinks about what a blessing it would be for someone to walk in at that moment. How easy it would be to leave if Leo would only make the choice for her. She helps Martin get his pants back on and wipes the sweat from his forehead. He just turned twenty, the same age she was when she married fourteen years ago.

"I'm not trying to pressure you into anything, Martin. I just know you want to get away, and I'm afraid you're staying for me. I don't want you to waste away on an old woman."

Martin rises slowly, still dizzy with pain and kisses her forehead. "Dougherty's never waste, Estelle."

Hearing the bosses snorting laugh through the thin walls, Martin thinks of Leo stumbling into bed with his wife, drunk, covered with sweat and too much cologne. He'll fall over her and in an instant it'll be over and he'll fall asleep, but she won't.

Estelle will go take a shower, then lay awake for a few hours before finally drifting into an uneasy sleep. Before they started seeing each other, Estelle described the scene in detail, and Martin felt heartbroken whenever he thought of it.

"You have to promise me something."

"OK."

"You have to come and see me. You have to come all the time. I'm not talking about late night hook-ups. I want you to come talk to me. I'll cook for you and we'll be together, whatever you want. We don't have to say anything if you don't feel like it. If you promise me, I'll go for it."

The sensation of butterflies in the stomach has become so foreign that it startles her. "Martin you don't owe me…"

"Yes or no Estelle?"

"Alright, I promise." He leans in and kisses her and she grips him tightly trying her best to conceal the small tear running down her check. Finally, she releases him and looks to the ground.

"Estelle, stop…"

"I know, I'll stop."

He climbs to his feet and helps her up. "I'll quit tomorrow."

"There'll be an envelope with some money under the front fender of the broken down Freightliner."

He turns to leave, and thinks about the past; not his, but Bodie's. He thinks about the time when a man could have grabbed a woman like Estelle and led her away to another life, but not anymore.

Estelle keeps her eyes on Martin and pays no mind to the fact that Leo has walked through the back door and into the laundry room. Before her husband even speaks Estelle can feel her teeth grind.

"Where the hell have you been? Is the princess of Bodie too good for my truckers company?"

She watches out the front window of the house and a small puff of black smoke spits out the tailpipe of Martins truck.

"Go back to your stupid party Leo." Walking past him and toward her room, Estelle savors the rush of flushed skin.

Chapter III

Small Town Bars

There are no towering roller coasters. No traveling concert tours. The turmoil of arcades and skate parks is as foreign as world famous art. In place of malls and gourmet coffee houses stand gas station parking lots, and the bored search out empty fields in the countryside where they can enjoy themselves far from authoritative eyes. Large shade trees surrounded by manicured lawns give way to the thin shadows of abandoned orchards. Well groomed bushes turn to waist high dandelions, foxtails and ironweed, leaving pant leg and sock saturated with sticker and seed.

Small towns have taverns. They're not pick-up bars or dance clubs. They do not accommodate the ruckus of young men and women. These are blue collar bars. These are the domain of old men. The latest music does not play, and the décor is anything but trendy. Small town bars held to the old ways when tribal elders gathered under the moonlight. They would discuss the past and make decisions on the future. Reading the stars and speaking to their gods, venerated men would decide on the fate of their people. Like those ancient leaders, those frequenting these off the map dives have lived, they have suffered. Their credentials are their broken hearts and tired faces. Mostly men are here, passing whispers between each other. Hushed words about the past and their hopes for the future might mean nothing outside the walls, but within them they carry the weight of tradition.

In the cities, the bars are ruled by the young, and even if one is searching for quiet, they must tolerate the noise. In the small town, those not yet old enough to drink are forbidden from walking too close to the front entrance. They must cross the street and never look through the door. There are no dance clubs, and restaurants never tolerate people speaking louder than a whisper. If they want to dance they must do so around a parked car with the radio turned up, hidden away from the eyes of the town.

They're mirror images, one preserving the old, the other creating the new.

Chapter IV

Artistic Obscenity

Jonathan takes the last bite of Santa Rosa and tosses the pit to the cement. As far as flavor, it's all downhill. He watches the stone skip across the ground before dropping into a storm drain at the center of the gymnasium plaza. Maybe the discarded seed will take root in the small layer of dirt, chewing gum and decaying sunflower shells covering the bottom of every campus drain. One day, when the variety has been forgotten, the last tree of its kind will live under the cement of Bodie High School; a hidden Santa Rosa bonsai.

Martin spits on the ground and watches it dry. "Why does Velarde want us to meet him here?"

"Maybe he's feeling nostalgic."

"After we graduated I made a vow to never set foot on the grounds of Bodie High."

Jon steps over to the water fountain in front of the high school gymnasium to wash his sticky fingers. "You've been on campus since we graduated. We helped set up for county track and field championships last year."

"And the year before that we helped clean up after open house during janitors strike."

"So what's the problem?"

"All three times I broke my word because Velarde wasn't paying attention and ended up getting himself caught up in helping out with some stupid event."

"You don't know that's what this is about."

"Yeah I do."

Jonathan leans against the gym and slides down until he's seated on the cement. "Well, whatever he wants he better get here quick because he's five minutes late and it's a hundred and two. I spend six days a week working in this heat, and I'm not spending my off time cooking in this concrete purgatory."

Martin stomps back and forth, half muttering to himself. "It wouldn't be so bad if he would occasionally find people to help out when we need it."

Jonathan listens to the uneven pattern of Martin's stride. "Why are you limping?" he asks.

"Oh…when that branch hit me in the face I fell over and tweaked my groin trying to catch myself."

"You outta know better than to pick a fight with an oak." Jon laughs. "Anyway, are you going to tell me why you quit Bodie Trucking?"

"Since when do I need to justify anything I do!"

"Since March seventeenth 1994."

Martin rubs his face hard and the small scratches tear open. "I don't know how many jobs I've quit, and you never gave a damn Heffron?"

"I didn't see it coming, that makes this a curiosity. You always start enthused, as though you finally found your place in the world, then slowly you get disillusioned. This gets worse and worse until finally you walk. As far as I could tell you were still into the work."

"I guess you'll have to rewrite your book on Martin Dougherty."

"The word around town is Leo will make sure you can't find work. Then you'll be forced to beg for your position back. That or leave town."

"If I go back there, I won't be begging for anything."

"How you gonna pay rent."

"I got it figured. The money I got for my truck will get me by." The farmboy won't back down, until the futility of arguing is made clear. "I'm sick of it all anyway. I'm sick of my aunt and uncle's crap, and I was sick of the job."

"You've been sick of your aunt and uncle since you moved in with them, what changed?"

"Can you just drop the subject, Heffron?"

"If it's that bad, me and Laura would could put you up."

Jonathan leans his head back, closes his eyes, feeling his heartbeat slow. On this very campus he mastered the technique; only to keep from being sweaty in front of girls. Perhaps one day the wisdom of old age will reveal a more enlightened use for the talent. Even in this semi-trance, Jon hears the Firechicken roaring toward the school.

As the Firechicken comes to a stop, Diego watches Martin pacing back and forth, from the sun into the shade of the gymnasium overhang, then back to the sun. Contrastingly, Jonathan crouches against the wall like he always has, half asleep, disinterested as ever. It's only been eight days since Jon finished his final semester at Fresno State, and his summer tan has already reappeared. His long blond locks, bleached white by the sun, make his blue eyes stand out and even though he's still thick in the midsection, Diego knows a month on Ian Heffron's ranch will leave him svelte.

Diego gives quick glances toward Jon, but avoids Martin's piercing stare. Regardless of the occasion, Jon always wears the same tattered sandals with some jean shorts adorned with holes and long white strings hanging past his knees. It's always been somewhat of a scandal that Jon Heffron, a sixth generation farmer, refuses to wear pants for anything save for solemn events or cold months. Even at work, a time when farmers everywhere agree that long pants must be worn, Jonathan walks around in shorts and sandals. By July he'll have tan lines of the footwear across the arches of his feet and his soles will be brown and callused.

"Can't you put a pair of shoes and pants on Jon, just so I can say I saw you fucking do it?"

"It's hot. Besides the Yokut's never wore shoes in the Valley before the Spaniards came, even in the winter fog. They survived."

Martin steps back under the shade. "So what you got us into this time."

"Fuck you Marty, this wasn't my fault."

Jon opens his eyes, and can't help but smile.

"Who'd you run into, and how'd they finagle you into working for free. More importantly how'd you get the two of us involved?"

"Oh I'm sorry, I didn't know asking a friend for help was a fucked thing to do. Have the last three days without a job been so tiring that you're pressed for time? Shit, the farmboy put in ten hours of peach packing yesterday and you don't see him complaining."

"That's cause Heffron lives to work. If you gave him a choice between working and making love to Laura, you know what he'd choose."

Jonathan salutes Martin. "That's because I'm not that good in bed, so why waste the girls time."

Martin growls loudly. "Damn it Heffron I'm being serious!"

"So am I; I'm a lousy lay. Ask Laura she'll tell you."

"Heffron shut up! Velarde tell us what the hell we're doing here."

"This is really all my sisters' fault. She got in a big argument with my mom over some video she forgot to return that ended up costing thirty bucks in late charges. They were yelling at each other over it for hours. Just to get some peace and quiet I left the house and headed down to Lena Park."

"Velarde…please get to the point before I have a stroke."

"Anyway, on my way I stopped off at Alphonso's to pick up a breakfast burrito and some water and I ran into the principle."

"Here we go…" Martin turns away with an exaggerated air of disgust.

"God damn it Marty, it's not my fault! He was panicking. Someone painted a women giving birth on the side of the gym, and they got that church event here tonight."

Jonathan breaks his trance and jumps to his feet. "Are you telling me we've been sitting here for twenty minutes, and there's a naked women on the side of this building!"

"Yeah. It's on the other side right near the entrance. Wait up Jon let me…God Damnit."

Martin sighs at the sight. "If he moved half that fast in high school he'd have played in the city/county game."

Jonathan rounds the corner and rushes down the side of the gym. He always felt proud of the look of Bodie High School even if most made fun of it. The buildings might look at home perched atop granite walls of some deep Himalayan valley. Each of the thirteen buildings has a pagoda style roof complete with red tile shingles. Coming down from the roofs are not metal poles commonly found at California schools, but large cement pillars painted white. Acting as the backdrop to the pillars are wood plank walls stained dark brown. All that's needed are some Nepalese scribbling with a few well placed statues of Buddist deities draped in prayer flags and the Bodie High monastery would be complete. The architect, one Samson Feguntes, designed it in honor of the towns' once large china town that stood on that very spot.

Then, one summer Jon watched in horror as this large square monstrosity rose above his beloved monastery. A cement kaba covered with tan stucco with no significant features save for, the metal overhangs, a sliding double door entrance and towering black letters reading 'Bodie High School Miners'. Everyone in town marveled at its modernity and boasted that they now had the finest gymnasium in the Valley. As far as he's concerned, random vandalism can only improve the obscenity.

Its centerpiece, a middle-aged woman surrounded by vineyard holding a newborn child, is nowhere near as offensive as he'd hoped. The backdrop of bright green leaves with purple bunches of grapes makes the prostrate woman pop with a translucent glow. The vineyard blends into a blue sky peppered with perfect recreations of the towering white thunderheads that appear over the eastern Valley every spring. The woman's face is tranquil, but something about her closed eyes and furrowed brow says she wants to apologize to the child but doesn't know how. The baby lays laughing on the brown dirt in front of her, still attached to the umbilical cord.

Diego and Marty come up behind Jonathan.

"So this is it?" Martin says.

"Yeah. It's good isn't it?" Jonathan answers, not trying to hide his disappointment. "Whoever painted this is almost there, he's almost found his voice."

Marty pushes Jonathan lightly. "You call that good? It's garbage. And what kind of name is Bolivar?"

Jon looks down to the corner to see the small signature. "He was a revolutionary from Latin America. The country of Bolivia is named after him."

"Is that right?"

"Yeah. He was a fascinating figure."

Diego looks back up, trying to judge how high they'll have to climb to paint over the mural. In one of the vineyard rows near the top of the mural there shines a black sword engulfed in flame. A silver-winged angel clad in a triple breasted suit and dress shoes wields it. The glowing point of the sword like a star presses against the back of a kneeling farm hand. In the condemned man's hand is a basket of fruit which he offers to a small child with pale skin that contrasts with his own burnt, cancer riddled hide. Diego stares closely at the man's face expecting to see some sign of anger or fear at the forced attrition hanging above him, but there's none. Like the woman at the murals center, the man is content, but lacking any underlying feeling of apology.

"Man it is fucking hot! Let's get this done."

"What are we doing anyway?"

"Well if you hadn't run around the corner like a cheerleader chasing the quarterback you'd know the principal wants us to paint over this before that church thing starts. He left everything we'll need around the corner." Diego takes in the artwork some more as Jonathan and Martin collect the tools and supplies they'll need. It's not appropriate for a high school campus, there's no doubt of that, but it's fit for Bodie.

"Actually, it's too damn bad," Diego mutters, "I kind of like it."

Martin slams the ladder against the gym. "Velarde, are you telling me you'd be alright with looking at this thing before going to class each morning?"

"I would have rather looked at anything other than these damn walls. Every high school I've ever been feels like a fucking minimum security prison."

Diego runs his fingers across the mural. The rushed brushstrokes reveal the artists fear; scared of being caught but knowing that to give up without finishing would mean abandoning something sacred. Diego imagines the artist as someone recently arrived from a distant part of California; maybe even Mexico. They're lost in this new world where nothing makes sense, and they don't seem to fit in, so they find comfort remembering what they left behind before painting it on a wall.

"This kid may be the same guy who painted that picture of a farmer dying under the sun on the Olsen property. Remember Heffron, you were telling us about it the other day."

"That's right! He painted it on old man Olsons' big standpipe on the west side of his land." Jon takes in another look at the mural. "I bet it is the same guy. I didn't hear if he signed it Bolivar though. The style's exactly the same. Well done, detective Dougherty."

Diego feels sweat beginning to collect on his forehead. "Let's go check it out after we're done Marty."

"Can't. I got somewhere I gotta be."

"The life of an unemployed truck dispatcher never rests huh?"

Jonathan prepares the pressure washer, and spends a few moments cleaning the surface. The wall dries quickly and Jon pushes the bulky, outdated machine aside before covering the cement with the large canvas mat, making sure to tape down the sides so it doesn't slip. As he carefully stirs the paint and pours it into the trays he can hear Martin yelling at Diego about something.

"If you two are done flirting, Marty why don't you start painting the lower part and Diego you get up the ladder."

The two work quickly, even with Jonathan scolding them over putting the paint on too thin. In between the criticisms, Jon closes all the cans, cleans the brushes before the paint sets, and along with the pressure washer, puts it all away. He places some barricades along with a wet paint sign he finds inside the small hallway at the gyms entrance. He pulls caution tape around the work area and steps back to inspect the site.

"You know it's no wonder you never bothered painting the Firechicken Diego, because that is a really shoddy job. You can still see the mural, clear as day."

"Fuck you Jon, you haven't painted shit, and you're going to question my work. Get your farmboy ass over here and do it yourself."

"You're surprised. This is Heffron's MO. He strolls around looking busy, bosses everyone around, then gets all credit. You really should forget teaching and go into business Jon. You're a natural"

Jonathan walks over, ducking under the barricade and tapping Diego on the back. "Long night last night Diego? You look kind of flushed."

"Get your ass up the ladder Farmboy."

With a salute Jon climbs to the top step. He stumbles for a moment, and the ladder starts to pull away from the wall. He thinks quickly and remembers that his third cousin, Tom Heffron, died eight years ago in a fall from a step ladder. Jon relaxes as Martin's giant hand slams into his back, and in an instant the ladder is resting safely against the wall of the gym. Jon adjusts his ruffled shirt and begins to paint.

Jonathan reaches for the last of the uncovered painting, and Diego marvels at how easily the farmboy manages everything. Maybe that's why the Heffron legacy exists, as some specialized force of evolution, because the normal methods used by the world to break a man don't work on that family.

"You're never going to make it past twenty-five Jon."

"Well, not as long as you keep getting me stuck doing every odd job in Bodie."

Chapter V

Facing Legend

Tourists crisscross the Valley on their way to the ocean, mountains, or heading to the city of their choice, and every summer the intersection at Lac Jac and Mountain View Ave floods as these migrating herds pass." Inevitably some cross Harold Jung's apricot orchard, and here a slick of unattended irrigation mixes with fine dust, sending them spinning into the fields. These accidents have opened great spaces in the orchard, where healthy fruit bearing trees once stood. Soon, one of Leo's trucks will get trapped in the overflow and shortly after, Leo will own a small parcel of poorly tended apricot trees.

Quick turns of the steering wheel and Martin gets the Firechicken back under control. His emotions got the better of him, that's the only explanation for making a tourist mistake. Taking his frustration out on the accelerator, the old car leaps forward with a wail. His heart pounds and the red curls of hair bounce to the cadence of the beat.

Martin twists the steering wheel twenty degrees to the right and the cars horn sounds. "Damn it Velarde! How can you spend so much time working on cars, and not care about the little things. I swear if Leo comes out and shoots me I'm gonna to haunt you."

The car slides across the gravel of Bodie Trucking's front entrance. He parks in what might be the last space but the lines have faded; washed away by winter storms. Had he come to work that morning the lines would have been repainted yesterday. Only old, abandoned gopher holes and ant hills, exposed by the same showers, break up the plainness of the yard.

The line of fifteen Pacific Coast Redwoods (*Sequoia sempervirens*) separating the yard from Lac Jac Ave looks artificial; like a bad oil painting. The weather has turned, and the Redwoods emerald needles have gone bronze. Martin remembers arriving many a morning positive that he was looking at a row of dead trees. Leo yells at the maintenance staff incessantly each summer. 'I'm so sick of staring at those damn brown trees! I swear someone's going to get fired if you don't keep those things green.' They water the trees daily, and fertilize with carefully balanced potions. Yet with the first summer heat the needles of the forty-foot redwoods turn brown.

Climbing out of the Firechicken, Martin looks at the buildings and trailers that run perpendicular to Leo's house at the back of the yard. Unlike the twisted fondness he feels for the coffee colored trees, Martin's skin crawls at the site of the office trailers. Across from the trailers, white garages and sheds with red tiled roofs link with the old farmhouse to the north and the row of redwoods to the south giving the yard a look of a traditional Spanish town square. Only a small Catholic church topped by a thin steeple could make the image more authentic.

Martin visualizes the thriving vineyard of Thompson Seedless (*Vitis vinifera*) that once stood there. Leo removed the old vineyard, one of many that surrounded Bodie, to make room for his trucks. That was a decade ago, still every spring small vines emerge from the ground. The plants are in denial;

refusing to accept the land no longer needs them. For sixty years they dominated the landscape before being torn from it. A less stubborn thing would have accepted the truth. Just two weeks earlier, Martin and Jose spent hours cutting away that year's growth. The deep tire ruts, born from the mixture massive trucks and winter rains, cross the yard. With the ground dry and the vines removed, someone will smooth out the tire marks with the old tractor that came with the land.

Martin always enjoyed the hum of chattering men, and the lingering scent of fertilizers, alfalfa and leather saddles that came with the shop. Some truck drivers brought ramshackle chairs and tables so they'd have a place to relax between deliveries. Leo grudgingly bowed to public pressure, installing a swamp cooler to comfort those watching the old black and white TV during lunch break. As time passed it became more break room, and less maintenance shed, but everyone still calls it the shop. Functional tools that once littered the shop are scattered across the garages where the trucks are worked on.

The shop will be missed, but Martin feels overwhelmed at knowing he will never set foot in that muggy office again. No more countless hours answering questions for irate truck drivers and dim-witted customers. Maybe the nightmares of secretaries standing around him demanding solutions will end. Even if they don't; no more attending weekly meetings or answering phones. Then, best of all, no more Eric.

"You got guts coming here boy. Quitting just as we're getting into the busy season, I've never heard of such a thing. Leo was so angry when I gave him the message, that he said he was going to shoot ya for stabbing him in the back."

It was a given that Eric Masterson would be in the office, but where are the secretaries and dispatchers? Have they all left the office unmanned in the summer? It's unfathomable.

"The only thing I can't figure is what he saw in you. I think he thought it'd be nice to have a Dougherty on staff. I explained it to him many times; your uncle's the last real Dougherty."

Like a hard wind blowing over a lake, each syllable causes ripples of crawling skin to shoot across Martins body. That high, grating voice doesn't belong with a man of his build. He's short, but he's strong and even if he's getting old, he still represents the only state champion wrestler to come out of Bodie. Martin thinks of the time the two spent half a day tossing fifty pound bags of cement into a truck. Eric had just turned thirty-four, but it was Martin who spent the next day limping through his work, crippled by soreness.

"Don't worry boy. I didn't tell him you were coming in today. Figured I'd let you go in peace. Kinda think of it like a farewell gift."

It's amazing, the office is cleaned nightly, yet still smells like dust. Not the powder of the Valley floor, but a different kind. An old scent, like that found in the archives of ancient cities. The smell is there, along with the deafening silence of a tomb, yet even with a white glove nobody will ever find any dirt. Three desks are spaced evenly in the middle of the room. The walls, lined with file cabinets and paintings of generic Valley scenery, are covered in the cheap wallpaper meant to give the illusion of a log cabin. To the right is the table where Martin spent a day with Eric learning how to operate the dispatch radio. In ten minutes he had it mastered, but Eric hovered over him for a day. Next to it stands another table where a secretary taught him to balance the account book. What was that secretaries name again? He can remember the combination to the safe under the table, but try as he might Martin can't think of that pretty young girl's name.

"Masterson, I didn't stab anyone in the back."

"You didn't! I can't believe you can say that and keep a straight face. He gave you a job didn't he? He's moved you up in the company, even though you never earned it. He did the same for me, but I never betrayed him. I never would, they're almost like family to me, so I protect them. Hell, you even made it harder on the man's marriage."

"What are you talking about?"

"They've been fighting every night for the last two. Poor Estelle. Such a sweetheart and you gotta bring pain on her before you leave."

"Oh yeah, you're a real compassionate man Masterson. Divorced because you spent more time here than with your wife and kids. You should be on the cover of American Family Weekly."

"I never betrayed them! I never betrayed anyone, and that includes Leo. Not after everything he's done for me. I wouldn't ever do something like that, hell I never show him any disrespect."

"You think that's because you're some kind of loyal man. You don't stand up to Leo because you're a coward Masterson. For ten years you've sat in this office, and kissed up to anyone you think can protect you. People can say what they want about me, but they can't say that I'm afraid to face anyone!" Eric stands motionless, unaffected. "Hell I'm here right now. Why don't you just walk over there and call Leo and tell him I'm here? I don't give a damn about him or his shotgun."

Marty leans over Eric's desk until their faces are inches apart. He can smell Eric's back teeth rotting. "Give me my check, because I'm losing my temper."

Eric slowly rises to his feet and every muscle in Martin's body tenses on instinct. It's about damn time. "You can't talk to me like that boy!"

As the old hand takes a step forward Martin inflates himself. "I got nothing to lose Masterson." The sight of Eric trying to save his dignity is familiar, like when Martin punched a hole in the wall of his aunts' kitchen wall after losing a fight to Miguel Jimenez in seventh grade. When he got home, eyes swollen and lip busted, he needed to do something, so he took it out on some drywall.

"What does that mean?"

"Get my money Masterson, or I take it out of you."

After a brief standoff, Eric turns grabbing the folder sitting atop his desk. He digs through the file frantically and Marty notices Eric Masterson talking to himself. The whole scene has a strange eerie quality, and Martin jumps when Eric throws the check into his chest shouting, "Now you're done here. So get off the yard!"

Grabbing the check from the floor, Martin stares at the back of Eric's head long enough to make the room feel more uncomfortable before stepping out from under those horrible lights and back into the sun. Walking down the metal steps toward the Firechicken Martin wants to know what Eric mumbled under his breath. Stop worrying about it; enjoy the victory, even if it's a minor one. Ian says to always enjoy the minor victories. Of course, Ian also preaches to never dwell on the past too long or you lose sight of the future.

His future resides in an envelope tucked under the fender of the broken down Freightliner at the far end of the yard. It's a future full of the peace of sanctuary. He imagines lying out on his couch every day after work before getting up and cooking himself dinner. On some days he can have Diego and Jon over to drink a few beers. No more hiding in his room ignoring the constant bother of his aunt and uncle or having to explain his moods.

Then there'll be the days Estelle comes over. They can spend their time together without the strange smells, and disruptive noises of cheap motels. Nothing will exist outside his apartment, it'll just be them. He won't represent the ultimate fall of the Dougherty name, and she won't be the wife of Leo Radmonovic. They can pretend they're another anonymous couple, enjoying the moment.

Then she'll go home, and he'll remain free. He'll fall asleep comfortably each night in his own bed while she cowers in the corner of Leo's. His future will be bright at the expense of her misery. Would he even be able to sleep knowing what she's going home to; what would that say about him? Reaching under the fender to remove the tight roll of money, Martin considers the weight of discovery that would come with leaving Estelle behind. How many of these nights will end with Leo yelling at her for coming home with a smile on her face? How long could it last like that for any of them?

Martin looks at Leo's perfect farm house. Beyond it stand the mountains; the same ones Ulysses Dougherty looked at more than a century ago. Set to go prospecting the next morning, the town fathers asked if he'd become the new town marshal, and help them stand up against the violence that threatened the fledgling community. The story goes that Ulysses agreed immediately, not because he harbored ambitions of being a lawman, but because he felt duty bound to serve those who asked it of him. It's a lie. Martin knows Ulysses stayed because he would have been ashamed not to, like he was running away. He'll never be able to prove it, but Martin is sure that even as he agreed to wear the tin, Ulysses dreamed of mounting his horse to ride into the freedom of those mountains.

Chapter VI

As Fine an Occasion to Contemplate

Jonathan stands at the entrance of his row of tomato vines fighting the forgotten battle. It's a global conflict that has been waged for centuries. Jon defies the Sun's authority while imagining being one of the many whose lives are governed by alarm clocks set to arbitrary policies, conjured in glass buildings. Do they understand that they follow a code completely new to humanity. Do the masses realize that they are the freaks, not him

Jon looks through the dim morning light across half an acre of crimson fruit, refusing to begin the day's labor despite the heats growing insistence. Moments pass as rays of light assault him with greater force, demanding he work, every moment marked as a minor victory in an inevitable defeat.

Workers at the big plantations on the east side of the Valley harvest by machine. Giant mechanisms that pick green tomatoes sent to ripen in warehouses and cold storages. Slowly, Jon crouches down and picks his first tomato of the day, placing it softly in his bucket. He can still hear his father's voice, "Like eggs boy, treat um like eggs." Despite preparing the packing stations, his muscles have lost none of their morning stiffness, and after ten minutes Jon feels a slight itch on the middle finger of his right hand. He forgot his gloves. That small cut will burn with tomato acid for the rest of the day.

There will be time for talking and joking later when the heat forces a slower pace. In this morning cool, the only noise is the rustling of the vines as the pickers mine for fruit. The quick crash of tin buckets hitting the ground after a packer empties it is the only break in the silence. Dew covers the landscape, making the air smell the way it does right before a thunderstorm. In the distance, silhouetted against dark blue sky two scrub jays harass a Coopers hawk, darting and singing harsh complaints. The hawk flies below the still visible moon, before swooping down suddenly as though bouncing off the silver sphere.

Occasionally, the workers are startled by the loud whirr of Quail inadvertently driven from their hiding places amongst the vines. To pass the time, Ian's two dogs charge across the patch hunting ground squirrels and digging for gophers. They do so playfully, knowing they will soon feast on the scraps tossed down by the crew at break time. In the background, the light cooing of mourning doves acts as the harmony that links all other sounds. Jonathan looks to the left, glimpsing the shadow of a pair of coyotes heading back to their den after a night of foraging. The heat and humidity grow more intense and the acid from the plants burns Jon's hands while his arms go rubbery from the hauling of full buckets from the patch to the trailer. In front of him Jon see's red; long strips and round spots of bright tomatoes weighing down the vines. Then he looks behind him and the red is gone leaving only green. The taxed plants perk up after being picked, and even with the occasional broken branch and bent leaf, they seem grateful for his effort.

"Jon. Break." Ian snaps.

Jonathan walks over to sit under the blue tarp of the packing trailer. He remembers when Ian fitted it with the tarp thrown over a simple frame made from PVC pipe. He did it the day after Ian Jr. passed out from heat exhaustion.

"I hate the humidity." Jonathan huffs. "It just drains your energy. I've only been up for four hours, and I'm ready to go back to sleep."

"I don't remember the heat ever bothering you. Too much beer and hamburgers with your buddies?" Ian says with a smirk. "You need to spend a little less time at My Friend's House."

"That's got nothing to do with it. Ten days ago I was sitting in a seventy-five degree library studying for finals. I haven't been out in anything hotter than eighty degrees in nine months. I'm not acclimated yet."

"You've been back a week. You should be comfortable with the heat by now."

"Who said anything about heat, I said it's the humidity in those damn rows. Its ten degrees hotter down in those furrows than it is walking around. You'd know that if you'd pick up a bucket from time to time." Jonathan says glancing at the packers.

"It's not ten degrees hotter in those rows!" Ian laughs. "You exaggerate everything Jon."

"Yes it is *patron!,*" Hector Alverez says from his place on the tractor. "You watered the patch yesterday. I've told you many times not to do that when we go in to pick the next day. The wet ground makes the heat worse. You should water it tonight, that way it dries when we come back to pick later."

"Why, because of the humidity boss?" says Ian.

"Yes *patron*."

Even without looking up Jon can see Hector's eyes sparkle, bright as ever. He's put on weight, and grey has sprouted around his ears and across his thick mustache, but his eyes are still bright. Dragging fingers across his work stained shirt, Jon marvels at how Hector manages to work so hard, harder than anyone on the crew, while staying perfectly clean.

"Why didn't you tell me god damnit," Ian protests, already knowing the response.

"I tell you all the time, you don't listen." Every good king has that one advisor who can be honest without consequence. They can challenge, even tease their boss a little. Sometimes this person is a wife or child. Other times it's been a favorite general or artisan. This is the interaction that the crew watches under the blue cover of the packing trailer. They stand in awe as Hector Alverez mercilessly badgers the otherwise undisputed king of the Heffron farm.

"If you had it your way we'd still be farming those damn walnuts, boss. Anything to make things as easy as possible," Ian shouts up to Hector, still refusing to lift his head from his breakfast.

"It would be better today." Hector answers sharply. "What you should plant is almonds. They make money."

Then Ian Jr., the youngest in the family, asks, "We used to farm walnuts?"

"That's all this area was fifty years ago. Walnuts and grapes. Before that, Bodie was the biggest wheat grower in the world until the water table rose. After that everyone around here switched over."

"I wish we still did walnuts," the young man chirps. "Walnut trees are fun to climb."

Jonathan smiles his normal smile. "Right now, I wouldn't mind walking under the shade of a walnut orchard."

"There is nothing more boring than raisins and walnuts. I hated doing that crap, so did your dad Jon. There's no challenge in it. With walnuts, watering and waiting for the damn things to drop controls your entire life. Raisins are a little trickier, you've gotta watch for mildew, and they have to be pruned right. Really though, the biggest thing with them is hoping it doesn't rain while they're drying. It all comes down to luck, just guessing how long to leave them on the vine before laying um down. Heck, if I wanted to lay my life in the hands of luck, I'd take up poker.

"That's why we liked stone fruit; it more interesting, and you have a little more control over time. Though I guess in the long run we don't have any real control. Anyway, we started transferring the place to peaches and nectarines in 84' and by 1988 we were exclusively stone fruit. It's more labor, but it keeps you busy. There's nothing worse than waiting for sugar levels to get high enough to pick. Give me a good peach orchard any time." Ian looks down at his watch. "Jesus we've been on break for twenty minutes! Come'on get back to work!" The pickers gather their buckets and go back to their rows while the packers return to their stations.

"You're falling behind packers let's get moving." Ian's gravely shout contrast perfectly with the soft nature of his normal speaking voice. It's a persona, thinly veiled, which the crew loves because they know the real man.

Jonathan drops back into the rhythm of picking, driven by the increasing length of green behind him. Maybe it doesn't matter, there'll always be another row, and another after that, but better to focus on the little victories. Time passes quickly in the trance before the sound of Hector singing softly breaks his rhythm.

"How'd you already finish your row, Hector?"

"Why do you still come out here, Jon?"" Hector asks, making no indication that his mind focuses on anything but the work.

Jonathan tries his best, but can't answer without pausing. "Stop asking me that Hector."

"You've been in college for so long, spent all that money, and you're still stupid. You could have saved a lot of time if you had decided what world you wanted to live in," Hector says.

"I still gotta few months till I start teaching, so shouldn't I help out and make some money? Hell, this family's done enough for me, right? But once I've got the keys to my class-room, I won't have to do this anymore. In the case of this damn tomato patch, I'll be glad of it. I won't miss those itchy figs either." Jon looks up and sees Ian pestering Guadalupe about not separating the small tomatoes from the large ones.

"You'll come back." Hector pauses to kill a brown spider guarding a particularly large tomato. It's a problematic ma-neuver, removing the small arachnid without damaging the delicate fruit. There's been much discussion about what species of spider lives there, but regardless of the name, they do well in Ian's tomato patch.

"I won't be coming back Hector, no matter what anyone says. I'll make a decent salary, good job security and retirement. Not that good of a retirement, but better than what farmers get. I'll be working in an air-conditioned room, no more twelve hour days in Sun. Plus, you get all the holidays and summers off, un-like here. Man we've had to pick oranges the last three Christmas Eves, and we always work on Fourth of July." Jonathan's hears the volume of his voice rising. "I'll come and help when needed, but this is my last full time summer working the land."

Hector stood for a moment, wrenching the stiffness from his arthritic back. "I wish you could hear the heartbreak in your voice. You have to remember, you grew up eating the dirt. That's what makes it hard for farm boys to leave. They eat the dirt, and it's a taste that doesn't wash away easy."

"You're saying is we can't do anything else. That's not true. I may be a farmboy, but that doesn't mean I can't live anywhere else. Life is what you make of it."

"Farmboys eat the dirt; it becomes part of them, from when they're little kids. It gets in your blood and there's nothing you can do to make it go away."

Jon looks over the tomato vines separating him and Hector. "First of all, I'm not a boy. Second, that doesn't even make sense because if that were the case then there wouldn't have been as big a drop off in family farms as there has been in the last twenty, thirty years."

"That's the nature of business. It has nothing to do with what they wanted. Some moved on because they lost their farms, or to make money for their families. Then there were some who left because of family fighting. Too many arguing over the land so some get pushed out. None left because they couldn't take it, and none left because they wanted to. It killed a piece of every one of them to leave this behind."

The dirt, the heat, the stress; Jon feels sure that parting with these will not be difficult. What he'll miss is the joy of living within the rhythm. Not the pleasant pulse of Hector's philosophy, but the peace found in focusing on those quiet beats of life until they consume his thoughts. It's a skill only farmers and ranchers have mastered. Farmers embrace the monotonous parts of life as though they were a symphony. They let themselves be consumed by it until they feel nothing else. They can spend hours performing the most repetitive of jobs without a moment boredom. They can dig trenches without feeling burning muscles until the rhythm is finally lost at the days completion. It's a talent that takes years to learn and its mastery usually comes without any notice.

Jonathan feels a deep melancholy at recognizing that the life he will soon leave has imparted this rudimentary enlightenment. Not the spiritual freedom of the great sages or the peace of the prophets but an wonderfully simple insight not attainable for those who live apart from the land. They spend days intentionally avoiding the rhythm. He thinks of all the people who join gyms, clubs and sports leagues for no other reason than to avoid listening to silence.

"*Lunche,*" Ian bellows. The crew gathers their meals and without prodding, crawl into the back of Ian's truck to drive a few hundred yards to the Heffron Eucalyptus grove.

Thin rays of light shine through the sparse canopies giving the grove a surreal feeling. The crew trudges through foxtails, dandelions and stinging nettles covering the ground. Mixed in are the large white flowers and blue leaves of jimson weed. Coyote's dig their dens in the grove, and leave little mounds of dirt in all directions. It has been decades since the trees were planted and generations of coyote dens have created a rolling to the landscape. Red-tailed hawks nest in the upper branches, and every year a pair of horned owls returns to renew their courtship. The rest of the canopy is filled with robins and sparrows, which zigzag from the branches to the ground in search of seeds and grubs for their brood.

"Hey Jon." Ian says, "You've been neglecting this path over here."

Jon looks to his right at the thin, fading trail cut through the weeds. He doesn't know how many paths he's made through the years, but Ian might.

"Yeah, I moved to get some more privacy."

They gather at a small picnic table at the groves southern end. Jon's grandfather put the table there, maybe for no other reason than to justify the wasted land space. Ian passes a water bottle around so everyone can wash the acidic residue from their hands. Some of the old timers use fresh tomato juice saying the acid cleans the skin better than any soap.

"You want some?" Hector asks as he passes a bowl of *carne asada* and tortillas to Jonathan.

"I'll have one." Jonathan carefully puts a small burrito together using the ingredients Hector gave him. "So, are you going to tell me how I can solve my problem?"

"What problem?"

"What we were talking about. How I eat dirt, and am destined to life of depression and misery without it."

"*Cabron*, you don't understand anything. The dirt, it's a part of you and that's why you come back. The farming, that's nothing, just a job. You own the dirt, you control it; here you are a prince. Even if you become the greatest teacher ever, there is no way to replace that. Always in the back of your mind you'll know there's another teacher who could take your place. But there's no one out there that knows this land like you. To replace that feeling, you're going to have to find something that needs you as much as you need it. This farm is nothing without the Heffrons, it needs you. That's the only way it'll ever work for you Jon."

Eating his lunch, Jonathan makes small talk with some of the other members of the crew. Ricardo, who's worked on the ranch for three seasons, is especially talkative. His wife will soon be having their third child. Jonathan hates smoking, but he likes Ricardo. The crew sits under the eucalyptus trees, smoking cigars on a hot day listening to Ricardo talk about his children. Jonathan smacks his lips and knows the ashy taste of the cigar will keep his mouth dry for the rest of the day.

Jonathan looks over at Hector. "How much longer we got?"

Hector furrows his brow. "Two hours to finish the patch, an hour to unload."

The Sun shines directly overhead as Ian stomps his feet indicating the end of lunch. They climb back into Ian's truck, and he sticks his head out the window. "The thermometer on my dash reads a hundred and three degrees!"

The crew falls back into the rows and Jonathan returns to his trance. He imagines standing in the center of the produce isle at the Big Potato Grocery Store. Wearing one of those green aprons might feel stupid, but he'd be cooler. He'd be in the air-conditioned room making the same money in forty hours that he does in seventy working for Ian. He'd have days off, real days off in the summer. He could take lunch and breaks with Laura every day; they could even car pool in the morning. There'd be some customer complaints to deal with, but that's no different than the farmers' market. "What am I still doing picking tomatoes? I'm a college graduate," he whispers to himself. He could have a normal life…like everyone else.

By three in the afternoon the crew, drained from heat and humidity, works to secure the newly harvested boxes to the trailer. They're all driven by that smell of a day nearly complete, only needing to take the load to Ian's homemade cold storage. Jonathan throws lines of rope over the stacked boxes when Ian walks up behind him.

"You need to go to the shed and get the bin trailers ready. Take them to the Brittany Lanes, we're going to pack peaches tomorrow."

"We just picked those things two days ago Ian; they're going to be too green to get more than twenty bins. We should give them another day."

"I don't want to go in there either, but this patch is going to need picking again in two days with this heat. The Spring Flares are getting close, and I'm afraid if we're not careful we'll fall behind, especially with the labor shortage. We're not going to be getting any more crews this year." Ian pulls a bent cigarette from his pocket and lights it. "I'd rather deal with a little green tomorrow than fruit rotting all over the ground in two days."

Looking over his shoulder at the green field it's hard to imagine that in two days it will be painted red again with ripe tomatoes. Still, if Ian says the next pick will be ready, then it will. Covered in sweat and feeling faint, the sight of an acre of relieved tomato vines causes a soothing feeling to wash over him. The white string that strained to hold the loaded vines at dawn now hangs lax without the weight of ripe fruit. A modest feat, but the freshly reaped patch of tomatoes is his accomplishment.

Jonathans attention returns to Ian and something far less inspiring. Not that Ian's dying or even sick. For a fifty year old man with a lifetime of manual labor under his belt, most would say he's doing well. But there are more rings surround the eyes than Jon's used to seeing so early in the harvest. He gets tired, even the youngest get tired; but Ian has never been this tired in June.

"Well, if we have to pick then I guess we pick."

Something in his nephew's tone snaps Ian out of his malaise. "Come on, where's the spirit."

"I gotta go help Marty finish moving into his new place tonight. It's taken up the last three nights of my life. I'll probably end up getting three hours of sleep, so I was hoping tomorrow would be short so I could recover a bit."

"Laura going to help?"

"Why would she want to help?"

"Why wouldn't she? Besides, then you won't have to unpack everything. She's good at organizing things."

Jon laughs. "Give Marty's new place a feminine touch."

"You three boys could use some feminine touch." Ian tosses a tin bucket to his nephew. "So Marty's really going back to work for Leo?"

"He already has, started up yesterday."

Ian sighs. "Too bad. It would have been nice for someone to stick it to that son of bitch."

"You don't think Marty acted a little impulsive in quitting?"

"Yeah he did, but sometimes that's a good thing. Especially for a young man." Ian slaps his nephew on the back again. "You could be a little impulsive from time to time Jon." Ian thinks the same thing every time he slaps Jon; maybe it'll knock the old man out of him. There's a time for carrying an old spirit, but his nephew embraces it too readily.

"Yeah, I suppose if I don't, I'll never do my part for the family legacy right?" Jonathan salutes Ian and returns to tightening the ropes. If the load of tomatoes falls over during transport, he doesn't want it to be on account of poorly tied knots. "I'm really tired man, I bet I fall asleep on the road and crash into a power pole."

"There was a Heffron that was killed like that. He fell asleep at the wheel after working a double at the glass plant. Went right into those transformers outside of Dinuba. Knocked out the power for miles around. They say when the fire department pulled the body from the car, all the meat fell off his bones because he'd been cooked all the way through. They had to scoop up his remains with a shovel and bucket."

"Well I guess I'll be OK then. But I still need some sleep."

"Ah, you're young. Try doing this when you're my age." With a hard jerk Ian cinches the last knot and the trailer is ready to go. "I think I'll give you a B+ for the day. You lose points because of your incessant belligerence and poor leadership."

Jonathan looks over at the reddening Sun settling into the western horizon. In a few hours the blue sky will be awash by reds, yellows, purples and blacks as light filters through the dust and clouds. The air will remain hot; a reminder that the sun didn't lose, not really. Overhead, birds have stopped flying as large dragonflies of every color materialize out of nowhere. The insects take flight as the day ends, each darting movement mocking father Suns waning authority.

Chapter VII

The Dwindling Eucalyptus Forests of the San Joaquin

Fads aren't often associated with rural life. They may arrive, but only after being established or forgotten in their places of origin. By the time they get to the country they can no longer be called fads, but outdated examples of the status quo. The existence of a living past is another sign that the people are outsiders; dwellers of forgotten corners of a nation and not fully connected with exciting goings-on at the heart of life.

Other, stranger trends take root in these places. Not as famous as bell-bottom jeans or flannel coats, but they happen. The remnants of them can be seen even a hundred years after they first take root. Long after it was forgotten that Bishop William Taylor introduced the eucalyptus tree to California, the evidence of this fad is still visable across the San Joaquin Valley. The locals call them 'Blue Gums.' Unlike the slow growing pines and oaks of the area, which have excellent wood for many purposes, the Blue Gums rise rapidly in the California climate. All types made for great fuel during the cold and damp Valley winters, and some varieties made for excellent furniture and cabinets. Even many railroad ties that connect northern and southern California are made from the wood of Blue Gums.

Huge groves of the massive trees were planted all over the San Joaquin, as farmers were sure they would corner the market and make a fortune. Soon other uses were discovered. The odor of the trees drove off flies and mosquitoes, and so were planted around horse corals and riversides. Then eucalyptus leaves began to be crushed and processed to extract the oil. The trees were helpful, but like many fads, they were not as valuable as people hoped. Yet the groves still stood. Cutting the trees down and removing their invasive root systems was too expensive for many. The groves were whittled away slowly over the years, but reminders remain.

Chapter VIII

Testy in the Evening

Before the murky water of the Dead Man combines with the San Joaquin River, there's a low spot where the south side of Bodie stands. At one time, when the waterways of the Valley swelled with the spring, Dead Man's River would overflow at this point, flooding hundreds of acres. Flocks of waterfowl congregated there, along with the foxes, hawks and eagles that preyed on them. Cranes and blue herons hunted catfish and bass that flourished in the seasonal marshes. The waters supported fields of Tule reed so high that herds of elk could graze without being seen, and following their scent were packs of wolves and the occasional grizzly bear. On a high spot at the edge of the wetland, a village of Yokut Indians lived for hundreds of years. The village needed the floods; it needed the marsh. It survived on the fish and fowl as much as the grizzlies and wolves did. The Yokuts used the reeds to build boats and homes. They needed the grasses and brush to attract elk, rabbits and deer.

The Europeans that first came to this place needed something different. They needed the soil made rich by centuries of floodwaters. They needed land to graze their cattle and grow their wheat. The fish and fowl were nice, but they were luxuries worth losing for dry land. The predators that came down from the mountains were a threat. The elk were killed, and the reeds were replaced by fences. Where the village once stood, Bodie's first city hall was raised. Later, when the symbolism of have city hall sit on top of the small ridge became unimportant, the town headquarters was moved and an apartment complex was built.

Inhaling deeply, Jonathan smells the memories of the land as distinctly as the paint and plaster of Martin's new apartment. He can see the seasonal marshlands, the herds, and the flocks of birds that sound of thunder when taking flight. He can hear the cattle that came after the marsh vanished, and the shouts of the long dead vaqueros who tended them. Jonathan wonders if the first settlers felt any remorse when they changed the landscape, or were they as unmoved as those charged with tearing down the old hall?

Stretching out on the couch Jonathan cracks his knuckles which have gone numb from a day of hard use. "I don't get how people work nights. It's unacceptable. The dark is for eating, sleeping and sex."

Martin can't help but laugh. "Damn Heffron! You sound like a broken old man. Remember what your uncle always says. 'Don't worry about things you have no control over.'"

"How's that relate to me being tired from a fifteen-hour day? Besides, I haven't fussed half as much as Diego."

Ignoring the comment, Diego leans against the wall picturing the day that might have been. He can feel that wonderful contrast of blazing sun against cool mountain air. He closes his eyes and the perfectly rounded granite domes surrounding Cartwright Reservoir appear on the horizon. Pine dominates and wind rushes down the ridges surrounding the water. The thought of fresh trout grilled with pepper and lemon makes Diego's stomach growl. In the mountains, watching rays of light dance across the water, he might have washed down his meal with a cool beer.

Instead, he shadowed Martin down the twisted walkways of the flea market looking for that hidden gem. Diego looks again at the unidentified marks that pepper the couches upholstery; peculiar stains guaranteeing he'll never sit on the couch. Martin hasn't stopped talking about how lucky it was to find that old gray lounge chair.

"Marty listen to me, that thing is not a great find. It's not worth the fifty you paid for it. It's a filthy piece of shit. I'm begging you, do not say another word about that chair." Diego speaks through gritted teeth and aching belly.

Martin runs his fingers across the small rectangular coffee table like it's a prized example of antique art. The missing pane of glass at its center might as well be part of the pieces charm. He did manage to find a very stylish pair of vanilla colored lamps in the shape of rearing stallions, but they need rewiring.

Diego stares at the lamps and asks, "You know this stuff is all shit right?"

"This is coming from the guy who drives that rusty green hunk of garbage parked outside."

Puffing himself up, Diego retorts, "Fastest car in Bodie asshole, and you'll never drive it again."

Jonathan listens to Martin intently, the way an intern at a museum might listen to the chief curator giving a lecture on the buildings contents. Dark bags underscore the farmboy's eyes and he moves with hesitance of a man in pain. Still with that small smile and vacant stare, Jon doesn't look bothered by the fact that he should be asleep, instead of feigning interest in Martin's tour of garbage.

"It was a good haul Heffron, but I gotta say there's something about that flea market. It's a feeling that attaches like a parasite. You don't know how it got there, and you didn't see it till it's too late. By the time we left I wanted to kill someone," Marty says while falling into his stained couch.

Jonathan shifts in his seat. "You got to pay for progress." It starts as a simple twitch in the corners of his mouth. Quickly a small smile becomes that all too familiar grin. "I can see that first Spanish colonists standing at the border of the marsh all those years ago; staring out over the clean water stocked with fish and teaming with birds and elk. Then panning to see a thriving village of Indians with small children playing in reed canoes. After some time taking in the majesty of it all, it came like a shot. 'You know what needs to be built here… Garbage! Look at these poor, lost, primitive people swimming, hunting and living in perfect harmony with the land around them. Don't they see that the trees, animals and free flowing water are in the way of progress.' So they did what any of us would have done. They burned down the village in the name of God, dammed up the river, and drained the marsh so in a hundred years they could build a parking lot dedicated to the selling trash."

"Yeah," Diego says, "your people think you know everything, and all you've done is fucked the world up. What, because a white man invented the light bulb it makes up for every other fuckup in history?" Diego leans back into the nearest dining room chair, shifting his weight in a vain search for comfort.

"Like I said Diego, that's progress for you. Trying to deny it would be nothing short of avoiding duty."

What would Jon have felt his duty was if he'd been the one stumbling over the old man in Tijuana? Would Jonathan Heffron have said anything after seeing the look of shock on the man's face? "I'm not responsible for any shit thing this town has done and I'm not responsible for the way people behave at the flea market. I suppose I'm not responsible for anything but my fucking self." Diego feels a cool sense of calm wash over him that he has not felt since before Tijuana.

"You know who you sound like Diego."

"I don't give a fuck."

"You sound like someone who wants to believe something other than what he knows is right," Jon says with a salute.

Diego stares out the window into the thick air of the Bodie night. He can see the glow of the flea market shooting up in the distance and in that very instant some maintenance worker eager to get home flicks a switch and the sky goes black.

"You know Jon, we've been friends a long time, you really need to let all that philosophical shit you got from your dad lay to rest."

Jonathan rises from the couch, and it's the look in his eyes that brings it all back. Diego should get out of the way, and he knows it, but all he can do is think about Bodie Beach after Jonathan's last game on the high school basketball team.

Nothing but a small sand bar littered with driftwood and beer bottles, the beach always had a mystical feel, especially that night. Diego remembers cold, but there was nothing special about cold in the Valley winter. A blue moon hung in the sky, speckling the ground with eerie shadows as the glow shown through willow branches that strangled the Dead Man's banks. More than anything, Diego remembers the smell. January in the San Joaquin Valley always smelled the way water tastes, but on that night Diego remembers how that familiar crisp scent was replaced by the sour aroma of an old ice box.

Jonathan arrived late, and walked directly to Martin without acknowledging anyone. He had a typical content look in his eyes, but talked to himself more noticeably than usual. Diego saw him but Martin spoke first. "Hey Heffron, why you shaking?"

"No hot water in the gym after eight o'clock. Now, on top of everything else, I'm freezing."

"Oh. That's too bad."

"What is it?"

Martin started rubbing the back of his neck. "Well, you know that the friend I was telling you about..."

"The one I have to spend the night entertaining while you're off hooking up with some other girl."

"Yeah, well I just met her. She's kind of... annoying"

"Oh this is too perfect," Jonathan grumbled.

"I'm really sorry man, but Jacqueline was so cool that I figured she'd have cool friends.

"You figured she'd have cool friends? What planet do you come from Martin! When have you ever known a group of cool girls to hang together? If you meet a great girl she invariably has surrounded herself with friend's who can only be described as; Oh who cares."

Standing on the banks of the Dead Man Marty waited for Jonathan to stop talking when he answered, "Look man, I'm really sorry but I need you to take one for the team alright."

"I took one for the team tonight and we lost by thirty."

Martin frowned. "What do you mean by that?"

"I mean if I spend the whole night talking to this idiot, and you don't get laid, then I'm never doing a favor for you again. Even Laura said this is stupid."

"That's because she's jealous. You should just ask her out already."

"You know what Marty, that's a good idea. Maybe I'll go right now, and you can deal with this yourself." Jonathan kicked at the dirt in a questioning manner. He always toed at the ground this way, like the dirt might somehow save him.

Diego wonders if he'd been a more responsible friend, maybe things would have been different. All he had to do was head of Eddy Messi before he got to him.

"Hey Jon," Eddy said, "Go get some more wood for the fire. I figured you probably have a lot of energy left over from the game."

Jonathan lunges across Martin's living room, and Diego can't imagine turning away, but that night on Bodie Beach he did. How many times did Eddy tease Jon, even insult the Heffron family and Jon ignored it every time? So that frigid night, Diego turned away, back to his date standing on the banks of the Dead Man, and he didn't turn back until the sound of Jon's fists meeting Eddy's face cracked through night.

In a flash Jonathan pinned the star of the Bodie High Varsity Basketball team to the sand, using his left forearm to hold down Eddy's head, while he rained punches with his right hand. Diego was one of the first to rush over, but it was Martin who pulled Jonathan off. Marty didn't get there before Eddy's jaw snapped forcing him to miss the rest of the season. Bodie won no more games that year, and Jon was kicked off the team.

Those same massive arms that freed Eddy from further beating now restrain an irate Jon Heffron a few feet from Diego.

Diego looks at Jonathan's flushed face and shaking limbs. He can see every muscle in the farm boy's body is tensed. Even so, Diego looks in Jonathan's eyes and recognizes immediately that even though he's angry, Jon is in complete control. He's frustrated, tired and upset, but the long day of work followed by an evening moving furniture has not overwhelmed him. Jon would like to be fishing too, he'd like to be doing a lot of other things at that moment, but it doesn't matter to him. To Jon Heffron it's just another job.

"You know" Diego leans toward Jonathan as he speaks, "I get so sick of listening to your fucking smart ass comments. The only reason you're pissed is I've just said something you can't use a joke to hide from. You don't say ten minutes of real shit each day. Well guess what; it's time for you to deal with that shit with your father."

"You motherfucker! You think you can get away with that. You think you can say anything you want because of your family. I'll fucking kill you!"

"Calm down Heffron! He's still your friend!" Marty tosses Jonathan back down onto the couch. It's a humbling experience to be so easily controlled. His adrenaline at its highest; he pushes with all his strength, and Martin tossed him aside with one arm.

"Have you even heard a fucking word I..."

Before Diego finishes his sentence, Marty looks at him, raises his eyebrows, and says in a low, authoritative voice, "Quiet. You've said enough." Marty then looks back at Jonathan. "You're tired Heffron, why don't you go home and meet us at My Friend's House for lunch tomorrow."

"I've got work tomorrow." Jonathan turns to Diego. "You want to call that an excuse. Come by the farm if you need proof. Then we can finish our discussion."

Diego still doesn't move; he stands looking into his friend's calm eyes and how they contrast the frantic energy pulsating from every other part of his body. Diego knows this will sting Jon, maybe even ruin their friendship, but he can't help but feel good.

Jon leans in as close as Martin will allow and whispers, "If you ever mention my father again, in any context, you'll wake in the hospital." Jon turns and walks out slamming the door behind him. The windows rattle and a pile of papers on the dining room table fall onto the ground.

"Where did that come from Velarde?"

"I had to say it."

"That was messed up. Just leave him alone when he's tired." Marty takes a large swig of beer. "Hell of a way to open my new apartment. What's been the matter with you lately?"

Diego reaches into his pocket trying to find his phone, which rests on the pavement of the empty Bodie Flea Market. Even now it buzzes causing birds and rats to hurry back to the safety of the nearby river. Only the mother coyote, who keeps her den under an old sycamore is attracted by the strange blue glow and vibrations of the phone. She approaches slowly, taping the phone with her front paw. The glowing stops, and the phone rests. After a moment she licks it and decides it's nothing of value.

She walks toward the small pole shed at the center of the parking lot. She stops periodically as a scent catches her nose, but more often than not she leaves it behind. Four litters raised along the flea market, and some of the spoils she's brought back have proven poisonous. She gets to the side of the pole shed, digging through a knocked over trash can when the bright lights of an approaching car startle her. She quickly grabs a hotdog on the ground before darting back to the riverside where she stops and watches.

A door opens and someone steps out. The mother coyote puts her prize down and sniffs it. It's not enough, but the intruder will leave soon, so she waits. She watches as the figure in the dark opens the trunk and pulls out a box that rattles with the sound of rolling paint cans. Then a stepladder is pulled out and placed against the side of the pole shed. This strange figure climbs back into the car and the lights brighten, illuminating the rusting side of the building. She sniffs at the air, searching for some scent to explain the purpose of the stranger. After some time, she smells the sharp stench of wet paint and the sound of heavy breathing. The mother picks up the gnarled hotdog, taking it back to her hungry pups, hoping the foraging grounds will be free when she returns.

Chapter IX

As Good Time to Kill a Dentist

On July nineteenth 1889 a small mining town gathered around a hastily constructed gallows on Main Street. Dawn burst over the Sierra Nevada Mountains, transforming the condemned man from an insignificant shadow to an imposing silhouette rising in judgment over the crowd. All stood motionless, watching with quiet respect, but not mercy. It was an illegal killing, but justifiable. The man would hang for murdering the town dentist, who five days earlier had been removing the decayed tooth of a small boy. An opium addict, the dentist slipped, stabbing the boy in the back of the mouth. Lost in an opium-induced stupor he could do nothing but stand by helplessly and watch the boy die.

It was Ulysses Dougherty, by that time an old man, who informed Samuel Heffron that his son was dead. "Listen to me Samuel, I'm going to go arrest that son of a bitch dentist and put him on trial for negligence. I promise he will be punished."

Samuel stared at the plank floor his son helped him build to replace the dirt they had lived on for four years. He thought of the noise made as the boy chased his little sisters across the floor in play. Something about knowing that he'd never again hear the sound made him feel like innocence had left the world forever.

"I'm sorry sheriff, but if that's what you came here to say then you need to arrest me now." Sheriff Dougherty and Samuel Heffron sat in quiet for hours. The old farmer tried to picture every detail of his son, afraid the memories might disappear by morning. Across from him, on an old Victorian chair the Heffrons brought from New Mexico, the sheriff gazed out the window, questioning his duty for the second time.

Ulysses rose without speaking a word. He walked out of the farmhouse but stopped in the doorway and took a final look at Samuel. "I'm sorry things turned out like this for you Heffron."

The next morning the dentist was found with his throat cut. Samuel Heffron turned himself in, was found guilty of murder, and sentenced to hang. The good sheriff presided over the affair, but never in those four days did he look at Samuel Heffron. Even as Ulysses stood on the gallows reading Samuel Heffron's crimes to the citizens of Bodie, Sherriff Dougherty would not look at the convicted man. The lever was pulled and Samuel Heffron dropped like a stone, but the rope broke. He hit his head on the stage before falling through the hole and onto the ground below. He spent two weeks in a coma.

His deputy's tied Sheriff Dougherty to a desk so he wouldn't beat the gallows builder to death. When Ulysses, learned that Samuel had finally passed, he wept; the only time that an adult member of the Dougherty family cried publicly.

Running his tongue across his teeth, Jon Heffron sits in the waiting room of the towns' only dentist's office. It's been over a century, and none but a few remember the story, but the

Heffron's remember. Jon inhales the smell of fluoride wafting through the air every time a door opens. Trickles of nervous sweat run down the back of Jon's neck and down the sides of his stomach. The perspiration hurries down his side quickly, and he realizes he's lost weight. The sweat hits his pants and disappears. To pass the time Jon leafs through outdated magazines.

Across the waiting room, a weathered old farmer, stares at the carpet either because he's deep in thought, or because his mind is blank. Either way, Jon feels envious. Jon enjoys imagining that this old man, from some unknown farm in the Valley, has managed to achieve enlightenment. The best things happen in the most unsuspecting places according to Ian.

Sporting an old, plaid shirt with shabby blue jeans, this mystic farmer might fail to qualify for a Costco card. His steel-toed boots are caked in dirt and riddled with nicks and cuts. Powerful hands have a calloused, disfigured form that is no longer flesh, but closer to something carved from wood as wild hair falls shoulder length and is mostly gray dotted with brown. Covering his face is thick gray beard hanging to the middle of a wide chest. It's hard to see his mouth through the gray mat, but he may be smiling at times. This man is no mystic; only an farmer enjoying some lost memory.

"Jon Heffron."

Jonathan looks up to see a neatly kept dental assistant standing in the doorway holding a clipboard. He follows Gwyneth into one of the examination rooms.

"What are you getting done today, Mr. Heffron?" Gwyneth says as she holds out her arm to indicate what room to enter.

"I'm past due on a cleaning."

It's a typical dentist office, with white walls, bright lights and a small counter, neatly stocked with the various tools and chemicals of the trade. At the end of the counter is a small white trash can with a flip top and a hazardous material sticker on its side. Jon looks at the painting of a tranquil summer landscape no doubt meant to calm nervous patients. The signature at the bottom right hand corner reads S. Dougherty. His father owned a Sienna Dougherty painting. They're worth money, but Jon can't help but judge this particular piece underwhelming. Over the chair stands a large boom arm with the largest light ever used to illuminate such a small area. Thousands of watts to brighten the inside of the mouth. While trying to get comfortable, Jonathan elbows the empty tray to his right. In a few moments it'll be full of bloody tissues and dirty tools.

"You know, I've got an afternoon meeting with our congressional representative."

"Really!"

"I'm going to try to get him to fund the building of a giant black marble phallus in the center of town to commemorate Bodie's past as a haven for prostitution. The ancient Norse believed the phallus was the symbol of Frey, the god of fertility."

"Is that true?"

"Sure. I wouldn't go before a state representative and ask for a giant black wang in the center of town without doing my research."

She snaps on a pair of gloves. "What happened to the days of the quiet, gentlemanly small town people of Bodie?" Gwyneth laughs.

"If you ever took the time to read the history of Bodie, you'd know that those days never existed."

"OK sweetheart. Open wide. I'm going to stick this in your mouth. It's a kind of solvent. It'll make it easier to get the plaque off your teeth. I'll come back in a few minutes to take it off."

Jonathan concentrates on the sound of her stride as she hurries down the hall. He listens carefully as Gwyneth reenters the waiting room. He imagines the position of the door based on the pitch of the squeaking lower hinge. Gwyneth then guides the old farmer into the other examination room, her long step falling into perfect harmony with the man's waddle; like the slow thump of a bass drum accompanied by a quick tap of a cymbal.

"Come in here Mr. Kagan, and take a seat." Listening again, Jon hears Gwyneth undergo the same procedure with Mr. Kagan.

Jonathan represses the sudden urge to regurgitate the small amounts of pink paste that slide down the back of his throat. He controls the reflex, refocusing on the sound of the butcher paper wrinkling as Mr. Kagan settles into his seat.

"So Mr. Kagan, what's the occasion for a June cleaning? Our records show you weren't supposed to come in for another few months." The voice isn't Gwyneth's; it's too sultry. It must be Caroline.

"I've got a meeting today."

The slight tremble in Mr. Kagan's voice helps Jonathan paint a picture of the old man's face. His hidden smile instantly transformed to a sorrowful frown with a hint of fear. That gray beard betrays nothing, but Jonathan imagines he'd recognize the change. Mr. Kagan's already hunched over features sink further into the tan dentist chair forcing Caroline to reposition the lights overhead.

"Who's your meeting with?" Caroline asks.

"The bank." The brightness in Mr. Kagan's eyes deadens completely now and his voice drops to something above a whisper.

"Ouch. I hate going to the bank. I do as much of my banking through the ATM or the phone. I've even heard that the internet is a good place to do your banking, but I don't get computers."

The sudden crash of the instrument tray striking the tile floor makes Jon's heart skip a beat. The violent noise is followed by the distinct sound of Mr. Kagan lunging forward in his seat, but not rising from it.

"I don't know what I'm going to do."

Jonathan hears the soft whimper of the old man and knows what it means. It's not some obnoxious cry or angry howl. Jon remembers when he and Martin as kids playing together and Martin told him that his parents were getting divorced. Then he began to cry. Martin barely made a sound, but tears rolled down his checks, and Jonathan knew his friend was scared all the way to the bone. Mr. Kagan probably hasn't felt this way since his own childhood, but Jonathan can see the tears roll down until they disappear into his beard.

A door opens down the hall, and Dr. Armstrong hurries from his office to the room where Mr. Kagan cries and Caroline remains motionless, sifting through her training to find some reference that might help.

"What did you do Caroline? You were supposed to give him a simple cleaning."

"I didn't do anything Dr. Armstrong. I was just about to begin, and he started crying."

Caroline and Dr. Armstrong look down at Mr. Kagan hunched over in his chair. For his part, Mr. Kagan continues to cry quietly, but through his tears Jonathan can hear his barely audible phrases. "It's all I know. This bank turns me down and I lose everything. Who'd hire me? I can't do anything but run my farm." Mr. Kagan just rocks back and forth softly in his seat. "I couldn't get a job on someone else's place; I wouldn't be any good at it. I wouldn't know the land! There are so many things to know about that place, it's taken me a lifetime to learn. Whoever buys the place won't know. Won't care either."

"Someone will buy it and pull every tree. Every building on the place will be torn down to make room for more orchards. Our pond will probably get backfilled. Everything I've ever built will be erased in a month. Nobody will ever even know that I worked that land. My whole life…gone."

Jonathan can feel Mr. Kagan blush as he realizes what's happened. The leather seat begins to make noise again as Mr. Kagan climbs out of his seat.

"I'm sorry bout that." Getting down on his knees, he helps Caroline gather the contents of the fallen tray. "Do you think we can do this another time Dr. Armstrong?"

"Um… yeah. Talk to the secretary up front, and she'll reschedule you."

"I'm sorry I wasted your time today Dr. Armstrong."

"It's not a problem Mr. Kagan."

Jonathan turns to look at the old farmer leaving the examination room. Jon gives the smallest of smiles, one meant to convey, 'None of these people understand a thing of what you just said. But I do.' Even with his thick beard Jonathan can tell Mr. Kagan is returning with his own small smile saying, 'thank you.'

The burning sensation on his gums has now become unbearable. Jon looks up at the wall clock to see the time for him to spit has passed.

"Oh, I'm sorry Jon. Here, suck on this tube." Gwyneth, eyes red but not crying, hands Jonathan a thin white suction tube that he chews desperately trying to get rid of the torturing flavor.

Loud knocks of wingtip shoes fills the room. "Well Mr. Heffron, you come to us on an eventful day."

Jonathan opens his mouth, wanting to point out the inappropriate attitude Dr. Armstrong's taken toward Mr. Kagan's shattered world. That old man is losing everything, and to laugh it off as nothing more than the mornings entertainment is sinful. Jon Heffron wants to say this, but the suction tube holds his mouth closed like a gag.

"Gwyneth please hand me the…" but before finishing his sentence she snatches a small metal hook from the instrument tray and hands it to him. "Alright Mr. Heffron, I want you to keep that suction tube so whenever you feel you need to spit just bite down." Taking the tube in his hand, Jon thinks about Mr. Kagan and what he might have said if he had heard the good dentist's comment. Would he understand that Dr. Armstrong's attitude is a result of coming from a world where occupation and identity don't mix?

"Open wide Mr. Heffron, and lean your head all the way back."

"You really need to come in more often Jon," Gwyneth says. "You're going to have problems later in life if you don't have your teeth cleaned every six months. Plus it makes this whole experience worse."

"Ah-ha."

"You're a farmer aren't you Mr. Heffron?" asks Dr. Armstrong.

"Ah-ha."

"I have quite a few clients in Agriculture."

Why do people always talk to him about agriculture? Agriculture has nothing to do with farming. Agriculture is something you study in school. You learn farming by going to the field and doing it. Agriculture is a job. Farming's a way of life. Agriculture means managing the land, while farming means working it. He considers pointing this out when a sharp sting to his gums and the subsequent jerk of the head distracts him.

"Now try not to move Jon." Gwyneth says.

The grinding from the metal hooks made his whole head shake. "Ah-ha."

"From what I hear it's been pretty tough out there lately. How are you guys doing?"

If ever there was a question fit for agriculture, that's it. Are you still hanging on, that's a question for a farmer. Looking up Jonathan wants to see something of Bodie in the man. The dentist has worked in the town for three years, and nothing has rubbed off. Still, maybe he could understand if these damn hooks are removed. He can explain all this to Dr. Armstrong and the man would understand. Suctioning some more spit from his mouth Jon answers, "Oh-Ha."

"That's good. Gwyneth hand me a swab please." In a reflection of his protective goggles Jon watches his teeth get scrapped clean of a year and a half worth of buildup.

"You can see what I'm doing can't you?"

"Ah-ha."

"Well I guess I better not mess up", he laughs. "Do you know Mr. Kagan well?"

"Ah-ah."

"It's too bad isn't it, to see a man broken down like. Maybe it's for the best. At least this way the man can move on. He's well into his sixties, and still out there working long hours in the sun. Then he goes trudging through the mud, rain and cold in the winter. It'll be a difficult adjustment I know, but when he gets past the initial shock of change, he'll find things much easier for him. Please use the suction real quick Mr. Heffron."

Gwyneth cleans drool from the side of Jon's face and says, "Oh it'll be much better. I hate to see that poor old man come

92

in here, tired and worn out. he's done his part, now he should be enjoying his golden years."

Like a fish with a lure in his mouth Jonathan jerks his head, embedding the dentists hook in the roof of his mouth.

"Don't move Mr. Heffron! Just stay still while I pull it out." A sharp pull and the hook is removed. "That's why you have to stay still while I'm working."

The long flat stick used to keep his tongue from the wound transforms into a straight jacket. Dr. Armstrong could remove the device and let him speak, it would only take a minute and it wouldn't change the outcome, but they can't even give him this, and who needs such distraction. Better to scrape away the rough spots, wash away the unsightly discolorations, and demand he remain quiet in his discomfort. Ian, Mr. Kagan and himself need only stay in the past, condemned to silently watch the movements of the present.

"Aw 'ush or?" Jonathan mutters as a small trickle of blood runs down the back of his throat causing him to cough.

"A few more moments. We'd be done if you could keep still. You also need to keep your mouth open wider Mr. Heffron." Dr. Armstrong snaps. The man continues to work in silence for a few minutes. "You know Jon, maybe your uncle could hire Mr. Kagan, just part time. Nothing too difficult, only something to keep him busy. I'm sure you could find something for him. Think of it as giving back to the community?"

Perhaps Dr. Armstrong severed a vital nerve while stabbing the roof of Jon's mouth. Perhaps he is dying. No, the Heffron's have already suffered one death by dentist. As panic subsides Jonathan thinks about what Armstrong said. Give back to the community. Back to the community? Is it even possible, to give back to a community your family helped to create.

Casually grabbing the scalpel sitting on the tray, he tongues the wound again and repeats that phrase in his head. You can give back to the community, Jon.

A spray of blood covers Jonathan's face. He holds the terrified dentist in place with the scalpel now imbedded in his neck. With each beat of the heart another spurt splashes him in the face, but Jon doesn't flinch. Staring into Armstrong's eyes, Jon demands understanding in these final moments. Dr. Armstrong must know that he is going to die, not because of some senseless act of violence, but as justice for a crime committed. He's dying for taking Bodie away from his family and for taking it away from people like Mr. Kagan. Dr. Armstrong will die for coming here, and failing to respect who he is and what the town means to the people who carved it from the Valley soil.

"What was that you said Gwen? That Mr. Kagan will be better off without his land? That now he'll be able to enjoy himself?"

With a twitch of his arm Jonathan sticks the scalpel through her eye and she drops to the ground. Leaning back in his chair and closing his eyes, Jon imagines himself on the gallows, noose around his neck, waiting to be hung for the murder of a dentist. All of Bodie watches but no matter how hard he concentrates, Jon can't picture any of the faces in the crowd as respectful or understanding. Jon focuses but can't make the people in his dream look the way he wants. There is no sympathy, no understanding. Nothing but blankness.

Jonathan jerks his head again. "I told you not to move Mr. Heffron. You're going to end up in the emergency room."

"Please spit again Jon."

Chapter X

Amusing Fate

Sporting a stoic smile Ian, flicks a smoldering cigarette at the nearest interloper. For Gabriel it was a sack of sweating dynamite, for him a plague of goats. Pulling a peach from the branches overhead, he looks out at the horde devouring his tomato crop. He slices the peach using the pocketknife his father bought in San Francisco after the war.

The west side of the farm could always be counted on for good peaches. Over the decades four different orchards stood on that spot, and they all stood out. Closing his eyes, concentrating on the flavor but there's only goats; hundreds of them getting fatter by the second, their faces smeared with tomato innards.

He remembers his father, old Charlie Heffron, talking about the red fire brought on by overuse of DDT following World War Two. The birds fell from the sky whenever they sprayed. Later came the plague of mite, the tiny spider that found itself atop the food chain, living in a world free of predators. Overnight, the vineyards looked as though someone had taken a blowtorch to them, the whole Valley burned to a crisp by a microscopic plague.

As the last tomatoes disappear into bloated bellies, Ian thinks of the other story of Dad's life. The day Charlie came out of vineyard in front of the house with his cane cutters flashing. Ian remembers his mother's crimson blood filling the tire tracks, and the paleness of her severed leg. He can hear the helpless tone of his father's last words to her. "How many times have I told you to leave the canes alone till I get done?"

A cloud of dust envelops Ian, and he looks at his wristwatch. Ten minutes have passed since he called his nephew promising one of the greatest spectacles in the history of the Heffron farm.

"I've told you not to kick dust up?" His cigarette slips from between his finger and falls into the still wet irrigation ditch at his feet. "DAMN'IT!" He pulls out another and lights it quickly.

"Where the fuck did these things come from?" Jonathan shouts, blinking uncontrollably.

"God if your mother found out how filthy I let your mouth become, she'd never forgive me." Ian takes another drag and points at the goats with his burning cigarette. "It's the eleventh plague."

"Ian, how did this happen!"

"One of Joe Kapresians younger brothers is a trucker. He was running a load of goats up to Sacramento and stopped off for a rest. Last night one of Joe's kids snuck out for a look. They opened the doors to the trailer, and the goats got out."

"What time did this happen?"

"They don't know. The kids were scared and ran back into the house without saying anything. Joe came across these things about five minutes before I showed up to turn on the water."

"What are we gonna do about this Ian?"

Ian watches a pair of goats pass within a few feet of them, a mother with a kid in tow. He sighs again before pulling out a new Marlboro and lighting it. From behind the vale of smoke Ian watches Jon shift back and forth in his stance, unable to process the joke of it all.

"I guess I thought it would be funny in way."

"Ian…"

"This is my farm and I don't want you worrying about it anymore. You'll be teaching soon, so the time has come for you to stop letting this place dominate your life. I admit, it would have been nicer if you'd learned this another way, but most of the time you don't get to choose the vessels our lessons travel on." Staring back at the lit cigarette between his fingers hoping to decipher some augury in the rising smoke and falling ash.

"You going to Diego's party tonight?"

"Ya, so what?"

"Go have a good time."

The lines of Ian's face look drawn on while his hair and thick mutton chop sideburns are unkempt, their grayish brown shine, dulled. Those gray-blue eyes don't sparkle the same way even as his ears glow red. Ian has gained weight and looks less healthy for it. Even the small twitching of his right eye, the one he's had since the minor stroke five years ago has grown more noticeable.

Ian drags his cigarette until his chest burns. "You kids grew up too fast, and it's made you all too serious. It's something me and your dad always regretted."

"I can't believe you're going to bring my dad up right now. You should be pissed Ian! You can't stand there and do nothing."

Finally taking his eyes off the bloated goats and looking at his nephew, "I'm sorry I brought this to your attention the way I did. I should've thought about how'd you'd take it, but I don't need any of your shit today Jonathan. Especially any backlash because of unresolved issues you have with your father."

When Gabriel sat at the kitchen table, revealing that they would have to sell his farm, that's the only thing that compared. It happened in the living room in the month of October. The days had begun to cool, retiring the air conditioner until spring. The Sun hung low, and the living room was partially shaded by the Sycamore in the back yard. Those comfortable days were a perfect contrast to standing with Ian under that stifling peach orchard, and yet the scent in the air, the weight of the moment, and the look on Ian and Gabriel's faces were identical.

Jonathan remembers how angry his mother had been when Gabriel walked in. It was obvious he'd been smoking, but when he explained she became despondent. It was her job to motivate, to make sure dad always kept his feet moving, but on that day Yvonne Heffron sat across from her husband saying nothing.

Neither of them spoke so Jonathan took over. "There's more fruit out there than I've ever seen. It's a miracle the hail didn't touch the vineyard, or the persimmons for that matter. If we can get them in we'll be in good shape."

"Prices are in the toilet Jonathan. Unless it jumps by two dollars a box in the next week, we're done." He kept wiping his forehead like something itched.

"So, there's still a chance. No point in getting all down yet." Why did he get so angry? His father earned the right to be pitied, if only for an evening. Usually fate has the courtesy of varying the manner of catastrophe, but hail three years in a row? Frost, worms, even locust should have played a part in the downfall. The pharaoh suffered ten plagues for his sins. God found Gabriel Heffron worthy of only one.

Gabriel coughed that familiar cough. "It's over Jon! The price never goes up this time of year. If anything, it'll drop another dollar by the time the last boxes are shipped."

"Fine, if you're going to give up then the hell with it. I guess I shouldn't bother waking up tomorrow." Jonathan jumped to his feet and left his parents alone in the living room. Gabriel and Yvonne sat quietly staring at each other for some time.

Lying on his bed down the hall, Jonathan heard Gabriel rise from the table, and change sullenly down to the master bedroom. Stopping in front of his son's door the failed farmer might have been thinking a million things and Jonathan imagines all of them. He thinks of how his father looked on the other side of that door. He wore that stained pair of brown overalls and work boots; the soles just starting to peel back at the heels. Jonathan pictures Gabriel's watery eyes and weathered hands examining the picture of father and son hanging next to door. Maybe Dad wanted to scold him for being disrespectful. He may have wanted to hear his son say he was sorry and everything was going to be all right. Worst of all, he might have wanted to sit quietly together. That wouldn't have been bad, but the man never came in. He stood on the other side of that door, alone with his thoughts. He raised his fist to knock before dropping it down again. When he walked toward his room and lit a cigarette; it might as well have been the sound of a nail in a coffin.

Jonathan stands looking at Ian and somehow knows that it's how Gabriel looked on the other side of that door. "You're right Ian, I shouldn't cuss so much." Hesitating for a moment, he reaches out and pats his uncle on the shoulder before turning toward his car, not looking back.

Jonathan starts his engine, and carefully idles over the dirt road before accelerating onto the pavement. With the conviction of a dying man seeking salvation he heads for the Giant Potato Grocery Store, housed in a large cement building three miles from Bodie, marooned in the center of an old vineyard. Jonathan needs to see a smiling face, and hoping to erase the image of his uncle's mournful grin. The tires of the little Honda lift off the ground, and the whole vehicle pulls left as it bounces into the lot. Jonathan parks far from the store and strolls across the blacktop turned gray with the dust of the Valley.

Laura Theroux's 46' Willy's Jeep is parked in its customary spot under the street lamp. It's the Jeep her father built for the son he never had. She wanted an Acura, but how could she break the man's heart? Even when they spoke about it in the seclusion of Jon's apartment, she would murmur her hatred of that Jeep, fearing her father might learn the truth. Laura almost cried when she related the hangdog expression on his face when asked to sell the Willy's for something that could drive faster than twenty-five without the risk rolling over.

He walks faster as pins and needles assault the side of his neck. It's a privilege and a burden, knowing the significance in every subtle movement of another person. The slight lifting of an eyebrow means she's angry. The way Laura tightens her lips before she's going to cry. The best is the way she cracks the knuckles of her thumbs when jealous. These things might go unnoticed to anyone other than Jon Heffron. Hopefully there won't be any craning of the neck when he tells about how he spoke to Ian. Angry and sad are one thing, but disappointed is too much.

Jon enters the store to find Laura talking to an elderly gentleman at her check stand. Without taking the smile off her face Laura puts her hazel hair back into her ponytail. The old ladies talk about Laura's hair as a wasted opportunity. Some of the most beautiful locks the town has ever seen and she keeps them confined in a simple rubber band. Jon once thought the same thing, but the more people criticize it, the more he loves that ponytail.

She's wearing her favorite jeans. Some of these tears have held for years without getting bigger, like the possibility of abandoning Laura is frightening. Her simple tank tops are changed almost monthly, though nobody ever notices. Once a year she buys one pair of sandals that are worn even in the depth of winter, and one pair of sunglasses that she wears for a week before breaking it.

"I'm really sorry sir, but there isn't anything I can do. If you like I can get the manager but I'm afraid that he'll tell you the same thing." Her real smile would brighten the mood of the angry old man.

Instead he frowns, shifting his weight like he's stiff after a long flight. "Well, I would like to hear it from him for myself."

Laura continues to argue politely with the older man, who in turn grows more and more agitated, until the manager arrives.

"Good afternoon sir. How can I help you today?"

"Well, what I've been trying to explain to this young lady is that I bought this milk on Monday and it wasn't supposed to go bad until tomorrow, but smell it and tell me it's drinkable."

The store manager lifts the carton of milk to his nose and inhales a deep breath. He studies the carton critically, then smells it again. The manager put the carton down, saying in an authoritative tone, "I don't smell anything odd sir. Did you taste it?"

"Are you kidding me? Drink that stuff and I'll end up on the damn crapper for a week. You want to do that?"

"Do I want to do what?"

"Do you want to sit on the crapper for a damn week?"

The manager doesn't move. "Well, no sir I sure don't, and I don't want you to either. I'm simply saying that there's no smell, and the expiration date clearly says the milk is alright through tomorrow."

"I don't care what that stupid date says. I'm telling you that milk is no good."

Moving to the back end of the counter, Jonathan taps on Laura's shoulder

"Another pleasant day interacting with the wonderful people of Bodie." Laura whispers into Jonathan's ear as she gives him his customary hug. She gives great hugs.

"Who is that guy?"

"He's a relative of the Smiths. A retired businessman from Fresno who moved down here to be closer to his grandchildren."

"Maybe he just went to the flea market," Jonathan half whispers to himself.

"What?"

"Oh, just something Marty said to me the other night. So, what do you think about going to Diego's?" Jonathan asks.

"You came here to ask me that?"

"Yeah."

"What's wrong Jonathan?"

He lied to everyone for weeks; insisting he was all right. He mourned his parents, but he was coping. He never cried, his eyes never watered, his voice never quivered. Then, sitting under a guava tree on his father's farm, hours before it would be sold to a big packing outfit from the south side of the Valley, Laura asked how he was doing. Jon said he was fine in a practiced tone that had become second nature. She put his hand on his wrist and asked again. For the first time since his parents were killed, he cried.

That day, Jon found freedom in honesty. Not honest without being judged, for Laura certainly judges, but feeling free to accept the verdicts without resentment or offense. Even more refreshing is that once she lays down her decision, no matter how unsympathetic, he will feel free to accept it and still love her.

When he finishes talking she looks at him, raises her thin eyebrows and says, "You shouldn't have talked to Ian like that."

"I know."

She looks back at the old man still arguing about the milk. "You need to go apologize to Ian tonight, and ask him what you can do to help. That's all you can do. You should have known better after what happened between you and your dad."

"I know, but not tonight. Tonight I want you to come to Diego's with me."

"You never even apologized to Diego for attacking him did you?"

"No, but it'll be alright."

"You have too many forgiving people in your life Jon Heffron. It's spoiled you."

"Including you?"

Laura rolls her eyes, looking away.

"Do you work tomorrow?" Jon asks.

"Yes, and that's why I can't go to one of Diego's parties. Last time we went to Diego's house we didn't go to sleep until the Sun came up." Jonathan remembers seeing a drunk Laura dancing in the bed of Martin's truck. "I was hungover for two days."

"Come for an hour. We'll leave whenever you want. Plus, it would mean a lot to Diego, the party's for his grandparents' wedding anniversary."

"You sure Diego's going to be alright with you there?"

"That got blown out of proportion. You know how Bodie is. Everything's fine."

Laura turns to see how things are going with her manager and Mr. Smith. "I'll meet you there after work, but I'm taking the Jeep because you won't want to leave. Now go buy some champagne and give it to the Velarde's from the two of us."

"None of the Velarde's drink champagne, Laura."

"Jon, don't argue."

He buys a bottle of champagne destined sit in the Velarde fridge for months before ending up in the garbage. Walking toward the exit, the automatic door opens, and Jonathan finds himself staring at a Labrador/Collie mix followed by a collection of common mutts. They all stop in unison looking at him curiously without betraying their intentions. Valley dirt falls from their thin summer coats, making little piles on the clean linoleum floors of the Big Potato. This could be his moment to take his place in the family legacy. Jonathan Heffron, mauled by a pack of dogs in a grocery store.

Chapter XI

Only Temptation Remaining

There are people, maybe no more than a handful, who understand the benefits of sanctuary. Such a refuge is a gift; and like all great gifts those who possess them scarcely realize their luck. A hitch appears when one succumbs to temptation, transforming the sanctuary into a self-made prison. It's the monster Jon created, all the while knowing better. So often running from crisis, retreating to the Heffron farm and avoiding problems under the guise of sacrificing for the family livelihood. Instead of providing a brief reprieve to collect his thoughts, the cover of the land becomes a cultivator of denial.

Marching toward the massive Velarde home, Jon thinks of the opportunities he had to make things right, and every corresponding excuse. The Velarde's lived out of cars and trailers for two years until the massive barn was transformed into something habitable. Enrique tore off the siding, replacing it with fresh pine boards, insulation and sealing the inside with drywall. The bay windows went in next, then Oak double doors, and a sliding glass entry was put in the back. The original roof was replaced with redwood singles and the sides were painted white with emerald trim. He added plumbing, wiring and reinforced the second floor where he put all the bedrooms. Along the outer walls of the ground floor are the bathrooms, a kitchen, storage areas, an office and a one car finished garage. In the center of it all sits the large sunken living room. Due to its placement, there are no windows in the living room, so Enrique cut a large square in the roof and second floor creating the largest skylight in the county. Around the house he raised an enclosed deck that holds it all together, like a moat around a medieval keep.

It's on this deck that Diego talks to his cousins, posturing like a prince giving instructions to an ill-favored vassal. It would be so easy to climb back into the Honda, and return to the land. Better yet, Laura could have left work early to walk in with him. She'd notice him tense up, and watch the sweat start atop his forehead. She'd squeeze his hand in a reprimanding way, leaning in to whisper, 'This is your own fault Jonathan, now stop being a baby.' She'd laugh to hide the scolding. Passing through the gate of the newly finished picket fence surrounding the yard, Jon and notices a missing section.

"Remember me telling you about how that tree got in the way when we were building the fence." It's strange seeing a friend changed, especially when the catalyst is unknown. Jon takes in the transformation imagining what could have happened over eight days that would make him so unsure of himself.

"I doubt I was listening," Jonathan mumbles with that damn smile.

"Fuck off, you remember. Me and dad were building the fence, but when we got to the corner we couldn't sink the post because of the tree roots."

"That's right. You spent half the day sawing through roots just to dig one post hole."

"Well we cut too many roots and the damn tree died. Pissed dad off. Every time he walks by that stump he mumbles about how that was the biggest Digger Pine in the county. He said it was older than Bodie. Anyway it dies, so we hire this guy to come and cut it down. He said it was a combination of the cut roots and the heat wave that killed it.

"We figured he'd get that we'd want it taken down without fucking up that fence, he owns a tree removal service after all. He pulls up with nice equipment, and a truck with all kinds of decals on it, he even had a shirt with the company name across his chest. No need to point out the obvious to a man like that right. You know the company Jon, Hurtado Tree Company."

"Yeah I know them. The owners a drunk, but he's good."

"Well, maybe the booze is catching up with him because if he were sober he wouldn't have hired these jackoffs. They cut the tree and it fell on the fence that we spent a month building. To make it worse, it fell on that fucking post. What's so funny?"

"Nothing. There's absolutely nothing funny about that entire situation." Jonathan says with feigned seriousness.

"I get it. It's very funny." Diego frowns.

Examining the demolished fence, they remained silent, each trying to decide where to start. Without looking Jon feels the glare of Diego's family through the large, pane windows of the house. He can hear them all asking the question he's asked himself for days, how will Diego handle the presence of his friend?

"You wanna a beer Jon?"

"Alright," and Jonathan follows Diego up onto the raised front porch.

"Where's Laura?"

"Work. She's coming later though. That reminds me, I brought a bottle of champagne for you guys."

"Since when do we drink champagne?"

"Since never."

"Her idea?"

"Yeah."

Crossing the crowded living room into the kitchen and temperature rise twenty degrees. Large pots of soups, rice, and sautéed vegetables cover the stove and much of the countertop next to it. The room has been bustling with activity since dawn. On the small kitchen table two of Diego's aunts finish making tortillas. They'd been working feverishly for hours but now there was nothing but large covered dishes keeping the fresh bread warm. In the oven, three large pans of enchiladas bake. Hopefully they made the chicken enchiladas with the green sauce. Sweat forms on Jon's brow and a suffocating sensation twists at his chest. Ten women packed into one room but the only sound is soup simmering on the stove.

The Velarde back yard was an extensive putting green fading into the dust of California farmland. Only the small stage built by Diego helps designate the yards' outer boundary. Though nothing more than a redwood platform raised two feet off the ground, Jonathan remembers the excitement that spread when people learned a real stage was being built outside of town. A picnic table sat on the stage, allowing Diego's grandparents to watch the revelry unfold with the pride of royalty.

As Diego takes to another journey of the social butterfly, Jonathan hopes inviting eyes will find him, but the only friendly sight is the empty table under the oleanders. Heading to the table, his foot hooks an extension cord and as it tightens around his feet Jon imagines the power being disconnected and the festivities coming to an end. Only electrocution would save him. Contorting his body hoping to fall flat rather than disconnect the power. The cord tightens and at any moment the plug will give, it's inevitable. Jon feels the cord slip a half-inch toward his toes, and then a little more before it finally comes free from his foot. The music still blares so he quickly retreats to the oleanders.

Despite the familiar Velarde family rhythm, Jonathan notices the changes in the details. The extra inches in height on the younger ones, and the added width on the old. Over the years' faces have left to be replaced by others. Clothes and hairstyles have evolved, but really, it's all the same.

Diego's parents still dance slow to every song regardless of the beat. Javier has trapped three members of the family, telling the same story. A tale of great injustice, when he was not named to start his varsity year even though he was, in his own estimation, the best shortstop in town. The children have chosen the nights' victim, who they will tease mercilessly for the rest of the evening. It's never the same child, but it's a rite of passage. Some couples argue about this and that, while more harmonious pairs watch the amusing play performed before them.

Jon watches the mélange of unspoken traditions churn as the sun drops below the horizon, and the last rays of light paint the sky red and purple. Laura should arrive in a few hours, bringing his excuse. She has to wake for work in the morning after all. She'll pay her respects, and then she'll want to dance before leaving. Despite everything, he'll soon be lying in bed next to Laura. Before they fall asleep she'll chastise him for cowardliness, but that's all right.

Some of the harsh stares might turn away if Diego would just come over, then everyone could see the two friends laugh together. A quick toast to some unimportant event, that would be enough, then Diego could return to the way of the social butterfly. Jon becomes fixated on Diego, who stands with his back to the oleanders talking to his older sister and a few cousins. Once again flailing his arms around, Diego reaches down to pull up his pants that continue to slip from his hips.

"He's my friend, that's why he's here," Diego barks. "Hell, I've known him longer than I've known some members of this family."

"He threatened to hit you didn't he. Fuck that *puto*, I never liked him anyway." Angelina shouts, intently staring at Jon hiding in the corner. "If you're not going to tell him he to leave, I will."

"I've respected every friend, boyfriend, and in-law you've ever brought into this house, you'll do the same. Any problem with Jon will be taken care of by me! And you better tell everyone to give Jonathan the same respect as always, because the only reason he's here is because he respects this family."

"Why hasn't he gone over to congratulate our grandparents then?"

"Probably because from the second he got here everyone's been dogging him." Diego looks over his shoulder. "Where the hell did that fucking asshole run off too? Did any of you say something to him!"

"The pussy's sitting under the bushes crying," Angelina says, storming off toward her husband who stands near the dance floor smoking a cheap cigar.

Diego reaches past his remaining cousins to the ice chest. "So this is how we treat guests. I'll remember that next time one of you bring someone who pisses me off." Like an out of body experience Diego see's himself say this over his shoulder. Then, he's back, walking into the shadows of the oleanders, beers dangling from his fingers.

Diego slides a bottle to Jonathan who grabs it without looking up. "So what's up with you?"

"Goat's." In a world where people fight over spoiled milk the morning tragedy doesn't fit. The fall of the tomato patch is too grand, and Jon finds himself smiling at the idea of it all. While crossing the land he might as well be walking in another world with values that don't apply anywhere else.

Jonathan lifts his beer and adds, "Thank you Kapresian's."

"The Kapresian's are a bunch of assholes. Remember Freddy. He was a fucking piece of shit. Marty kicked his ass a couple of times."

"Broke his nose after the Fowler game our junior year." Jonathan had forgotten about the youngest Kapresian. "He was a loudmouth wasn't he?"

"Shit Jon, I feel bad. I'm a dick."

"Understanding yourself is a sign of impending enlightenment."

"I wanted to ask you something, but my little crisis is childish after that."

"I'm sure it is. It's alright though."

"Do you ever think of Tijuana?" Diego whispers.

"You want to go to TJ again?"

"No, I don't belong there. I just want to know if you thought about anything we saw?"

"Like what?"

"That UCLA student that got his face chewed off, or the homeless guy in front of the Rockadile." The night's temperature drops, and Diego's heart speeds up. His hands shake, forcing him to put his beer down.

"Look man, I didn't do anything with that hooker", Jonathan says.

"That's not what I mean God damnit! I don't give a shit about that. I was asking if you've thought about the other stuff, you know, the things we saw."

111

"Well, I haven't bought any gum since we came back. Does that help any?"

"It's all I've fucking thought about since we got back. Every time I see one of those old pickers sitting in the park at the center of Bodie, I feel like crap. Then I go out on dates with Isabelle, and I think that I'm no better than any of those other bastards."

"Wait a minute Diego, that's a little strong. I mean I can see feeling bad about a homeless man, though I don't remember the guy in front of the Rockadile"

"The fucking old guy sitting on the ground. You remember I started yelling at him."

"No. Why'd you yell at him?"

"Fuck if I know. If I knew I wouldn't be losing sleep. I screwed up a damn oil change at work two days ago because… what's the matter with you now?"

"I think your family's pissed because of that stuff that happened last week."

"Don't worry about it?"

"Maybe I should take off. I don't like that I'm bothering your family." He pauses for a second, not hearing Diego trying to comfort him. "The only thing is Laura might be coming and I told her I'd be here."

"Has Jonathan been whining like this all night?"

The smell of lavender perfume fills the air and Jon turns in time for Laura to kiss him on the forehead before traveling around the table to give Diego a hug.

"He's in one of his self-pity moods girl. As punishment, don't fuck him for a week."

"Dear God Diego! This is a party for your grandparents. You shouldn't make jokes like that tonight." Laura sits at Jon's side, and instantly repulsing the hateful eyes. People complained about her plainness, but something about Laura Theroux compelled everyone to treat her like royalty.

Laura immediately falls into telling how the manager of the Giant Potato was just about to give old Mr. Smith two free gallons of milk to get rid of him when a pack of dogs suddenly appeared and went crashing through the aisles. When the manager learned they were Mr. Smith's dogs that managed to escape from the car, he not only banned Mr. Smith for life, he promised to sue if he wasn't reimbursed for the damaged items. Diego catches Laura up on the story with the fence, followed by Jonathan and his day at the dentist. Through it all they laughed and hollered, repeating parts so they could carry on.

Finally, the pleasantness of conversation ends, and none hide their disappointment.

"Jon you promised you'd get me to bed, but first you are taking me out to dance. Then we'll go pay are respects to Grandma and Grandpa Velarde. com'on farmboy, off your butt."

Watching Jon and Laura dance, Diego thinks back to before they started dating and how Jon avoided dancing. None of the Heffrons were good dancers, but when Jon and Laura got together, that didn't matter. They'd jerk around and stumble offbeat to everyone's amusement. It's like watching toddlers hop around to tunes sung by Kermit the Frog. Diego knows he's never danced like that. He's surely danced better, but never like that.

The mothers have taken to lining up on the back porch. As if a rigid schedule had been set beforehand, one or two of them would return to the kitchen only to reappear with another plate of food. Every time a new dish appears they act like it's the first of the evening.

Barbeque smoke and the smell of bacon wrapped hotdogs fills the air. Additional picnic tables appear, and are immediately packed with men too drunk to do anything but drink more. Though cut in half, the dance floor is still full of young people gyrating between drinks, including Jon and Laura who decide to stay for one more song. Diego has witnessed this scene dozens of times, going all the way back to his childhood. Everything is familiar, except for two giggling teenagers standing over a small boy.

At seven, Jorge was already aware of the advantage of drunken adults. The boy revels in the removing of itchy clothes and running between dancers, careful to attract as little attention as possible. Then he rests alongside the teenagers invited by Angelina's husband.

Stepping out from the shadows, under the yellow full moon in the sky, Diego passes Jonathan who only turns when Laura taps his right shoulder, directing him to watch. Jon thinks nothing of it at first, only the butterfly heading for another flower of entertainment. Then he and Laura watch Diego nearly push his cousin Joaquin over, moving toward something in the distance.

Storming toward Angelina, Diego grabs his sisters' arm and spins her around. She'd have fallen over but for Diego holding on.

"Do you know your son is watching two idiots smoke pot and get drunk?"

"Who do you think you are putting your hands on me?" Angelina pulls her arm away from Diego's grip and slaps him.

"You're pissed at me! You slap me in the face while those two disrespect our father's house."

Angelina's husband steps forward to separate the two siblings. "Let's calm down."

"Don't think for a minute that you get to say shit to me just because you married my sister. You brought those two assholes here and look what…" Diego's head snaps to the side from the force of another of Angelina's slaps. Before Diego can say anything more Jonathan pulls him from the crowd.

"Come on man, you don't want to take this any farther." Jonathan tries to pacify his friend, but Diego can only berate his family for failing it's youngest member.

Jonathan gets them around the side of the house before releasing his hold. He looks at his friend in the moonlight. Diego's not even that angry, he's disappointed and upset, but not angry.

"How could they be so fucking ignorant? They didn't even care as I told them to their faces."

Jonathan keeps Diego in front of him. "Could you bring my car around to the front Laura, we're getting out of here."

"I'll take my car," Diego says quietly.

"Well I'll come with you then. I'll get my car tomorrow."

"I'm not a fucking child, Jon."

"Never said you were. But come to my apartment anyway. We'll have a few drinks, and I'll make us something to eat."

Turning toward the Firechicken Diego whispers, "I'm not hungry."

Jon watches his friend walk towards the Firechicken parked under the only tree left in the yard, an old Gingko that felt too sophisticated for the simple yard. Diego climbs into the driver's seat and sits motionless talking to himself, and a curtain in those large bay windows moves. Laura honks her horn, and Jon walks to the Jeep as the music starts up again in the back yard.

"I thought I was driving him to the apartment?"

"He wants to take the Firechicken."

"We won't be getting to bed early tonight I guess," Laura says.

"I'll meet you back at the apartment."

Jon watches Laura drive away in her unloved Jeep before looking one last time at the Firechicken, which still sits motionless under the Gingko tree. He wants to knock on the window and tell Diego to let it go. He wants to tell his friend to apologize for everything and forget whatever offense his sister committed. Jonathan wants to tell Diego it's not worth it, and leaning forward to take a step toward his friend before heading the other way. He walks slowly down the driveway toward his car, hands in his pockets, looking down at his moonlit shadow in the soft dust of the Valley.

Chapter XII

The Firechicken

In 1968 a man moved from San Felipe to Tijuana after selling the cantina that had long supported him. Loading his remaining belongings into a truck, he headed north on a cool summer morning. He bought a small house near his grandchildren then walked seventeen blocks to purchase a brand new 1968 Pontiac Firebird. The twenty-year-old ford flatbed was fine for the village, but he lived in the city now. It took a week, but this retired bartender drove that car down every street and alley in the city. He still walked around his front yard with nothing but underwear and refusing to eat anything but tortillas and beans. It didn't matter, by owning that car the old man had conformed.

Later he made another choice, this time following his family to the small town of Bodie California. The car came with him. He found these new neighbors more agreeable than their counterparts in the city, still he judged them unworthy of the beautiful machine. The Pontiac was too much muscle for a puny town. So quickly it fell into a state of perpetual disrepair. This old man, who had treated the car as his most valued possession, did only the minimum to keep it on the road. When the paint faded and chipped he didn't renew it. As the fabric ripped, he blatantly refused to mend it. The people of Bodie did not deserve the effort or money the car required.

Then, after a long life, the old man died leaving nothing behind but the barely running automobile. His surviving sons decided the car meant little to their father so it should mean less to them. Then, on the day it was to be transported to the wrecking yard, the old man's favorite grandson made his own choice.

"Don't get rid of that car. We used to work on it together; he wouldn't want you to just destroy it. Let me take it and I'll fix it up myself." So, it happened that the old man's thirteen-year-old grandson took up ownership of the dilapidated 1968 Pontiac Firebird.

For the first time since it roared down the streets of that infamous border town the car was truly cared for, and never was it more loved. The car was a tool for the old man. For the grandson, it meant something more, and he went to work. He rebuilt the engine several times and worked for free at a transmission shop so he could learn how to repair his own. By the time Diego Velarde got his driver's license, the 68 Firebird was the fastest car in Bodie.

Then, the time came to begin work on the cosmetic end of the cars restoration, but for unexplained reasons the grandson stopped. The chipped, faded paint remained. He refused to replace the cracked dashboard, or the broken headlights. He didn't even bother fixing the spring that had punctured the upholstery, though it kept tearing holes in his pants. Everyone asked the grandson why he didn't complete his project. With nothing more than a shrug, he'd answer, "I don't fucking know."

One fateful day, standing with his friends in the high school parking lot, Jon Heffron shouted, "We always go to My Friends House let's get some Chinese. Come on, we'll take the Firechicken."

Diego's Firebird died that day.

From then on it was the Firechicken.

Chapter XIII

Blessed Admonishment

Isabelle's cramped three-room bungalow sits near the aqueduct north of Bodie. As a boy Diego would go there with Martin to fish for channel cats, though nobody ever saw one in those waters. Spinning the steering wheel of the Firechicken until the horn sounds, Diego looks into his review mirror, and the top of the My Friends House sign at the center of town. Not an impressive sign, but still the tallest manmade structure between Fresno and Visalia.

A light illuminates the front yard to show Isabelle Martinez in the blue mini skirt he bought her, paired with a black lace blouse, and matching stilettos. She turns to lock the door and Diego peers through the living room/kitchenette into the cluttered bedroom and bathroom scarcely the size of a portable toilet.

Isabelle jumps into the Firechicken, and the springs give a disapproving moan. Leaning in and kissing the side of Diego's neck she whispers, "How was Kings Canyon?"

"Oh, it was great. Hiked into Paradise Valley, and sat around a camp fire all night."

"I thought they didn't let people make fires up there anymore," she smiles.

"Yeah well, we took a chance, and got away with it." He slams down on the accelerator and spins the Firechicken back toward the center of Bodie.

"We should go camping," Isabelle shouts with a spasm. "I've always wanted to camp on the beach."

"Why would you want to camp at the beach? They'll be people everywhere."

"Not Bodie Beach. We could spend a long weekend in Big Sur."

"Sounds like heaven, but Alex won't give me time off now." How do people like Jon and Martin do it; how do they manage to carry the weight so easily. "Where do you feel like eating?"

"Let's go to a movie first. *Fabric of Life* starts in Hanford at eight."

"What was this movie about?"

"It's about a single father raising a daughter while working at a textile factory in the late eighteen hundreds."

"Alright." The Firechicken's dash reads five o'clock, meaning it's almost seven. The sun will fall below the eroded tops of the Coastal Mountains. He should have apologized, maybe that would've prevented the family meeting. Soon someone will make the clumsy transition from small talk to the topic of his behavior. Grandpa will say his grandson wouldn't have ended up this way if they'd stayed in Mexico. He'll say they've all been raised spoiled Americans with no respect. Dad will counter with the examples of his murdered brothers, and how if the family had stayed in Mexico more Velarde's might've been buried young.

Mom won't say anything, only cry softly to herself. Angelina will keep her voice quiet whispering into their whimpering mothers' ears. She'll say Diego thinks he has the same rights in the house as the people who own it, inquiring why he still lives at home, when she moved out at eighteen. Angelina will guide Mom down this line before finally getting to the point; that it's time he move out. She'll ramble on about the impossibility of growing up while living with his parents. It'll be late when Mom finally breaks into a loud, animated fit claiming her beloved son is on drugs. She's been waiting for him to become an addict ever since she saw that news special on how the Valley has become the Methamphetamine capitol of the world.

"Will you stay on the road Diego!" Swerving in time to avoid hitting an old abandoned telephone poll, the Firechicken squeals and shakes.

"What's the matter with you?"

"I'm just tired." Diego turns and looks at Isabelle. "You look beautiful tonight." Without even acknowledging him she stares into the empty streets. "So, what's this movie about again?"

"I just told you?"

"I've had a lot on my mind. Tell me again." Diego remembers his Papa Velarde in the hospital. They'd all relied on the old man, and even is the end, he remained the center of the family. Papa Velarde was dying, and still they came in, asking for help, updating him on the family drama, and Diego watched it all knowing that's what killed him.

"You've been a mess ever since you went to TJ."

Almost losing control of the Firechicken for the second time, Diego considers pulling off the road and walking home. "How'd you know I went to TJ? I never told you."

"Yeah so what. You and the *huero* went to a whore house in TJ with Mauricio, did you really think word wouldn't get around Bodie?"

"Goddamnit, I should have known Mauricio would spread the word the moment we got back. I know Jon didn't say nothing, no way. Marty would have kept his fucking mouth shut."

"Can't you stop saying fuck all the time?"

"Why?"

"It's just too much fuck."

Diego wants to scold her, or at least pout a little, but he can't help but consider the point. "Ian Heffron told me there's nothing worse than being repetitive. I believe him. God people like that are boring. But fuck is different, it's one of those words that always works, and never gets old." He breaths a heavy sigh and his vision blurs for a moment. "You can never overuse fuck."

"Forget I brought it up," Isabelle snaps. "And for the record, Marty doesn't keep secrets better than anyone else in this town."

"Dougherty's always keep the secrets that matter. They're probably the only family in this town you can say that about," Diego says half to himself. "You know what girl; can we go and eat first. I haven't had anything today and I could use a bite."

"Where you want to eat?"

"I don't know." Diego revs the engine and suddenly gets the feeling that Isabelle is looking at him. "What's up?"

"Let's go to the Dead Man instead."

"Is something going on down there."

"No."

"Sounds perfect." Diego accelerates through the streets of Bodie, and crossing the corner of Madera and Seventh he relives beating Ryan Nelson for telling their third-grade teacher he cheated on a math test. At least that was the reason he gave, truthfully he'd been looking for that fight ever since Ryan called his family a bunch of wetbacks. A sudden right turn, and Diego finds himself on Tule Ave where the plaque to the Dougherty family stands. He thinks of the day he defaced it with a stolen can of spray paint after growing tired of the relentless talk about the famous Dougherty family. In the center of the park stands the leaning fountain, where he and his friends would play the shanking game after school, running around for hours, stabbing each other with pencils and yelling 'shank!' with each hit. This always ended predictably enough; someone draws blood, then a fight.

Then there were the other stories, the ones he wasn't a part of. He learned them all, and in time he told them with the same frequency as his own. Like the giant tree stump at the center of Main Street and Canyon Ave that once was a giant Valley Oak. When it died, the town didn't remove it down because it was there during the founding, until a branch fell, killing Earle Heffron's wife two days before he returned from the Great War. Still they left the stump for posterities sake. Then there was the Griswold's Tire shop that had once been a disco. It was the only time anyone tried opening a dance club in Bodie. It closed when the owner announced he wouldn't play Johnny Cash because he considered the music outdated, and nobody fucks with Johnny Cash in this town.

He was practiced at telling his stories, and could do so with such ease that only upon finishing would he realize he'd been talking. His tone and mannerisms having become rehearsed like a stage actor doing his hundredth performance of the same play. The strange part is those other tales; the ones born decades, even centuries before his birth. It took some time, but he soon found that he voiced them in the same way. He used the same movements, the same excitement as if they'd occurred right before his eyes. That was the way of the town, eventually the stories come together to become yours.

Crossing city limits, entering black countryside, without distinguishing landmarks, but Diego knows. He can see the outer rows of grapevines illuminated by the passing lights of the Firechicken. Even this is a reminder; a reminder of a time when driving to the countryside was an adventure akin to traveling to another land. 'Dude, we've been driving for a while, I think we missed the turnoff.' Then a few panicking moments later someone would shout, 'Do you see that, that shining sign in the distance? I think the dirt road's just past it.' Then the next five minutes were spent driving ten miles an hour down unknown country roads looking for the party. It's safer in that indistinguishable black soup than on the streets of Bodie, but the openness of the farmland made the younger Diego vulnerable.

Diego has mastered the darkness, navigating to the beach by feeling how long he's driven in a certain direction, and soon they arrive at the patch of dirt that once sustained a riverside meadow.

How is it she ends up on top of him? How did that happen? The dark night has painted Isabelle a gray-blue color, a living thing of beauty carved from marble. In the rearview mirror, Diego sees the distant yellow glow of Bodie rise, slowly fading as it gets higher, until snuffed out by the bright red slashes of a wildfire slowly spreading across the Sierra Nevada's. Above the roof, stars fight to push through the rising ash and the slow, summer river seems saddened by their absence.

Isabelle slips off her blouse, tossing it aside. Diego runs his hands up her lower back but stops when he comes across the smallest of imperfections. It's the scar she received while playing with her little brother Jorge as children. George almost ran into a barbed wire fence their uncle erected at the end of his property. Isabelle managed to stop her brother from being tangled but got hooked herself. She stood, hooked for twenty minutes trying not to cry, afraid that doing so would make her brother feel guilty.

Diego thinks of similar games Angelina and he played as children. Why'd he have to be the one to finally take it too far? It was simple and perfect at the time. Tie a little string between a tree and a bush where he knew Angelina often went to sit. Then climb to the top of the house and peer down from the roof, watching patiently. Sitting in the Firechicken, Isabelle pressed against him, Diego has to suppress the urge to strike himself when he remembers laughing as Angelina fell to the ground. Then the panic he felt when she howled with pain, blood streaming down her arm.

Quickly, Diego lets his hands drop to rest on Isabelle's hips. The first things he ever noticed about her. It'd been raining, but all of Bodie was in the football stadium watching their girls' soccer team play for the Valley Championship. Isabelle wasn't the best player on the team, but the captain nonetheless. He saw her hips first, moving up and down the pitch, her wet uniform clinging to her. Mud stained her socks and shin guards and she sported a fresh black eye courtesy of an elbow in the first half.

She was fierce; determined to accomplish something transcendent. Even when they fell behind by a goal late in the second half Isabelle remained unshaken in that purpose. She led her team by will, encouraging, calming, and in those last moments she won them the Valley Championship on a penalty kick.

That day Diego watched those hips torque and spin around. He watched them whip back straight as the ball headed into the corner of the net. Isabelle's eyes focused with a resolve he'd never had, not for anything. He could visualize the contrast as her unflappable demeanor turned joyous at the realization of the accomplishment. It was beautiful the way she ran toward her teammates, and shared her glory without any pretentiousness.

Diego didn't see any of it that day. He didn't see any of her, but he saw it all now in that black night by the Dead Man. He saw everything about her and at the same time, everything about himself. He was not the man for her, but he wanted to be.

An instant later, and Isabelle is back in the passenger seat of the Firechicken, trying to rub out the pain from the back of her head. She sits up quickly adjusting the remains of her clothing. "What in God's name was that Diego?"

The crushing weight of emotion forces his eyes shut. He feels inadequate, afraid, happy and frustrated. "I can't do this right now Isabelle."

There's silence and Diego looks at the glow of the foothill fire in his rearview mirror, and hearing Isabelle gather herself. The Firechicken doesn't make a noise as she moves clumsily toward him and whispers in his ear, "Don't fucking worry about it."

Chapter XIV

The Ice Sauna

The sound of his wife's voice drifting from the open window is muffled by the muggy night air, still Parker Lyon walks toward his precious Ice House.

"There's nothing wrong Parker, now come back to bed before you catch cold." The dried food distribution business in Denver went under in six months. He forgot to lock the doors to the livery in Sacramento, and half his clients' horses ran away in the night.

"Parker, leave it alone, and come to bed."

"I'm –j-j-j-just g-g-going to walk through real q-quick, and I'll be right in."

Walking toward the front door of the Ice House, a breeze rustles the leaves of his ever failing vineyard. He spent the day watching children run behind his trailer. For ten minutes they followed him shouting, and he pretended not to hear. Waiting until the last moment, Parker pulled his trailer to a stop, re-assured his horse and hopped down to hand out the last few splinters of ice to the town kids. As he rode home, he savored the shouting that followed. "Thank you Mister L-L-Lyon." It bothered his family when people mocked his stammer; at one time it bothered him too. Since he started delivering ice around Bodie, Parker couldn't help but feel the teasing was born from love.

His wife calls out again. "This is why I want you to stop letting people in that building. All it does is cost you sleep. You're too worrisome a soul to allow it Parker."

"Just ge-ge-get on to bed now and I'll be in sh-shortly."

Leave the extra money out of it; they could surely do without. The joy of watching those Heffrons argue about their twisted fascination with death was worth a bit of sleep. Had he never started letting people sit in the cool of the Ice House for five cents an hour, Parker would have steered clear of the Heffrons forever. The way death seemed to follow them frightened Parker and his wife. Then the family started coming to the ranch, flanked by their children.

Parker avoided their exchanges at first, but it was no good. Seemingly normal people speaking excitedly about the horrific deaths of loved ones? Only Jennifer Heffron felt bothered by the subject matter, while the rest reveled in the legacy. They feared above all else that they might be the one to break the cycle. Then Jennifer's little son Earnest asked her, "Mommy how do you think I'll die?"

"You see what you're doing! Brain washing my son with horrible ideas; you should all be ashamed. If you dare pass this lunacy to Earnest, I'll leave this Godless town forever," Jennifer barked as she stormed back to the Heffron wagon.

Another short breeze and Parker suddenly realizes how tired he is. A quick peak inside and it's back to bed. He turns the handle and pushes only to find something blocking the door.

Chapter XV

History

The shed must be ready by six forty-five, then it's off to the Pluot orchard before packing starts at nine-thirty. Forty bins of Spring Bright nectarines will fill much of the afternoon, or maybe it's the first pick of Elegant Ladies. It's become a blur. Knowing this Laura remained insistent; apparently it's something they need to see together. So, they drive north up Evanhart Ave, looking for the back road into the east side of Bodie, and then toward the rotting remains of the Ice House.

It's unfair how Ian always says, "You don't really wake up til nine Jon. You're here, but you're not up til nine." Certain parts of him are very much awake before the sun rises. Does anyone ever acknowledge how serious he is during this first part of the day? He's never funny at dawn; not that sympathetic either. Laura once called him a morning cynic and an afternoon optimist. Of course, his temper is always awake, but not his sense of tact, that sleeps in.

The Rodriguez family now owns the land. Before that, the property belonged to the Thomas brothers, who acquired it from whoever took it off the bank nine years earlier. A twenty-acre plot, woefully devoid of stability. Perhaps that's what saved the shell of the Ice House from the steel teeth of a bull-dozer.

The car skids across the gravel and Jon struggles to climb out of the Honda, his legs still raw from yesterday's fourteen-hour day. Laura moves unencumbered through the blackness. A short breeze, like a breath, rustles branch and leaf of a nearby almond orchard, and Jonathan watches the shadowy movements of the flora surrounding the Ice House. Foxtails and dried patches of Bermuda grass cover the river rock that plagues the land north of town. Once home to a large tributary feeding the Dead Man, it dried up long ago, leaving only smooth, round rocks behind.

Clearing a path between the blue-gray foliage of the Iron Weed Jonathan thinks about the stinging nettle and puncture vines under his feet, but Iron Weed is the only thing worth hating. They carry no points or poison but left to their own devices they grow six feet tall and spread as rapidly as any grass. Even the strongest herbicides won't kill them once they've passed a foot in height. Jon recalls spending days hacking at the stubborn plants, along with the tired arms, sore back and the blistered palms.

Through this forest, Jonathan finds the aluminum ladder and gives it a shakes. Still stable after all these years. They climb up and crawl across the wood shingle roof, avoiding the holes and weak spots like in high school. Finally they get to the railing that once held the pulleys and hooks used to move giant blocks of ice onto waiting delivery wagons. They slide across the long scaffold, making sure to keep splinters from piercing their legs.

The foothills surrounding Bodie are streaked with overlapping rattails of flame. It's technically three separate blazes all started around the same time on the nineteenth of June. Now they've combined into one giant inferno hovering over the long flat of The Valley. On the first day twenty-seven houses burned down. Jon thinks about the distant relatives he's met once or twice from the hills, and wonders if they're as hard-headed as the Bodie Heffron's. If so they'll stay in their houses as flames consume the world around them.

"I'm not saying I'd rather be here than in bed, but you were right when you said it was beautiful."

In places where the fire lines are thinnest, they resemble delicate strokes of a fine paintbrush dancing across black canvas while giant mounds of glowing coals dot the image. Firefighters from all over California have been summoned to the Hills, and Jon concentrates on the scene, hoping to see the flashing red lights of fire engines climbing toward the inferno.

"What made you want to come out here anyway?" Jonathan asks.

"I wanted to get something good out of those fires."

For three days bellowing smoke has blanketed the eastern horizon. It delays dawn each morning for a good half an hour. Even at their brightest, the black fog turn the sun's golden rays' ruby. Each morning Laura washes her Jeep, only to find a thin carpet of soot at day's end. At times she pretends it's not Bodie anymore; that she's on vacation somewhere where the sun hides behind smoke.

Looking at the red and orange flames in the darkness, Jon wonders if concentrating on a single spot long enough will allow him to see the fire march slowly up the hillside. In places the fire lines pulsate, but this could be an illusion. Then again, it could be a house burning?

Laura scoots in closer as the last chill of darkness rises. It's the little shot of cold that the Valley delivers right before sunrise, and if the horizon were not blocked by towering pillars of smoke, the sky would be turning blue over the Sierra's.

"What are you guys doing at Ian's today?" She leans in a little closer, and he smells lilac. "I know you're tired Jon."

Putting his hand around her waist Jon whispers, "No this is good. I've been looking at that smoke for three days."

"Uh-ha."

"We will be going to bed early tonight though right?"

"Oh Yeah."

A sudden flare in one of the fires causes that familiar feeling of guilt to turn his stomach. "Did you ever hear the story of how the Heffron's closed down the original Ice House?"

"No I haven't heard that one," Laura sighs.

"During the summer, the Heffron's used to visit once a week to cool off. They'd been doing it ever since Parker Lyon started renting sitting spaces in the cold. One day Lily and Sal Heffron are in here with some twenty kids. The rest of the adults had gone to Fresno, except for Jennifer Heffron I think. That's a lot of heads to keep track of. Anyway, most of the adults had gone shopping for something or other and Lily and Sal stayed behind to watch over this slew of kids. At some point they decided to bring them all to the Ice House.

"So they head to this place and pay their fee, and have a nice time. An hour goes by and it's time to leave. It's starting to get dark and Parker wants to close, so he kind of rushes them out the door. In the the confusion, little Ernest Heffron gets it in his head that it'd be fun to sleep in the Ice House. Sleeping in a cold room probably sounded pretty good to a kid who'd grown up without air conditioning. Ernest hid behind a stack of ice, and nobody noticed. The rest of the family piled into the wagon, and headed back to the ranch. Parker closed up the moment they left, and went into his house without walking through the place.

"The door was locked from the outside and Ernest couldn't get out. He died of hypothermia. Probably the only person in the history of the San Joaquin Valley to ever die of cold in August. Parker found him leaning up against the door. They say he tried to bring Ernest back for twenty minutes before he gave up. Parker was so traumatized that he sold the place a month later and moved to…Bakersfield I think. The Ice House spent the next twenty years bouncing from one owner to another before the invention of refrigeration drove it under for good. It split the Heffron's up. All those who went to the foothills sided with the parents who lost Ernest. Even after all this time the foothill Heffrons haven't forgiven us down here. And now their houses are probably burning down.

"You know Lily Heffron was my dad's grandmother. She said she never forgave herself for what happened to Ernest. The idea that it was the nature of the Heffron legacy never brought her comfort. Dad said she was a wreck until the day she died."

"Hum."

"What's the matter?"

"Nothing."

"You didn't like the story?"

"I don't like any of the stories about the Heffron's dying."

"It's the family legacy."

"It's depressing. Especially the way you all revel in it."

"I don't know that we 'revel' in it."

"You all do. Every Heffron I've ever met glows whenever they have an opportunity to talk about dead loved ones."

"Sorry. I didn't know it bothered you so much."

She squeezed his arm softly. "It just makes me sad to think that the best thing you have to look forward to about this town is the day you leave it forever."

134

Jonathan thinks of his parents' death and for the first time in a long time, he feels sad." In a strange kind of way, he thinks of them as really being gone. He'll have to be at work in another twenty minutes. Pulling Laura closer he inhales cool, ashy air and in the waking dawn of the Valley they watch the foothills burn.

Chapter XVI

Dead Fish

The Salmon Festival was born in the autumn of 1923 to honor the run up the Deadman. It wasn't long before someone suggested moving the festival to mid-summer, as September already had celebrations marking the end of the harvest. Then the dam was built, right at the point where the Deadman drops out of that beautiful glacier-carved valley in the Sierras. That mountain mansion of nature was flooded, and the waters of the Deadman stopped flowing at their previous levels. Year-round water remains near Bodie, but never reaches the San Joaquin River and with the closing of this liquid corridor, the fish vanished.

Martin still remembers his grandfather speaking of the Salmon. Every year as the fall colors emerged, buried memories of the run would shine in the old man's eyes. Emphysema had made walking across the living room an ordeal, but grandfather would fidget with excitement when recalling the fish fighting the current, searching for home. He would go with his friends to the muddy banks and spear Salmon as they heading for ancestral hatcheries. They would gather their flopping haul in baskets and when their mothers could use no more, they'd return to the banks and hunt more.

They should have changed the festivals name, but people have always proven more stubborn than Salmon, and Martin takes comfort in the thought. It reinforces the knowledge that the choking ash and blackened sky will not drive people from the park. Rescheduling the festival from its natural date did not drive away the crowds, neither did the dam, why should the falling remains of far off forests.

Passing faces smile and laugh as vendors sell deep fried foods, and carnival games for two dollars a turn. Women greet each other with the excitement of long lost friends even if they saw each other only a few days earlier. They happily chatter, stopping only to hand money to children pleading for one more game.

The men stand aside whispering to each other. These same men work together, eight hours a day, year after year. They see themselves in the same clothes, sharing two breaks and a lunch together, where they talk about the same things, becoming friends in a way. Then after twenty years of knowing each other, they cross paths at a little festival in a small town. The natural pattern of their relationship broken, they become nervous strangers stumbling through conversation, wanting to get away.

Martin Dougherty wanders on, looking at each encounter as another version of this same dynamic. He gets to the end of the first row of booths, and stops in front of a small platform. On top is a table with seven chairs all facing the small crowd gathered below. In each chair is a citizen of Bodie, mentally preparing for the annual eating competition.

The year before contestants raced to discover who could eat the most tacos in five minutes, before that, who could devour a three-pound pizza. The competition was a mainstay of the festival, but Martin never watched. He turns south, looking to cross over to the next row of booths.

Distracted by loud bells and whistles, and the sight of a young boy jumping up and down excitedly, Martin barely realizes he's slapped away two fingers digging into the middle of his chest.

"You're Dan Dougherty's boy?"

The worn middle-aged man remains motionless but for a weary tremor in his lower lip. His long brown hair has a natural curl, and the shade of the locks match the gold tooth flashing with each spoken word. The oversized leather jacket with worn jeans give him a gaunt appearance and his shoes, an old pair of combat boots mask his short stature. The way the man's eyes dart around, as though waiting for an ambush, feels familiar to Martin.

Still, he takes a step back before pulling a cigarette and lighting it. "We've met."

"Paul Villanuevo. I was a friend of your fathers from San Francisco."

"Of course, Paul! God it's been years. What brings you here?"

"Passing through. Got a piece of work with a contractor down in San Diego."

Martin hands a cigarette to Paul, lighting it as the two stand quietly for a moment.

"Your dad used to talk about the festival for salmon that don't run no more. Said it proved how stupid this town could be. I'd tell him not to be bitter, and it's not fair to judge something just because it's not for you." Paul takes a drag and looks around at the congregation that he knew only through tales told while sharing a bus bound for Mississippi. "Guess Dan was right. It's pretty stupid."

"Dad's always been too hard on this town."

"He judged them as they deserve."

"I don't know what gives a drunken deadbeat the right to judge anyone."

"That man never drank more than any other Dougherty I met, not that I met a lot of um."

"Just a deadbeat then."

Paul shakes his head, flicking his half-finished cigarette to the floor.

"Sorry Villanuevo. I know you and Dad went through a lot together."

"And I know your family's supposed to stand for something, some kind of ideal of what's best about this place, but let me tell you that the best thing a Dougherty ever did was done far away from here. When you combine it all up, he probably spent a year of his life on the road, traveling from one city to another, fighting injustices. Not one of those things he bleed for benefited him one bit. He wasn't suffering under the weight of segregation, and he wasn't ever getting sent to Nam because of that gimpy knee. But each time buses ran outta San Francisco heading to Mississippi, Dan was on one. He made four trips down there as I remember, and the third time he got beaten so bad he ended up in the hospital for two weeks. Did you know he was at Kent State?"

"Yeah, I heard that story," Martin huffs.

"Kent State wasn't a story, Woodstock was a story. Kent State was something real, and your old man was there. Then he comes back, and these people judged him. Why? Because he decided to stand for what he believed. Or was it because he drank too much, and they like their heroes clear eyed and well dressed."

"Well at least he fought for someone, even if it wasn't his son."

"Yeah, your Dad didn't do right by you, or your mom. If you want to hate him I guess he earned it. But don't let that blind you to the whole picture of the man. This town wouldn't understand cus they're all too busy throwing parties for dead fish." Paul pulls a shiny silver flask with the word "further" etched across the side, takes a belt, and puts it back.

"See ya round Martin."

A break in the cloud of ash allows a few rays to reach the festival. Not enough to brighten the landscape to its usual glory, but it's more than Bodie has seen since the fires began. Martin turns from the vendors, heading toward the only reason he came.

Martin should have gone to lunch with Jon and Laura, but he'd been snared with an obsession fueled by small town boredom. When there's nothing to do the mind will sometimes latch on to anything that break the monotony. At the end of the day the vandal was something new. Even if it wasn't particularly interesting, it was different. By the time Martin reaches Bolivars new mural the gap in the smoke has closed and the festival turns back to grey.

A man, aged no more than thirty years, stands at a dusty crossroad wearing a large flat brimmed cowboy hat as black as the duster falling to his ankles. Small splatters of mud with torn threads dangle from the bottom of the black coat. A pair of ornate spurs make his heels glitter like stars. He's sickly pale, the only color a thin trickle of blood runing down the back of his neck, and disappearing behind the heavy collar of the duster. His weathered hands hang loose, but something in the perfect spacing of the fingers says they're ready for what might come down either path. Then there's the shorthaired tan dog with the black strip down its back, crouching at his side with an annoyed stare, as though it knows something its master doesn't.

A sky painted like the best desert kaleidoscope imaginable with large, black clouds rising above the coastal ranges. The contrast between the sky and rounded mountains, which are blue before turning dark as they fall toward the floor, is painfully real. Coming out of this darkness are the two roads glowing, as if they produce their own light.

Martin mimics the man, going so far as imagining how the face must look; then he tries to match it. He continues until a piercing squeal interrupts the revelry behind him.

"OK ladies and gentlemen, we've got a few people that have some things to say, then you can all get on with the festivities."

Martin turns from the mural, and strolls to the statue of Lena Dougherty. She stands in bronze dulled by the ever-increasing fall of ash. The artist created a version of Lena in a tasteful dress that was popular at the time of her death, but Martin knows she always wore pants. The plaque at the base of the statue explains how Lena drove the brothels from Bodie, and this monument, built at the expense of the town, is a show of thanks to her many sacrifices. Martin uses the lip of this plaque to rest his feet before lighting another cig.

The Mayor steps to the microphone as the last remnants of the eating contest are swept away. Mayor Enrique Ramirez's, whose life in the public eye began when he turned sixteen, before that he might not have even existed. A member of the baseball team that went undefeated, and won the state championship, he set a league record for steals that year which still stands. The idea that this short, pudgy man was once a master of the base path is unfathomable, but the trophy cases of Bodie High School proves it.

In seventy-two, about the time he began to lose his hair, Enrique Ramirez got hired by the Bodie School District, home of the worst education the Valley had to offer. Within a few years his programs made them respectable. As his eyesight took a turn for the worst, Enrique parlayed this moderate success into a position on Bodie's town council. Back then, he wore a suit but now the Mayor dresses like someone about to step out for a jog on a cold morning.

The blasphemous decision to support the hiring of the first outsider to hold the position of Sheriff should have sunk Enrique's political career. Instead he's the first since Cyrus Dougherty to serve as mayor three times.

Taking another drag, Martin scans the crowd. Their faces all sport smiles accompanied with small laughs coming at the appropriate moment. Everything about the scene is absurd. Maybe twenty of the hundred and fifty who have taken the time to fain interest in the speeches voted in the last local election. Of those about eleven picked Enrique.

Martin listens to the wheels turning in the collective consciousness of the crowd. They want the talking to stop. He got reelected, what more can he ask for? They don't want to hear from Leo either. He'll surely speak next, being the primary contributor to this year's festival. Leo even paid for the stage so the luminaries of the community could posture from a platform befitting their rank.

The sight of Eric arguing with his ex-wife stops Martin leaving in leaving disgust. They divorced over a year ago, ending a seven-year marriage that had never been happy. Their neighbors said they bickered all night, and when they entered any room together the climate turned sour. By all accounts, the only good thing that came from their marriage was a son named Kevin who everyone called Ketch.

Nobody knew the specifics of the arguments until the day she appeared at Bodie Trucking with Ketch. She drove into the yard at full speed, nearly running into an outbound truck. Pulling up to the office as Eric came out with a handful of work orders, they say Ketch yelped with pain at being flung around by his irate mother.

Ketch was crying because he knew what was coming. His father forgot to pick him up at school again. It was alright as far as the boy was concerned. Dad was an important person. He had responsibilities, but for some reason mom never understood this. At one time they fought because she wanted dad around the house more. Something had changed, and now mom didn't want him around at all. She said so in front of all dads work friends. She was tired of being second fiddle to a job; whatever that meant. They were getting a divorce. Ketch didn't know what the word meant, but grew scared because he knew things were going to be different.

That was a year ago, and now Ketch understands. As his mother and father fight in that quiet, practiced way that's become their hallmark, the boy looks around at all the people watching the mayor talk. Then, he catches the stare of Martin Dougherty. They met a year ago while Martin was an ump for his little league games. He liked Martin; all the kids did. He was much nicer than most of the adults at the little league park. So Ketch waved, running over to the statue of the lady that died a long time ago.

"Hi Martin."

"How're you Ketch?"

"Good."

"Everything alright?"

"Mom's mad at Dad again. He was supposed to take me fishing at Dinkey Creek. The paper says trout are biting."

"Why aren't you going?"

"Dad has to run a emergency load to Anaheim. He's taking me with him though."

"Your Mom would rather you go fishing."

"She says Dad only cares about trucks. I tried telling her once that Dad needed to do his job or the people over in New

York wouldn't have any food. Dad has important work to do. She started crying, and ran out the room. I don't say things like that anymore, I just let her yell at Dad."

Martin flicks his cigarette. "I think your mom just wants you to have fun." Hearing Leo's voice Martin comes to a conclusion. "You know what Ketch, I think loud speakers were invented so those whose main ambition is to be heard can force themselves on the ears of people who don't care."

Then he hears that piercing accent of Eric Masterson. "Ketch, we gotta hit the road."

"Bye Martin."

Martin watches as Eric drags his son through the crowd. Eric has his head down, the red of his neck shining like a fresh sunburn. Martin jumps up and trots toward the father and son.

"Hey Masterson, wait a minute."

"I'm busy Marty-boy. What da ya want?"

"Look, why don't I run the load to Anaheim."

"What! I can do it myself."

"I'll do it."

Eric stood silent looking flustered.

"Com'on Masterson. Take a day off; go fishing with your kid."

"Oh, I get it. Another person telling me how to raise my son."

"I'm not telling you…"

"Damn right you're not. You came in, and made yourself the personal hero of Leo, saving the company twelve percent. Now you're going to teach me how to raise my boy!"

"Call it a professional courtesy."

"I'll call it you trying to take from me what I've earned. Stay outta my business Marty-boy."

With Eric off in a huff, his son's little legs desperately trying to keep pace, Martin turns back to the stage where Leo yells with excitement. He stares at the scrawny businessman intently, and can tell Leo is doing the same. Martin hates Leo. He hates the mayor. He hates the flock of sheep surrounding the stage pretending to care. What's more he wants Leo to feel his hate, all the way from the back of the crowd. So Martin Dougherty breathes fire at the man speaking, imagining the falling ash having come from his own lungs.

Chapter XVII

Rising Smoke and Empty Mines

The smell remains, but after climbing over the smoke, Marty and Estelle are under clear skies for the first time in eleven days. When the fires started Martin could distinguish nothing but the generic scent of ash. Now, like an expert connoisseur, he recognizes the aroma of smoldering Oak and burning grasses. A fresh breeze comes from the north, and Martin knows that a grove of *Aesculus* burns somewhere nearby. A day earlier the pleasant fragrance of smoking *Calocedrus decurrens* filled the air before vanishing behind the more pungent odor of flaming *Arctostyphylos*.

After several seconds of hurriedly rifling through her purse, Estelle pulls out a pen and ties her hair into a bun.

"I shouldn't complain, but taking a trip into the mountains while they're burning down is pretty stupid."

Leo's car comes to a stop at the end of the dirt road. The wildflower bloom ended two weeks ago, leaving only dead stems as a reminder that a short time ago the hills of Bodie were washed in color. The grass is gold, and with another week of heat it will turn brown, unless it's made black by the fires. The hills above the mines have green leaves of Oak and Pine along with silvery-gray granite boulders to give the landscape character, but none of this exists within the boundaries of the old mining complex. Martin picks up the ice chest and follows Estelle toward a shady patch right of the mine. In the thick air, the fifty-yard walk becomes inhuman, leaving him panting and faint. Trying to catch his breath he heads toward the nearest structure of the decaying enterprise.

Martin steps into the small shack outside the Miller mine entrance. The old blacksmith's shop connected with the assayer's room at its northern wall. He looks through the warped single paned window into the countryside beyond where piles of smashed rock alongside scattered remains of abandoned tools lie everywhere. Old boilers, broken trailers and huge mounds of tangled cable encircle the long bunkhouses. At the base of the hill, where the first strike was made, is the foundation of the mill that burned down in 1892. Ninety miles to the east, on the floor of the Valley stands Bodie, but the town was conceived here.

Martin see's Estelle's reflection in the window and says, "Nobody's gonna look for us, and the fires are supposed to be moving the other way. I thought it'd be somewhere we could go instead of my apartment. You know kind of have a romantic walk through the hills."

"It is romantic."

"I thought it was kind of a…couple thing to do." He turns back and looks around the shack as she walks up behind, grabbing his hand.

"That sounded corny," he says.

"It's very sweet, but you might regret not going to work today."

"The only people that will regret my absence are the secretaries. I can't believe Leo gave me the day off during the busy season."

"Well you did raise efficiency by twelve whole percent."

"I guess."

"You know whoever's been leaving those murals all over Bodie painted one on the back of the shop last night."

Martin shifts his feet but stops short of turning. "Did anyone see who did it?"

"No. Everything got closed last night. Kirk went home at ten, and said he saw nothing when he left. He locked the gate and went home. When Jose got to the yard in the morning he went around back to start preparing the trucks, there it was."

"What was it?"

"Remember in the cartoon version of Alice in Wonderland when Alice fell through the rabbit hole. She was going down, with all those objects falling with her. It was like that, but the objects were all weird stuff, not like in the story. Drug stuff, a dead body, guns, knives. It was really disturbing."

"That's the fourth, no fifth time he's hit something in Bodie."

"Well Jose's probably finished painting over it by now. It made me think it might improve the look of the yard if we were to get someone to paint some appropriate stuff all over that building." She sighed heavily and Martin knew what was coming next. "I told Leo and he snapped that it was a stupid idea because it'd make the place look unprofessional." She feels his muscles tense.

"He shouldn't speak to you like that. Why does he think he's…"

"I don't want to talk about Leo today baby. I shouldn't have even brought it up"

Estelle pulls herself close, kissing Martin on the shoulder. At that moment, when anyone else would already be kissing her, he stands patiently. When their relationship was new, Estelle used to reassure him with a whisper or some other little hint. Now she waits. It's cruel, to stand by passively while he struggles, but how can she not relish being with someone considering nothing at that moment but her desires.

They fall together and Martin's drifts. Before her, his mind would always wander back to his first dream. His friends all imagined being super heroes or famous athletes, but Martin thought of being a descendent of miners. The Dougherty's never made it to the mountains, they stayed in Bodie. This undeniable truth reminded to him by every street, building and park his family helped build.

Slowly his thoughts have moved from the safe joy of imagining the unattainable to the frightening reality of the possible. It's more upsetting than all those ridiculous dreams and like a schizophrenic indulging in peyote, being with Estelle makes it worse. With each kiss Martin finds himself falling farther into himself, closer to the a path separate from the Dougherty's that lies within his reach. Secretly, Martin has always asked for the opportunity, now the responsibility of following a road apart seems too hard to face.

Even resting in quiet satisfaction, a time when Martin used to think of nothing, he envisions the possibility of a simple life.

"Isn't this the area where Gabriel and Yvonne were killed?"

"No, they were about three ridges over, and up higher."

"You sure? I think this was the spot, or at least near here."

"No." Martin stares at a section of land about twenty-five yards away, riddled with the workings of generations of California ground squirrels. On the highest point of the most northerly edge of the colony stands a solitary mother kicking dirt and emphatically waving her tail toward a clump of dried grass. She jumps and gyrates occasionally making small squeaking noises without taking her eyes off the weeds. The purpose of their excitement becomes clear when the loud rattle of a western rattlesnake pierces the air.

"I used to go to the place they got killed all the time. Whenever me and Velarde wanted to smoke dope, that's where we'd go. It's right below this grove of *Seqouiadendron giganteum*."

"What?"

"Giant Sequoias. There's this little creek it runs between the trees, and in this one spot it cascades over granite boulders into a waterhole. We'd go down, swim in that hole and smoke weed. Diego and I spent hours in that water, talking to each other like we knew something about the world. For my money, there's no better place in the Sierra's, except for the Minarets."

"Jonathan never went with you."

"No, even back then he was working in the summer. In the fall and winter it was always to cold. I don't know why we never went in the spring. It doesn't matter now. Me and Velarde haven't been back since Jon's parents were killed."

Estelle slides closer to Martin. When they died, it didn't feel right. I remember every Heffron that died during my lifetime, and even when it made me sad, it always seemed to fit. But all these years later, I still can't quite understand what happened to Gabriel and Yvonne."

Estelle pulls her blouse back over her shoulders and tries to comfort him, but gives up when she recognizes the trance.

"Mr. and Mrs. Heffron used to come here all the time. Not this mine specifically, but to this area. This was where most of the gold was. The Noonday mine was just on the other side of the ridge over by that gate we passed. That was one of the bigger paying operations. The Heffron's spent most of their time at the Bulwer mine, up a little farther from here. It's near the north fork of the Deadman after it drops out of the basin above.

"There's really nothing left of the mine itself. The entrance is still there, but it's caved in after ten feet. I think the reason they liked it there was because it's the only one with a standing mill. All the other mills have burned down or fallen apart, but the Bulwer is still there. They liked walking around the old building even though the area's just a collection of grassy hills dotted with an occasional pile of granite. Still, whenever they spent the day in the mountains they'd pack a little picnic and go to that old mill.

"That's where they were headed the day they died. They'd gone by Big Potato to pick up some stuff for sandwiches, but forgot to get a bottle of wine. Mrs. Heffron loved her red wine. They stopped at the bait shop near Pine Flat to pick up a cheap bottle. That was the last time I saw them. It was the last time anyone saw them, as far as I know.

"There'd been a full moon the night before, and I'd been fishing overnight at Pine Flat. Didn't catch much, and on the way home I was going to pick up some hair of the dog. I walked out that bait shop as Mr. Heffron walked in. He stopped and looked at me, then he saw the beer in my hand. I mean, he didn't care. He knew I drank; hell he knew his son drank. Still, I didn't like him seeing me buy beer, especially at a bait shop at seven on a Sunday morning. I explained the whole thing, but didn't feel justified. He'd known me since I was a kid, and the whole thing made me uncomfortable. We talked a little; I don't remember about what, but he told me he was going up to the Bulwer mine with Mrs. Heffron. They'd just found out they were losing their place the day before.

"Out of pure nervousness I told him he should go to the spot where me and Velarde used to smoke. He told me they'd just go to the same old spot, and I should have left it. What did I care where they went, but the awkwardness of it made me press him. After a few minutes of badgering he said he'd think about it. He told me maybe a change of scenery would be fitting, seeing as they'd be discussing what to do now that the farm was going under.

"Six hours later I got the call from Laura that they were dead. They'd been killed in some kind of explosion. I figured it had to be the Bulwer mine. When I found out it happened at my spot, I ran to the bathroom and threw up. They'd gone to where I told them, because I was ashamed of being caught buying a beer. If I'd not been so proud they'd have gone on as normal, and Heffron might still have his parents."

"Have you ever talked to anyone about this Martin?"

Martin begins putting his clothes back on. "You can't tell anyone Estelle. If it ever got back to Heffron, he'll never forgive me."

She puts her hand on his back, and feels that his shivering in the ninety-five degree heat. "The only thing Jonathan could be angry about is that you waited so long to tell him. He wouldn't blame you for his parents' death. That was a terrible, terrible accident. You can't put the responsibility of such a thing on yourself baby."

"Estelle, I know the Heffron family legacy better than anyone except for the Heffron's themselves. Hell, my family was there when it all began. Even if I hadn't done what I did, they'd have died somehow, but I sped it up; I denied Heffron one last chance to speak to his father."

Estelle moves closer and wraps her arms around Martin's neck. "Martin are you hearing what you're saying. You didn't send Gabe and Yvonne there, and you didn't take anything from Jonathan."

"The day before his parents died, Heffron and his dad got into this argument about the farm being sold. He didn't mean anything by it; he was only scared. Who wouldn't be. That was the last time he spoke to his dad. Heffron could deal with death, that was going to happen, he just would have liked a little more time, you know, so they could have gone out on better terms. If I hadn't been so full of my own little hang-up's, so concerned with the opinions of dead relatives, Heffron would have had that chance. Instead he's going to live the rest of his life with the burden of knowing the last words he ever spoke to his father were in anger."

"Martin, look at me."

Martin doesn't try to stop her from sliding her arms under his and resting them on his chest. She holds him tight whispering into the side of his neck.

"Marty, you have a chance to help one of your friends better understand what happened to his parents. If Jon's really tormented with guilt, then maybe knowing more about how they died will give him peace."

"What if Heffron hates me for the rest of his life?"

"Wouldn't you rather he hate you than himself?"

It would be a good time for a breeze. Just a slight one, and only for a few moments but the air stays still. "I'm sorry to put all this on you Estelle. I wanted to bring you here to escape. Not to give you one more thing to lug around."

"It's nice to be able to carry something or someone again."

Martin thinks of Ulysses at that moment of truth. He needed to kick that horse, and he'd be in these mountains, it was the whole reason he dragged his family from Illinois. They were going to the mines where they would make their fortune, and live the rest of their lives comfortably in San Francisco. But Bodie wanted him to stay. They begged him to stay and help, to be the man they needed. Martin always thought if he'd been in that position the choice would've come easy. Now, faced with the same decision, he can know what the old man felt. As hard as it was, Martin promised never to make the same mistake. He'd never turn his back on the mountains.

"Let's leave this place together."

Estelle hesitates briefly before she giggles brightly, but still doesn't release her grip. "I wasn't planning on walking home."

"That's not what I was saying."

She's thought of the possibility many times, always stopping the idea before it germinated, telling herself such a thing would be too difficult; that the choice in and of itself would tear her apart. She convinced herself that the best thing to do was enjoy the fling, ending it once Martin suggested taking it farther.

Her head still pressed against Martin's broad back, she can feel his heart beat harder with each passing moment. She has an answer; in fact she's had one for a long time, her silence a result of the shock at her own certainty. "I'm ready when you are."

"Really?"

"I don't want to spend the next ten months talking about it Marty. I won't be able to handle it. If we're going to do it, we have to do it soon. Do you understand?"

"I understand."

A shadow moves across the ground before disappearing. He turns around and kisses Estelle softly on the forehead but gazes up at the billows of smoke from the approaching fires. It was supposed to be contained in this direction, but the thickening dark makes Martin believe otherwise.

"We'll leave on the fourth."

Chapter XVIII

The Last Charge of the Bad Man

In the depth of winter, moisture from the San Joaquin soil rises, creating banks of Tule fog. Named after the reeds that once grew around the lakes and ponds of the Valley, the fog appears quickly, cloaking anything within a few feet. The fog comes, and life goes on. Each morning thousands travel the roads of the Valley on the way to work and school, vision be damned. Car after car slam into pileups hidden in the mists until it's too late. There are years when these wrecks claim dozens of lives, but even before the automobile the Tule fog killed.

After seven years of murdering, high jacking and looting across the San Joaquin, federal marshals along with local law enforcement cornered the Bad Man from Bodie five miles outside the settlement. From the east rode twenty Marshals, while a posse of thirty citizens led by Ulysses Dougherty approached from the west. In the middle stood The Bad Man himself, with the exhausted remains of his gang. Hidden by the fog the legendary band of outlaws didn't see their enemies bearing down on them until the last moment. They had eluded the law for months, ever since the governor of California (pressured by the railroads) created a task force to deal with The Bad Man and his gang. Outside the town that named him, The Bad Man was finally cornered on the fifteenth of December, 1891.

They might have escaped, using the fog to cover their movements; they could have gone through town, and from there, to their hiding place in the canyons of the Sierra Nevada's. He couldn't let it go though, not The Bad Man. He turned the remaining members of his posse, and charged the marshals who were galloping toward the gunfire.

There are different endings to the story, and everyone has their favorite. In some versions, he and all his men were killed, proving that justice always prevails. Other's tell that all his men perished, but The Bad Man escaped to Mexico to live the rest of his days a respectable country gentlemen. Some say he was captured alive, but because Ulysses Dougherty respected him so, he was secretly released. The story is fading, and will soon be forgotten on the town, but when old timers send their loved ones into the fog they say, 'Watch out for the Bad Man.'

Chapter XIX

Confessing

The Valley sun reflects off white gravel; wrapping the work-shops of Mr. Wisnewski in a luminous haze. Here and there the last visages of auburn trim clings to sheltered corners and shaded eves. The once groomed gardens have surrendered to bermuda grass and puncture vines, which struggle to keep green in the dry soil. A decaying shell of a great city built by a vanished civilization, not quite in ruins but well on the way. Like the Mayan pyramids, everything will soon be swallowed by wilderness then forgotten. Even the bright gravel will eventually be replaced by Valley dirt.

Diego has chronicled the degeneration like he might one day compose a history of the place. *The Rise and Fall of the Great Wisnewski Empire.* The workshops went first, and with them the throngs of pilgrims who visited when news spread that the school district cut Mr. Wisnewski's beloved auto-tech program. His students assumed the man would throw himself into restoring the hotrods that won him fame. Collectors longed for the day when Alistair Wisnewski would end his teaching career and make his hobby a full time oc-cupation.

Instead his shop became a time capsule, with his final project, a restoration on a 1950 Buick, sits unfinished in the center of the shop. Weeds and ground squirrel burrows chip away at the foundation while rust streaks the walls. The rollup doors are frozen shut and dust carpets the once pristine interior.

The yard and house fell into disrepair shortly thereafter, as Mr. Wisnewski's sudden fall from sobriety drove away his wife. With her departure the well-groomed olive trees grew wild. The gardens of roses and California wildflowers are overrun with weeds, and the lawn died long ago.

Diego walks up the stairs to the front entrance, making sure not to trip over the loose board on the second step. He moves the screen door that dropped off its hinges before tapping lightly on the bell.

"Who is it?"

It's the closest he'll get to an invitation so Diego enters the dusty home, slipping on an old newspaper. He remembers visiting in high school, thinging it too perfect then, and now it resembles an abandoned frat house.

"It's your favorite student," Diego chimes.

"Well Mrs. Fitzpatrick, it sounds like you have a cold."

"Patricia may be your most successful student, but don't tell me for a fucking moment that I'm not your favorite."

"Well, favorite student, I don't want to be bothered today."

"If you're working on something, I'll leave," Diego says as he finds his mentor working a bottle of cheap wine.

"I've told you to stop bothering me."

"You also told me not to put a 383 stroker in the Firebird. I didn't listen then either."

"That model was the most beautiful of the 60's muscle cars, and your granddad kept it virtually original. It needed work, but you shouldn't have altered it. You should never alter perfection."

"You've customized dozens of cars in your life."

"Thirty-one."

"So?"

"I never altered the perfect ones. '57 Chevy or the '50 Mercury. Those you leave alone."

Diego walks over to the half empty six-pack and grabs a cold beer before falling on a large lounge chair covered in car magazines. "So how ya doing Mr. Wisnewski?"

Mr. Wisnewski takes a long drink of wine. "You've lost weight."

"Thanks."

"So, what's wrong?"

Mr. Wisenwski spins a small crank, opening the bent Venetian blinds, allowing slivers of light to shoot through the room, revealing a thick cloud of dust, and Diego feels stifled by the airs sourness.

"Maybe I just wanted to improve my appearance."

"The men of this town have many vices, vanity's never been among them."

"We're assimilating into the wider world."

"If you were, you wouldn't be wasting time with those idiot friends of yours."

"What's your fucking point?"

"You're either sick, just finished being sick, or something's happened that's made you lose your appetite."

"You know what, let's go out to the shop and talk about it."

"I'm tired of you trying to herd me into doing what you think I outta be doing."

"Nobody's herding. But men talking about this kind of shit should be working, otherwise it's girly." Diego rises, grabs two more beers, and another bottle of wine before starting for the door. "Com'on teach, you gonna turn down lecturing an old student."

"How 'bout you just sit down, and tell me what's on your mind since you're the one who came and disturbed me."

"You're no fun for a drunk."

"If you're going to insult me, you can just leave!"

"You're fucking over sensitive too." Turning to leave Diego slips again, hitting the ground, sending a new cloud of dust bellowing into the air. He reaches behind his back, finding a small box, no doubt the cause of the fall. He turns it in his hand before flipping the lid.

"This is a silver star."

"Where'd you get that!"

"Where'd I get it! Where the fuck did you get it?"

Mr. Wisnewski crashes across the living room, snatching the box from Diego. "It's nothing."

"When we were kids, Jon showed me the one his great uncle won at Guam before he got killed in that munitions explosion."

"You don't know anything about it."

"Don't be an asshole, tell me how you got it."

"Why should I! You refuse to tell me why you've lost weight."

"That medal is probably a better story."

"You haven't lived long enough to know a good story."

Diego cranes his neck wringing out the frustration. "Fine. I'll tell you, you tell me." He waits for a response and for a moment as a small sparkle returns to the broken man's eyes. A teacher always believes they have the answer. It's part of the job description, a compulsion born from living with an identity rather than working a job. So, Diego obliges, and tells Mr. Wisnewski everything.

Barely listening to a word, Mr. Wisnewski watches Diego speak frantically. The old teacher takes a breath, thinking with sadness that this is what it's come to for the young. They've been trapped by a great disconnect. It's all compartmentalized, with nobody contributing anything that hundreds of others don't already provide; yet people must feel needed. They do what they must, taking solace in brief moments when they can help each other, pretending it means more than it really does.

"So that's everything." Shuffling in his seat, Diego feels exposed, even with leaving out his recent failures in the bedroom.

Mr. Wisnewski drags himself upright, then stumbles out of the room. His passing disrupts the patterns of dust, and Diego amuses himself watching the dancing particles. Returning with two more cold beers, the old teacher hands one to his student.

"I'm going to tell you bout that medal."

"No advice!"

"You want to hear the story or not?"

"Fuck. I got nothing here."

"I was two years in, and I'd seen a lot of combat by the time I got this. We were flying ammunition into some marines stationed out in the countryside. Could have been any other American outpost. A staging ground for forays into the jungle chasing whatever we were chasing. We made four runs that day, us and three other birds. It was a two-hour round trip when you count in loading and unloading the supplies. Routine, especially by the standards of the last month. There hadn't been much activity of late, in fact I don't think I'd heard a shot fired in weeks. That was the way of things in Nam, you'd have a month of total boredom punctuated by a few hours of hell.

"We were heading home after the last run. I was half asleep but still made out the pop. It might've been the second shot that woke me, I don't remember. The smell of burning oil and gunpowder registered before anything. We'd been shot at plenty, but it's the first time my bird got hit that bad, still I didn't think much of it. The whole chopper shuddered with a violence. We were taking fire from below. Probably someone waiting to ambush a night patrol coming out of the outpost we spent the day refitting. When they saw us flying, they decided to take some shots at us for the hell of it. We started going down, and I held on as tight. I saw the chopper to our right burst into flames. Two friends were on that bird, and I never saw them again.

"We landed in a small rice field. Most rice patties were in large open areas, but this one was just three, maybe four acres, surrounded by thick jungle.

"Nobody in our crew was hurt, but we were shaken up. Except for our pilot, Lee. With all the spinning and smoke he somehow managed to land us perfectly. He was on his third tour, Old Lee. He was really kind of a hippie, though he had a temper. He was always getting reprimanded for not cutting his hair, and belittling the cause. He supposedly wrote anonymous letters to General Abrams calling for America to pull out and go home. But they couldn't get rid of him, he was too good. He kept signing up for more tours.

"Lee asked for a diagnostic, quick and dirty. He sent the rest of the guys around the border of the jungle to scout and listen for VC coming down on our position.

"I learned how to fix things by repairing old lawnmower engine, and now I had to patch up a shot down helicopter in the middle of the jungle. It felt like forever, and Lee paced around the chopper. He wasn't nervous; just strolling around, passing the time while I looked for the problem. I can imagine the man walking the same manner at a deli while waiting for his order. Finally, I found a small gearbox below the top rotor damaged beyond repair. It was a miracle, a crash landing, and all I needed was one little part and we'd be airborne.

"Lee decided we'd hike out, at least a day and half. We were gathering our stuff when, in a moment of clarity, I realized that if we could find the other downed chopper we could get its gearbox and fly home. So, me and another member of the crew, this young kid named Sandy, we walked north in the hope of finding the other wreck. Lee wanted to come, and to be honest I would have preferred it. He had more experience than Sandy, but if something happened to our pilot we were cooked, so he stayed with the chopper.

"We walked for fifteen minutes unable to see more than a few feet in front of us. The damn air was so thick I thought I'd pass out, and I was in good shape back then. I can remember ever rustle in the bush, and every birdcall more clearly than my wedding night.

"Maneuvering through the jungle we found the wreck, and by the grace of God the gearbox we needed was undamaged. I got the part and double-timed it back to the rice field. Just as we get back Sandy's skull exploded. Lee dragged Sandy's headless body into the chopper before returning fire while the other crewman jumped behind my M-60 and laid down cover fire. While this is going on, I climbed on top of the Hughie and replaced our busted part."

"I stood on top of that thing for eight minutes, taking heavy machine gun fire, and not even a scratch. Hell the guy firing my M-60, I can't remember his name now, he was killed about two minutes into the fight and Lee took a bullet in the shoulder and one through his right calf. Once the gear was fixed, Lee got us out of there. He almost bled to death, but he made it in the end. He even signed up for a fourth tour, but got shot down and killed during the evacuation of Saigon.

"When we got back to base this reporter got hold of the story and ran with it. It didn't make the national newspapers, but Star's and Strips published it. It was enough to get me a purple heart, even though I wasn't hurt other than a few scratches picked up in the bush, and that silver star." Mr. Wisnewski takes a drink of his beer. "The medal means nothing, but what I learned that day did."

Diego pulls himself forward in his chair and puts his unopened beer down on the coffee table. "I don't know that the medal means fucking nothing."

"I didn't do anything that wasn't done before or since by others."

"What did you learn?"

"What?"

"You said you learned something. What was it?"

"I learned the importance of serving a purpose, Mr. Velarde. At least that's what I thought when I got home. I remember the day it hit me. I'd been home two weeks, and was working on an old Cadillac that was in as good condition as your Firechicken there, and I realized that maybe I made it through that day because I was doing what I was put on this earth to do. I was being a mechanic, and was sparred."

Mr. Wisnewski looks closely at Diego. "I know it sounds strange, after all I wasn't really saving lives, or making the world a better place. I was just a grease monkey teaching subjects that aren't respected in society, but I served a purpose, insignificant as it might have been. Of course, now it doesn't matter does it?" Mr. Wisnewski takes another swig of beer wishing it were whiskey.

"So, what are you saying I need to do?"

"Discover your purpose Mr. Velarde, and serve it regardless of how unimportant it may seem at the time. Then spend the rest of your life praying the day never comes when you don't serve that purpose anymore."

Diego picks up the beer, not intending to open it, but to put it back in the refrigerator on the way out. "So all I have to do is find my place in the universe? Thanks for the fucking help."

"Well I'll help get you started by saying that regardless of what it is, you're not going to find it bar hopping in Tijuana."

"When are you going to start serving your purpose again?"

"I served mine."

"Ian would say 'It's only done when you're dead.'"

"The Heffron's are all insane. I'd sooner follow the advice of a derelict."

"They'd probably consider that a compliment, but that doesn't mean they're wrong."

Mr. Wisnewski sighs and looks at his student for the second time since he arrived. This young man, his favorite student, will no doubt be the one who finds him after it's over. He'll take it bad. Always so sentimental. "I really wish you wouldn't come troubling me all the time Mr. Velarde."

"Tell you what, when I show up at this place to find I've interrupted something more fitting a man of your purpose, I'll leave. Otherwise, see you next week."

Diego walks out, careful not to slip for a third time. At the door, he sees a flash on the small table under the front window. He looks quickly behind him as Mr. Wisnewski walks toward the kitchen. Diego grabs the polished .45 caliber pistol, and slips it under his shirt.

Chapter XX

When That Day Comes

"If I'm not under arrest, why do I have to sit in the back like a criminal?"

Officer Gerald Ramis coughs a weary laugh and says, "You've been in the back of a police car plenty of times."

"I should shut up and feel at home then."

"You're the most fearless person in the town. At least that's what they'll be calling you soon enough."

"Why's that?"

"When a man sleeps with the wife of the most influential person in town while working for him, well what else can be said? And why would a man with those credentials fear being seen in the back of a squad car anyhow?"

"I never had sex with Estelle! I barely even know her. I talk to her when I'm..."

"According to Leo you did. I don't think the Dougherty name will protect you this time Marty. Not that I believe Leo's quite as mad as everyone says, but there's no denying he holds sway."

Martin leans forward until his nose touches the cage thin metal cage. "I don't need a name to protect me from Leo Radmonavic." Sitting back, Martin watches as they pass the fenced off remains of Sushi on the Run. They've almost finished the soft demo, leaving nothing but the skeletal remains of an underappreciated icon of the community. There was nothing quite like it in the Valley, but it's all gone now.

"Well, what did she say?"

"Who?"

"Estelle."

Officer Ramis hesitates for a moment. "That's why you're being brought in."

"You're arresting me because Leo said I had sex with Estelle? This is a bunch of crap Ramis." Got to calm down a bit. Not too much though; Ian always says that's a sign of guilt. Ulysses would probably agree.

"I told you, you're not under arrest. We just need to talk to you about something."

It was sure to come, he knew it the first time he made her smile. Eric and Leo were interviewing for the new secretary, and Estelle came in. He told her where Leo was, and a look of embarrassment and disgust came over her face that Martin didn't understand. Later, after learning Leo was sleeping with the new hire, he got it. Martin began chatting with Estelle whenever they crossed paths, and soon she was smiling. One day she laughed and he knew, before anything happened he knew. He could have walked away without taking it any farther, but that first simple kiss would have become known. The story was already written, Estelle Radmonovic, darling of Bodie, seduced by the fallen Dougherty.

Still, only a few more days and they could have been free of it all. A few more days, and Jerry Ramis would have arrived to find an empty apartment. At that moment Marty would have been with her, driving down a lonely highway heading over the Sierra's. In time people would have realized what happened, and it would have been the talk of the town for months, maybe longer. It wouldn't have mattered though, because they would have been gone. Maybe one day, many years in the future, Jon or Diego would have stumbled upon them living on some ranch in a forgotten corner of Wyoming. They would have talked what the sensation created by affair, and Marty and Estelle would have looked at each other, smiling at the silliness of it all.

That was a dream, and now only the details need to be learned. Did Leo find out from Estelle, or did she tell someone without his knowing. Has word already spread? What would be the best from Leo's perspective? Certainly not public rumors, that kind of embarrassment would send him on a rampage. Finding out from someone in the company, or directly from Estelle would give Leo a degree of control; but which would be best? Martin wonders whom he'd rather learn from, his wife, or one of his closest friends?

Arriving at the parking lot of the police station he sees the second most famous vehicle in town. Only the Firechicken is better known than that gray seventy-six Silverado. It's fallen into disrepair, but Martin would take it in an instant.

"What's Mr. Wisnewski doing here?"

"He wasn't here when I left," Ramis answers.

Jerry pushes thru the double doors and waits for Martin to enter the reception room of the police department where three cops surround and irate Mr Wisnewski."

"Damnit the boy stole it I'm telling you! Now get out there, and do your job!"

"Mr. Wisnewski, please calm down and explain yourself in a clear manner. We can't arrest someone without evidence. Now how do you know Diego Velarde stole your gun?"

"I already told you that!"

"Tell me again."

"I left the pistol on my front table just a few hours earlier, and then that damn kid came by, bothering me like always, when I just want to be left to die in peace. He stayed around, bothering about the war and his little problems with cannibals and whores from Tijuana. Then he left, and now my pistols gone and damnit I know that little son of a bitch took it. Now I want you people to do your sworn job, and arrest that Judas!"

The police officers stand by patiently, but it's Officer Torres who speaks first. "Do you usually leave guns laying next to your front door Mr. Wisnewski?"

"It's my gun! It's my house, what business of yours is it where I leave it. That traitor of a student stole it, that's what matters!"

"I'm just trying to understand what it is you meant when you said you wanted to die in peace?"

"What, what does that…"

"Have you been drinking Mr. Wisnewski?"

"So, what if I have. How does it change that my…"

"If you drove here drunk at eight in the morning, and your accusing one of your former students, a man with no criminal record and a spotless reputation in town, I think it's a perfectly correct question. Now, without more insulting words, have you been drinking?"

Everything he's given to the town, to the school, to his students, and they still want more. That was tolerable for as long as he had something to give, but why more now. They want him to clean up, for what? They want him to act respectable, for whom? Now they want answers, by what right! He gave everything and asked for nothing in return. Even when they took the program away, he didn't cry or complain. He could have left that board meeting accepting the end before returning with a shotgun, but he didn't. He only wanted to leave it all on his own terms.

"You bastards. You Goddamn bastards!"

"Now Mr. Wisnewski…Stop! Grab him"

As quickly as Mr. Wisnewski lunges at Officer Torres, he's wrestled to the ground and locked in hand cuffs.

"Let me go! He stole from me. They all stole from me! You're all sadists. You love watching me suffer, and you want me to stay around for your amusement!"

Watching it from a distance Martin feels he's attending a strange play. The man writhing on the floor couldn't possibly be the one who dominated campus with his long stride and booming voice. Even students who never took his classes stepped aside, and here he is being dragged around on the ground like rampaging animal.

Ramis takes the side of Marty's arm. "I'm going to stay here Martin. Go down the hall and into the last interrogation room on the right, and wait there until the Chief comes."

"What's going to happen to him Ramis?"

"Half the force took his classes in high school. He'll be taken care of."

"What about the whereabouts of the gun?"

"The chiefs from L.A. I don't think he'll lose sleep over a missing gun…as long as Mr. Wisnewski doesn't have it. Oh, and please don't make me look like an idiot by letting you go on by yourself."

Martin remains silent passing through the halls of the police department before entering the last interrogation room and sitting in the empty chair facing the door. It's the third structure to house Bodie's police department. The first burned four years after the founding when the town sheriff, one Ulysses Dougherty, condemned a town whore for the murder of one of her customers. Hanging a murderer was nothing new. This time however, Ulysses misjudged the devotion of Susan Turner's clientele. How could he, a Dougherty, have known that the relationship between a man and his whore was such a powerful bond? The night before the hanging, four of these men broke into jail, rescued Susan and burned the building to the ground. Susan Turner was taken from the San Joaquin Valley, and never seen again.

The second station was built over the charred ruins of the original and served until 1923. Like all the major municipal buildings the Police Department was built next to the train tracks. One night a southbound locomotive jumped the tracks and smashed into the side of the Police Department at forty-five miles an hour, crumbling it to its foundations. Remarkably, the officer on duty survived by jumping under a large oak desk. The man sleeping in the cell wasn't so lucky. Peter Heffron was waiting for his trial on bootlegging charges when the roof of the building fell on top of him. The next morning Bernard Dougherty, the best trial lawyer in the state, was to go before the county judge (his older brother Stephan) to work out Peter's release. Jon's told the story so many times that Martin can't pass the building without thinking of Peter.

By 1925 the current police station was finished. Seventy-five years, and several renovations later, Marty sits in an interrogation room waiting to meet the latest Police Chief. Sure he's wanted to meet the man. The Chief moved from Los Angeles a year earlier in the hope of raising his young daughter in the relative safety of a small town. He was a novelty, and novelties were always interesting.

The door opens and a large heavyset man enters. His tanned arms look red, but while adjusting himself in his seat the chief's sleeves lift and Martin can see the pale white of his natural skin. His black hair, natural features along with the roasted skin give him the look of a member of the Comanche nation, but Martin doubts he has an ounce of native blood.

"Good morning Martin, I'm Chief Kearney. I want to apologize for disturbing you in such a dramatic fashion, and I promise not to take up too much of your time. I just have a few questions and then you'll be able to go." No need to wait for a response indicating that Marty understands. "First off, when was the last time you had any contact with Estelle Radmonovic?"

"At the last company party, about a month ago," Marty answers coolly.

"How long have you been having an affair with her?"

Rapid-fire questions, that's how they catch lies. "I never had an affair with her. I don't even know her that well."

"You've been working at her house for over a year, yet you don't know her very well?"

Martin starts to shift in his seat, but stops himself. "I don't work at her house, I work at her husband's truck yard, which is near her house. If she comes out to the yard for something, or she addresses me while walking around her front yard, I make small talk out of respect for my boss."

"You call that no relationship?"

"That's no more a relationship than anyone in Bodie has with her. This isn't Los Angeles. Everyone's on a first name basis with everyone, but that doesn't mean we're all having sex with each other."

"I'm just asking questions here, there's no need to make it personal." The Chief looks back down at the sheet of paper. "Why did you abruptly quit Bodie Trucking?"

"What does that got to do with anything?"

"Leo thinks it's because you broke it off with Estelle, and she didn't like it. You were feeling uncomfortable with the whole situation, so you quit."

"I quit because Leo thought he could insult my father in front of the entire company and get away with it. I walked, later on we talked it out, and he offered me a raise with a promise of promotion. I made my point, he understood it, so I went back to work."

"You're close with your father are you?

"No, but he's my father. Now I want to ask you some questions if that's alright with you?"

"Watch the attitude Mr. Dougherty." Chief Kearney doesn't raise his head and his face shows no emotion at all. There's no sweat on his brow and his fingers still hold the papers lightly.

"I may be a loser Chief Kearney, but since coming to Bodie my family has produced three sheriffs, four lawyers and a district judge. So, don't think I'm some ditch bank trailer trash that doesn't know his rights. You asked me to come in without any explanation, and I did. You're acting entitled to answers without grounds for asking questions. You're accusing me of having an affair with a married woman, but treating me like a murderer. Now, tell me why I'm here or I'm getting up and walking out that door, and we both know there's no way you can stop me." Even Lena would be proud.

"Two nights ago Leo Radmonovic called saying he hadn't seen his wife in a day. She officially became a missing person a few hours ago. We're going public with it today, but before we do we want to make sure she's not on a weekend retreat having neglected to tell her husband."

Marty feels his boldness melt away as the Chief explains the situation. "So, why would you think I have information concerning her whereabouts?"

"Because if you had, or are having an affair with her, or even if you just talked to her while she walked around her front yard, you might have an idea of where she is. I've seen it before. Now, can I continue with my questions or is there some other legal formality I've failed to observe, you coming from such a 'distinguished' family of law enforcers." The Chief remains stern in his manner, his training required it.

"Yeah, I talk to Estelle sometimes."

"Talk?"

"Yes, it was just generic small talk at first. Nothing memorable. After I'd been there a few months we started talking about other stuff."

"Flirting."

"I don't know how to flirt. No, she started mentioning stuff about her marriage. That they fought all the time. I didn't think much about it at first because every married person I've ever met complained about their spouse, especially those in love. She'd fuss about Leo, and I'd do my due diligence, sympathizing and it wasn't long before she really opened up. First thing she brought up were the infidelities. From what she'd said he'd slept with every woman that'd ever worked for him. After awhile she started bringing up other stuff."

"What stuff might that be Mr. Dougherty?"

"Just about how abusive he was. I don't mean physically abusive, more in the way he'd talk to her. He beat her down any chance he got, telling her how stupid she was, and unattractive. He blamed her for their not being able to have kids, I think that's what made her feel worse than anything, like she didn't matter. She hated her life there. I just think he'd driven her so far into a hole she never had the courage to leave."

"Perhaps he beat here as well. That's been known to motivate even the most frightened people to run."

"He never hit her."

"How can you know that?"

"I just know."

"So you don't think she could have just up and left."

"Not without help."

"Do you know of anyone else she could have confided in?"

"Maybe, I don't know?"

"Well, it's very possible she met someone who built up her courage and got her to leave. Sadly, that usually never turns out well."

"Why's that Chief?"

"Because women in that situation usually run off with the first man who comes along and tells them they'll make it all better, and the men that pitch that line usually hunt for women in Estelle's situation."

The Chief jots down more notes, and the walls of the small blue interrogation room close in. All the possibilities that seemed certain hours' earlier collapse under the undeniable truth that Estelle left him. Occam's razor proves the weight of simple truths, and Ian always put his faith in simple truths. Estelle didn't love Leo, she couldn't have. Then the hours crept by, closer and closer to July fourth. The confining fog that clouded her vision for eleven years began to roll back, but the freedom she'd dreamt of was nowhere to be seen. There was only Martin Dougherty, the great pretender, staring back from beyond the haze, and she felt herself traveling from one prison to another, but there was no going back.

"Well that's all the questions I have for you at this time Mr. Dougherty, unless there's anything else you can tell me." The Chief says.

"If I think of something I'll come talk to you," Marty says. "Are you going to tell anyone around town about this?"

"Would that be a problem?"

Marty sighs heavily and rubs his forehead, feeling the unevenness created by the small, fresh scars from the branch that struck him a few weeks ago. "I guess it doesn't matter, but I'd like to know anyway."

"The only two people who know about what Leo said are Ramis and myself. I told him not to talk about the investigation with anyone. My impression of Leo Radmonavic is that he won't want this to come out any more than you."

"That's true, but as for Jerry, he's a local, so that won't matter."

"I'll have someone give you a ride to work, I understand you're late."

"Can they take me to My Friends House instead? I don't think I want to see Leo today."

"Tell them I said to take you wherever you want, and if I can offer some free advice."

"Sure."

"Find another job."

Marty gets up and walks out the door. His legs are weak and his head hurts but he betrays none of this to Chief Kearney who finally raises his gaze from his papers. "Thank you chief and I apologize for my attitude. I really do respect your office and…"

"You just remember to come to me if you hear anything, no matter how trivial you think it is." The Chief calls the front desk, telling them to drive Marty wherever he needs to go, and to send Gerald Ramis in to see him. He sits in the empty interrogation room going over his notes when Officer Ramis comes in. "Jerry, I don't want you talking to anyone about what you heard today. Especially what Leo said about Martin."

"No problem Chief."

"That's not good enough Jerry. I don't care how much you think you can trust somebody, do not say anything. If it gets out about Marty and Estelle, I'm not going to take the time to find out if you were the one that leaked it. What I will do is make sure you never work in law enforcement again. I may not be a local, but I do know a lot of very powerful people that can make your career as an officer non-existent anywhere in this state. You'll be back out in the fields picking nectarines."

"Take it easy Chief."

"This thing could be bad Jerry. I won't have it fucked up because you Goddamn people in this town are so bored you can't keep your mouths shut. Don't say anything or I'll tell Martin you sold him out and that whatever he chooses to do will be done with total immunity. This is the type of thing that could ruin that boy's life, and I don't want to see that happen... if I can help it."

"I'm not going to ruin Martin Dougherty's life."

Chapter XXI

Stolen Land and Sushi on the Run

The best Cherries ever grown in the San Joaquin Valley came from an eighteen-acre plot halfway between Fresno and Bodie. The last crop was harvested in the spring of 1941. In 1942, the Tsukamoto family was forced from their renowned cherry farm and sent to Manzanar. Some Japanese farmers were lucky enough to have neighbors willing to maintain their lands until they returned. Most did not. The Tsukamoto's sold cheap before the land could be taken for nothing.

After the camps closed in 1945, the Tsukamoto's worked five years as laborers in the Southwest and in 1950 they come home to Bodie with enough to buy another plot. They could have returned to farming, but they needed something grander, something that would tell everyone that in spite of it all, they had conquered. So, they bought a small gas station and converted it into a drive thru sushi joint. The menu that hung over the window was adorned with an ornate mural of a cherry farm with the words, "Greatest Cherry's in the San Joaquin!" Against all odds and logic, it survived for forty-five years. The family lived out of the back, and did side work all over the county to compensate for the fact that their little restaurant never made money.

After forty-five years, Sushi on the Run finally went under. Many had sound economic reasons for the fall. They talked about the rise in the cost of insurance, and the strains of modern living on small business. Nobody was critical, but they admitted that a town the size of Bodie could never support such an enterprise. Ian Heffron had a different theory.

"That family was betrayed. Their land was stolen. When they came back, it wasn't because they wanted to move on, if they had they would have gone back to farming. No, they wanted to stick it to everyone that stood by and watched that sin happen without so much as a word in their defense. So they opened a business that had to fail, and then kept it going just to prove they could."

Chapter XXII

On Imagination and Chance

Stepping through the heavy doors of My Griend's House, the black, windowless walls and high ceiling transform the interior into a deep cave stretching on forever. In one corner stands a big screen TV so old and faded that even in the dimness the picture is a blur. Directly to the right, a long unoccupied mahogany bar, above which is a mural depicting a famous gunfight Jim Florentine read about before moving to the historic town. It hangs above the bar, destined to fade away like needless history. Only Diego, who'd accidently overheard Jim mourn the wasted beauty, takes the time to appreciate the mural.

Soon the tightly packed redwood picnic tables step out from behind the veil of darkness. Built from redwood planks, each table has a lamp made to look like the oil lanterns of the mining days. The long wooden benches are unforgiving, but nobody complains. Instead they shift from one spot to another in an endless search for comfort.

Like the beautiful bar, the black walnut flying buttresses lining the eastern, and western walls ruin the carefully crafted simplicity of My Friend's House. There're ten of them, five against each wall, perfectly spaced and losing clarity in the increasing dimness. One imagines that if the back of room were lit, hundreds of identical buttresses would go back as far as the eye can see. Shaped like their stone counterparts, their bases jut out eight feet from the wall before climbing to within sixteen inches of the ceiling. Under the last buttress along the eastern wall, a velvet couch permanently reserved for Jonathan, Diego and Martin. A mahogany bar with black walnut buttresses coupled with picnic tables, bad carpet and tasteless beer advertisements. A simple restaurant trying to be something grand.

Left of the entrance is a narrow passage leading to the game room. The jukebox pushed against the west wall amplifies the tightness of the hallway. Several pine air fresheners hang from the ceiling, stubbornly preventing the scent of the bathrooms from drifting into the rest of the restaurant. Most of the albums in the jukebox are classic hits, or recent pop songs chosen for the sake of pleasing teenage customers.

What does the back room look like? Was it really the same as in memory? Are the inviting flashes of the arcades, and pleasant aroma of deep fried food still at work? There was a time when nothing could replace the youthful commotion of that place. Even without the buttresses to impress the eye, Diego remembers that space as…exciting. Large arcade games take the place of beer lights and novelty mirrors, but still they float in those ever-present shadows. The worn pool table in the rooms center stands immovable like the whole foundation is built around it. A great light hangs over the pool table. Not some stained-glass piece like in billiard halls, but a full crystal chandelier. Diego can still feel the dancing particles of light being flung across the room by the suspended cluster of glass.

Back then he could have imagined My Friends House as a place he'd never been and his fellow patrons as more extraordinary than they really were. Instead he see's nothing but a roomful of people from Bodie, but not really. All commuters recently arrived for the cheap housing and safe streets. None bled to build the town. None cared about it.

Diego looks down the narrow hallway that connects to the game room. Directly across from him stands that glorious game from younger days. Memories of countless hours spent in front of that consul flood his mind. With a smile, he remembers how Jon, Marty and he would wager on games. What was the last tally?

He buys three fingers of bourbon, and strolls down the hall toward the battered console, hoping to temporarily recapture a sliver of simpler times. Taking the joystick in hand he feels years of pizza grease embedded in the plastic. Obscene phrases and drawings cover many parts of the arcade, but even this looks to have stopped some time ago. In the games prime, lines of young boys waited for their turn but now it's not even worthy of updated graffiti. A quarter falls and it begins.

As Diego starts the second round of the fourth level, watching his Mau Tai warrior battle the bearded Russian monster, he feels a tap on his shoulder. "Hey, there she is! How's it going Rene?"

"Don't pretend you're excited to see me. It's insulting and weak." She looks at the pocket watch hanging from her belt; the conversation has already taken too much of her time. "I hear you've given up the mechanic's life, and are breaking into gun running."

"This fucking town."

"Have you seen Mr. Wisnewski?"

"I went by the jailhouse today hoping to talk to him, but he wasn't there."

"They already released him?"

"Nope. They transferred him up to the psych ward in Fresno. He's been put on seventy-two hour suicide watch."

"How're you doing?"

"The best teacher I've ever known is suicidal, and accusing me of theft."

"Sorry for asking such a stupidly obvious question."

"It's only stupid because I have no fucking clue of how to feel."

"Anyway, I was wondering if you talked to Jonathan today."

She couldn't be more than five foot four with an athletic figure. Her flawless olive skin with raven black hair has a natural wave to it, which she straightens, highlighting with pink streaks. She wears green contact lenses to cover her dark brown eyes, and her ears are heavily pierced. Though people often comment on her excessive makeup, she wears very little. The silver ring adorning her right nostril and the matching stud in her belly button crosses the line of decency. To help accentuate her piercings, she has several tattoos exhibited always. Most focus on the large angel wings that start at her shoulders and end above the small of her back.

Diego wonders how his incarcerated mentor would react to Rene's black tank top, modified in the back to make her angel wings more visible. He'd certainly frown at the small white letters that spell the word *sinner* across her chest. Then there are her blue jeans with holes held together by patches and safety pins. The first time his parents saw her, they remarked that she wore her jeans too low. When Diego told Rene, she explained that raising her pant line would hide the tattoo just under her belly button. On this night she has a pair of surprisingly tasteful leather sandals, but she usually sports a pair of black, worn cowboy boots.

"Jon was just here, but Marty needed a ride from work. Why, were you supposed to see him tonight? Maybe have a little pity love to console him. You know, he just had a big fight with Laura."

"There're a lot of reason's I'd fuck a guy, but never for pity. That's why you'd never have a shot. Oh-oh I think I touched a nerve." Rene smiles. "If you've got self-confidence problems I know a free mental health clinic in the City taking on charity cases. Then if you still feel lonely, it's right around the corner from Castro. I'm sure that would do wonders for your self-worth."

"What kind of shit psychiatrist has to work at a free clinic?"

"I've come to accept, even if I don't agree with, the ignorance that causes people to laugh at San Francisco because of irrational fears of homosexuals and liberals. What I've never managed to figure is how you can poke fun at people trying to take care of each other. Here you are, a car mechanic, drunk on a week-night, playing an outdated videogame, and making fun of an Ivy League trained shrink who's dedicated his life to improving the mental health of those who couldn't normally afford care."

His face burns red as every vein in his body ignites. His hands shake violently causing his warrior to be quickly de-feated. Diego turns, ready to tell Rene that she should return to The City only to find she's vanished. It's her trademark, but whenever he mentions it people accuse him of being paranoid, or in love. Returning his attention back to the game, he drops another quarter. After ten minutes and two more dollars Diego retires from the game. Finishing off his bourbon, Diego stagers toward the couch.

Crossing paths with one of the high school students working that night, Diego orders another drink before falling into worn folds of velvet. After fifteen minutes of boredom Jonathan and Marty arrive. Jonathan first walks to the counter for a pitcher while Martin takes the seat next to Diego. When Jon catches up he can't help but frown.

Begrudgingly, Jon takes a place in a wooden chair across from the couch, and fills three frosty glasses before distributing them. Diego looks at Martin and in as sincere a manner as he can muster asks, "So how are you doing my man?"

"Haven't slept. Then there's all the damn questions coming from each person whose path I cross. Leo's gone into hiding, and I'm basically running Bodie Trucking myself. Even Masterson, Mr. Company Man himself, just sits in his chair all day mumbling to himself."

Jonathan sips his beer and tries again to get comfortable. "Well, at least Leo has an excuse; his wife is missing."

"He never spared a thought for her while she was there! Why get sentimental now!" Martin thinks of the time Jon snapped after his parent's death. One of their schoolmates asked how he was doing, and Jonathan lost his temper. It took three people to hold him back, and he got sent home until the school counselor deemed him safe for the rest of the student body. Everyone sympathized, but as Marty searches the faces of his friends, he finds no such understanding.

"By the way Jon, Rene wants you to call her."

"What for?"

"Fuck if I know," Diego says. "She just said she wants to talk to you."

Martin wonders, against all his will, what the other Dougherty's would do. It's perverse, almost masochistic, the way he's always hated them, hated his last name; especially when it's been of benefit. Still, despite every effort to the contrary Martin knows he'll never be free of the past that wasn't his. He could move all the way around the world, to some forgotten place where Bodie doesn't exist, but still he'd ask; what would a Dougherty do?

Rubbing his head neither the exhaustion nor frustration leaves so he'll let it run its course without a fight. His pride doesn't matter, nor fear of heartbreak. What matters is Estelle. It's what all of them would have done, every Dougherty stretching back to the beginning would be out there right now doing what's needed. Instead he sits drinking beer, pretending nothing has happened. All those private, self-righteous ravings about Leo's treatment of her; the way that man made sure everything came before his wife. How can he now claim to be better? Maybe she's gone forever, or maybe she'll be back. Regardless, he doesn't deserve her.

"Fuck it man, I'll go get um myself."

Martin comes back to reality in time to watch Diego stumbling toward the kitchen. "Where's he going?"

"Our friend Diego is upset because he's been trying to order cheese sticks for the last ten minutes, yet can't get service. So he's taken it upon himself to march into the kitchen to find some for himself."

"He could use some cheesesticks. If he loses more weight we're gonna have him checked for tapeworm."

Together Martin and Jon watch Diego stumble across the floor. They aren't ashamed nor do they take amusement in the proceedings, it wouldn't be fair. Diego once watched in silent horror as Jon pissed off the front porch of his house in broad daylight during a Thanksgiving Day party. Martin still blushes when he thinks of Diego finding him weeping at being cut from the wrestling team his sophomore year. The worst part was how sympathetic Diego always acted, making sure never to use those moments of weakness against his friends. So, Martin and Jonathan stare with a kind of excitement, taking pride in each minor achievement, all the while knowing they can never use this to embarrass Diego.

Diego maneuvers through the swinging doors into the cooking area, where he stands frozen in panic. The light shining off the white walls and steel counters creating a haze that sobers him in the worst way. Sweltering heat from the industrial pizza oven makes him long for the relative cool of the Valley night. The horrible clamor of the dishwashing machines, and food processors makes his bones ache, but he must have cheese sticks. At the back of the kitchen he discerns what can only be the entrance into the freezer. He refuses to stop; even though finding the frozen delicacy doesn't mean he'll know how to cook them.

Taking a step forward, Diego stumbles and falls to the ground so suddenly that he doesn't have time to brace himself. He immediately recognizes the taste of blood in his mouth.

"Fuck, I gotta stop drinking." The shock of the fall has forced a moment of clarity, and he's now sure that the shape at his feet is in fact that of an unconscious man.

Diego pulls himself upright with the help of the stove. Drunk enough to feel no pain, he still understands his hand is burning. Kicking open the swinging door Diego swallows a mouthful of blood.

"Somebody needs to get the fuck in here!"

Chapter XXIII

Right is Somehow Wrong

Light fades, draping the floor of the mayor's office in shadow. It's only been a few moments since Mr. Florentine made the proposal, but already Enrique Ramirez has made his calculations. Mayor Enrique Ramirez, the man who saved Independence Day.

"Well Mr. Florentine, I have to say, this is a very generous, and much appreciated offer."

The high school principal slides his chair a few inches to enjoy the lengthening shadow. "Yes Mr. Florentine it really is. If you're willing to make such a…contribution, I can't tell you how much it means to the community."

"So long as you agree to continue putting on the firework show, I'll donate all the night's proceeds at My Friend's House to the high school. If I do as well as last year, it should not only pay for the show, but also give the school a little extra to play with. Do we have a deal?"

The mayor lets the slimmest of smiles get through only to feel it vanish when his sight drifts to the old man.

"You haven't said much Elroy."

"I'm not even sure what I'm doing here."

The mayor leans back until the big leather chair squeaks. "You've put on the fireworks show for as long as any of us can remember. You're here because we want you to continue. I'd have imagined you'd be thrilled to learn that you'll now have the funding to do so."

Elroy shifts in his stance. The principal is behind the move, and Mr. Florentine is willing to fund it, but custom demands they stay and listen to the old man. "I'm going to be down at the football stadium by myself, sending fireworks into the sky, surrounded by empty bleachers. Meanwhile the rest of Bodie will be at My Friends House eating and drinking, not even paying attention."

Mr. Florentine stands up. "Elroy, they're already doing that, but this way your show will get the money it needs to continue. If this proposal isn't accepted then there will be no Independence Day celebration in Bodie."

"Leo Radmonovic agreed to pay for the show, and keep it as it is, as long as you close your doors for a night."

The mayor snorts loudly. "Leo has already done enough for the town. This gives another citizen a chance to give."

"I'd be happy to close My Friend's House for the night, and offered publically to do so, but everyone got mad at the idea. Some even said they wouldn't go to the celebration anyway."

"It's not the same. Goddamnit! Sitting at some bar, eating a hamburger and drinking a beer. It's about being in that stadium, the whole town, all looking up at the same time. They stare along the flat of the Valley, and in the distance are all the other shows, and at that moment the whole San Joaquin is bound together at once. You tell me Mr. Florentine, how's that still true with the distractions of imported beer, T.V. and deep-fried food. You can't. This'll keep the celebration going, but it'll be dead in all the ways that matter."

Another squeak as the chair moves back forward. "Does that mean you won't do it Elroy?"

"It doesn't make a difference one way or another. There're plenty of other people who could do it, but I guess it might as well be me."

"Elroy, I'm a newcomer to Bodie and I know there are some who don't like My Friend's House, but I promise I'm not trying to destroy anything."

"Son, I've got to the age where I don't care what people are trying to do. My whole life, every time someone does something wrong they stand up to say they were trying to do something right, as though that makes it OK. I don't care what you're trying to do; I only care about what you're doing. Now Mr. Mayor. I think you've humored this old purist enough for the voters, don't you?"

Mayor Ramirez could only nod.

Chapter XXIV

Could This Be the One?

"There's the turnoff," Marty says. "I can't believe the Firechicken got us here without bursting into flames."

"Are you going to be an asshole all night?"

"I had something to do, and if you hadn't been pestering me, I'd be doing it right now."

"Is this the same thing you've been doing every night for the last week?"

Nothing's been done. He's looked into Leo, Estelle's family, even everyone who works at Bodie Trucking Company. He's talked to friends and grilled people who didn't like her. Pointless action, like farmers firing acetylene canons into the air during hailstorms, and for the first time he truly wants advice from all those Dougherty's. All those memories, forced on him the way some parents force vegetables down their children's throats, and all because a Dougherty should know such things. And now, when he should reap the rewards of those torturous lessons, there's nothing.

Martins fist slams into the side window, bending it to the point of breaking. Only the tight confines of the cab prevent his fist from punching through the glass completely.

"What the fuck Marty!"

"Sorry."

"You want me to just take you back to your place?"

"No."

"If you're just gonna be prick all night."

"Park the car, I want a drink."

"Damn, they really went all out on this thing. We should call Jon and tell him to get out here."

"No point."

Swerving, Diego avoids the rotting carcass of a dog. "I know I shouldn't have said anything that night at your place, but I still say he needs to get over that shit with his dad."

"He'd be happier."

The pole shed is sixty feet long and thirty feet wide, but the ends are covered in plywood and painted white. The long sides are open except for the poles supporting a rusting metal roof fifteen feet above the gyrating crowd. The scent of fermented berries ground into the pavement by generations of workers tastes fresh, though the shed hasn't operated in years.

Along the roof hangs strings of tee-kee lights and the poles have been wrapped in Christmas bulbs. Against one wall stands a simple home stereo system plugged into a pair of large speakers. Tables covered with assorted bottles of hard liquor are on both sides, and water coolers filled with punch and vodka teeter on their edges. A half dozen kegs of beer, each sunk in a large barrel of ice, act as the crown jewels of the libations. Between songs, dogs and coyotes howl their disapproval at the fireworks bursting across the Valley sky. To the east, colorful explosions occur against the backdrop of the worst wildfires in the history of California.

"Missed out on free drinks," Marty grumbles. "You drive like a girl Velarde."

"You didn't even want to come, so stop bitching."

"Well if I have to be here, I at least want drinks."

"Useless white boy. No fucking car of your own, and you still think you can insult my driving. Besides I thought we were cutting back."

"Well I'm…in the mood tonight." Martin whispers.

"Just get us some beer, I'm gonna talk to Rene."

"Why do you want to talk to that freak?"

"Shit Marty, I don't know why I talk to you."

Navigating morphing paths between pulsating bodies, Diego becomes mesmerized by Rene's unaffected posture. Planted in the center of it all, holding a burning joint between her middle and ring finger, Rene makes it clear to everyone, 'you can go around.'

When he gets close enough Diego leans in and whispers, "You've been waiting for me."

She looks at him taking a long drag. As though they all agreed beforehand, the crowd steps back to escape the heavy smell of reefer spiraling around them.

"I've been waiting for a good song."

"Ian says denial's an ugly thing."

"He says the same thing about delusion."

Diego laughs and thinks for a moment he can detect a faint smile.

Rene turns back to watching the crowd but still addresses him. "If it's none of my business, say so, but I was wondering if you've been sick."

"Sick."

"Yeah sick."

"Why's everyone keep asking me that?"

"I noticed it the other night at My Friend's House. You've lost weight."

Diego looks down at himself, maybe for the first time in years, seeing more ground than usual. "No I haven't been sick. It's been fucking crazy at work though."

"Maybe you got a virus in Tijuana."

A light tapping on his shoulder and before he can turn Martin thrusts a cup of beer into his bandaged hand.

"How've you been Rene?" Martin shouts, already stinking of alcohol.

Taking an exaggerated drag, she nods to Martin. "I've been alright."

"It's rare to see you slumming with the dregs of Bodie society."

"These aren't the wastelands; the wastelands always sport the best music."

Taking a big gulp of beer, Martin's face begins to twist. "Why don't you go smoke that stinking weed somewhere else?"

"So, what's new with the whole Estelle disappearance Diego?"

Diego cringes at the bitterness of the cheap beer. "Nothing. Just that she's a missing person."

"It's Leo. He either chased her off, or sent her away, or worse," Rene says, breathing smoke.

"What makes you so sure?" Martin snorts.

"It's always someone close. Either that or she just ran off."

Martin feels bile rise in his throat. "They already looked into everyone at Bodie Trucking, including me. You don't know what you're talking about Rene." Tossing back the rest of his beer he crumples the plastic cup in his hand. "I shouldn't interrupt though. Go ahead, let's hear your proof."

"I don't have to prove anything to you; you either believe me, or you don't." An explosion of fireworks bursts behind and three perfect rings of smoke float slowly from her silhouette. "Estelle had a small collection of friends around town, but they were nothing but bubble headed housewives who enjoyed hobnobbing with local royalty. Only Leo had a reason to chase off his wife."

"What reason would Leo have," Martin says swallowing a lump in his throat.

"Maybe she wanted a divorce. Maybe he didn't want to give up half. Maybe she was stealing from him. Maybe she was banging a truck driver behind his back. Or like I said, maybe he just treated her like a dog for so long she up and left. Whatever the reason, Leo was at the center of it."

Martin opens his mouth again, but what's there to say.

"I gotta go. It was nice talking to you Diego. Oh, tell Jon to call me." Rene turns without looking at Martin, who watches angel wings sway delicately as she strolls away.

Diego looks at Martin. "You have to admit it, she's fucking interesting." Even with Rene and her joint gone, the crowd stays away from Diego and Martin who take up her place as the centerpieces of the party. Martin slides away to refill his beer, and returns holding a shot.

Diego might not have noticed the waving had it not been for the obscenely oversized wristwatch which flashed with the light from the hanging Christmas bulbs. Diego points Mauricio out to Martin who immediately shouts, "Get over here, and bring a couple beers."

Mauricio meets them in the center of the dance floor and asks, "Damn, what have you guys been smoking?"

"Rene was here," Martin growls.

Handing them the beers he addresses Diego first. "You've gone into hiding since we got back from Tijuana." Mauricio gives Diego a friendly hug, which is returned half heartily. He then extends a hand and greets Marty while respecting his policy on public shows of affection.

"Alex's been on our ass about catching up at the shop, so I've been stuck doing overtime."

"I figured the two of you would be at My Friend's House with the other *pinche gringo*."

"Mr. Florentine's in the hospital, so they canceled the event. Didn't you hear?" Marty asks.

Mauricio shakes his head. "I've been in Florida, man. Is he gonna be alright?"

"Yeah. He had a heart attack, but they say he's gonna make it." Diego looks at Martin, hoping nothing is said about his role in Mr. Florentine's survival.

"So why'd you go to Florida?" Martin asks, taking another swig.

"My parents sent me to Miami as a graduation present."

"They sent you to Miami for a graduation present?" Diego asks.

Mauricio nods.

"It took you six fucking years to graduate with a communications degree, and you were a fulltime student." Diego adds.

They laugh and Mauricio asks, "So where's Jon anyway?"

"You know Jon, always gotta spend the holidays with his uncle."

"Well this year it's probably more important because of Ian's farm. Farmers have always been weird about the land."

"What you talking about?" Marty shouts.

"I was talking to my older brother, he's in charge of Ian's loan at the bank. I guess Ian couldn't pay back the entire loan for the second straight year and the bank is gonna take the farm. I don't know, it's none of my business."

"Well, you brought it up so you might as well finish."

"Ian came to the bank hoping for one more year. My brother had to say no, unless there were some stipulations added to the contract that Ian didn't like. They talked for a while but finally Ian blew his top. He screamed profanities in the direction of random people and kept saying that nobody would take his land without a fight. I guess it got pretty bad.

"You know my brother didn't want to do it. My family's been doing business with the Heffron's for three generations. When Gabriel was killed, mom cried for three days. But, we just can't compete with the big outfits anymore so we aren't taking as many chances, even with locals."

"You haven't talked to Jonathan about this?" Diego asks.

"I haven't even seen Jon since TJ."

Better men than Jon and Ian exist, Diego could think of a few, but the Heffron's paid for their sins every day. Jon lost his parents, his inheritance, now something is taking away the last thread of his heritage. It's easy to blame the bank, but it's not the bank. The bank's only the vessel. There is something beyond, something hidden stripping, bit-by-bit, everything that makes up Jonathan Heffron. Soon all Jon will have to look forward to is taking his place in the last surviving family tradition.

Though maybe he understands now. That sick, twisted smile accompanied by a twinkle of the eye they all get when speaking of the family legacy. It's almost a physical excitement whenever a Heffron gets to discuss those moments when family and death shake hands. It could be downright appalling, to be thrilled talking about the painful loss of loved ones and ancestors. It went against everything his family taught him about the departed. But the Heffrons could see the writing on the wall, so they embraced most fully that which nobody could ever take. They would all die bloody, and even with the land gone and their way of life destroyed; nobody could take away the legacy.

An orange flash brightens the night and Diego watches Martin turn and walk away without saying a word. Generations of Dougherty's and Heffron's have been friends, and this is how Marty finds out that Jon's family is done farming?

Traveling across the stained concrete floor toward yet another drink, Martin thinks of hours spent in the Heffron shed. During the last World Cup Ian rolled a small black, and white television out so the crew could watch the Mexico and US games. Jordan Dougherty worked on the Heffron farm for a few years during the great depression. Then there was Samantha, who paid for an entire year of college by painting every structure on the Heffron land. Did these contributions not entitle him to some information?

"Nevermind! It's not my business."

Returning to the open space, Diego and Mauricio have moved on to nothing of consequence, and Martin tries getting lost in the pointless discourse, longing for distraction. He tries to ignore the sorrow and fear of Estelle's disappearance, only wanting a short reprieve, but is crushed by the loss of the Heffron farm. Even his most reliable escape, that ever-present dream he inherited from Ulysses, burns to the east.

"Hey Diego, go get me another beer."

Diego turns to Marty and shouts, "I'm talking. Get your own a fucking beer."

Mauricio sees an opportunity and takes it, "I thought you liked doing things for Martin and Jon."

"Blow me."

"I'll come over next weekend and help you and your dad re-shingle the roof."

Diego grabs Marty's cup, and gets them more beer.

"Where's your wife?" Marty asks Mauricio.

"She went to her parents' house for a Fourth of July party. She said she'd drop by later."

"Why didn't you go?"

"I've been married into their family for three years and they still treat me like an outsider. At this point, I figured I should accept it, and do my own thing."

"That'll bring em around."

"Here's your beer lazy fuck." Diego says thrusting the Dixie cup into Martin's hand.

"Come with me while I smoke a cigarette" Marty says.

The mercury falls and those under the canopy of sheet metal become animated; an army of partygoers waking from a trance. It's been too uncomfortable for anyone to enjoy the festivities, so the crowd moved only enough to justify being out. A night rhythm takes hold as hordes of flying insects arrive to dance their own patterns around the lights, and the energy grows with each fresh explosion overhead.

Diego watches his friend sway, sucking down yet another cigarette. All around are bursts of colors as every small town sends volleys of fireworks to heaven in honor of the country's birth. Closer still are illegal rockets launched from people's backyards. These burst overhead, and though they lack any splendor, Diego finds them no less patriotic. Only to the east, where the Bodie firework show should be, is the sky black. Not the natural black of night, it's something deeper, swallowing up any light getting too close to the eastern horizon. Diego glances at Marty to make sure he's not getting into trouble then closes his eyes to inhale deeply. The scent of dust and ripe fruit fills his lungs. It smells like July. Another breath and he detects the slightest whiff of sulfur. There must be a vineyard somewhere nearby.

For Martin the scene has become nothing but a mass pulsating in the distance. The scents have all been wiped clean, replaced by burnt tobacco and the music of laughing party-goers has turned to a record spun backwards. A girl standing ten yards in front of them comes into focus. It's her silver earrings. Nothing distinguishes her except her dark red hair tied in perfect pigtails. She's clad in a red tank top and jeans with plain brown flip-flop sandals that do nothing to keep the heavy dust from turning her feet a dull brown. The tank top is just short enough to allow anyone interested to notice she has a very slight potbelly.

"I'm gonna go rub that girl's belly," Martin says.

"What?"

"I'm gonna go rub that girl's belly."

"Who you talking about?" Diego begins to worry that his friend might be serious. For some inescapable reason, white people make the worst kinds of drunks.

"I'm talking about the red head with the belly."

"She doesn't really have a belly."

Marty mumbles something Diego can't comprehend and staggers toward the group of girls with right arm extended.

"Don't be fucking stupid man," he says in a laughing tone.

Marty then bursts into a fit of laughter, as he shouts, "Get out of the way!"

"Come on, let's get another beer." Diego says.

"Great idea!" Marty leads the way to the kegs, complementing Diego on his foresight the whole time.

Diego imagines laying on the hood of his car, getting lost in dancing colors mixed with swirling ash. Instead he shuffles Marty between smoking cigarettes, and a constant supply of fresh drinks but always keeping to the outskirts of the party where he can insult people without fear of reprisal. Diego listens half-heartedly as Martin drifts between vague attacks on faceless groups, and general philosophical ideas he finds revolting.

Together they remain on the fringes while Marty smokes his second to last cigarette, once again facing a group of girls. Just like before, the liquor fog clears and Martin picks an individual from the group. He looks over her shape, and feels certain that it's how his beloved looked at that age. The feeling grows until sickness nearly overtakes him. With his elbow, he jabs Diego in the ribs, and says, "Look at that there man, young, tall, with a nice ass. What could be better?"

Quickly the girl spins on her heels, and stares a hole through them. Diego looks at the tips of his shoes, which are just peeking out from under his stomach.

Martin and the girl lock eyes for a moment before Marty turns to Diego and says, "How about a pretty face?"

As quickly as she faced them, the young girl spins back to her friend's, pretending she heard nothing.

"I think she heard me," Martin laughs. She turns again to see the monster collapsing with joy. If only she would look to the left a little, she'd see his friend mouth an apology. Instead she turns away, maintains for the briefest of moments before bursting into tears and running toward the darkness. Her friend's, having taken to flirting with some young Bodie boys, follow shouting confused questions after her.

Diego decides to go after them. To hell with Marty, if he's going to act like an animal he can walk back to town. Before he leaves, he'll do whatever he can to comfort the young girl. After he strokes her shattered self-esteem, he'll call Isabelle. Maybe they can meet somewhere. That'll be nice, just to talk for a few minutes before going to sleep. To hear her laugh will be better.

Suddenly Diego's' feet lift from the ground, and he levitates for a moment before touching down again.

"Out of shed! It's going to burn down!"

Diego spins to see the last sparkles of purple disappear into the dust. Red and orange flames jump between rafters and creep down the sides of the shed. The crowd hurries from under the catastrophe, except for two teenagers who return to grab the last unopened keg. Future leaders. It takes a moment, but Diego realizes immediately that Martin Dougherty is not running in the same direction as all the rest. Diego stands at the edge of the blazing structure watching his giant friend run back and forth across the shed screaming.

"Heffron! Where the hell are you! Heffron!"

Diego sprints to Martins side, trying to tackle him but instead he's smashed onto his back. "Velarde, have you seen Heffron we have to find him."

"Jon's not even here!"

"Don't you get it Velarde? This is it! This is the thing that's going to get him." Martin turns to run some more, looking for the friend who at that moment is in no danger of burning alive. "Heffron get your ass over here!"

"Jon's not here you fucking lunatic."

"I have to save him! I have to save someone."

Acting on instinct Diego kicks Martin's massive legs out from under him. Diego jumps and grabs the back of Marty's curly hair and uses it to slam his head off the cement floor that's glowing from the inferno raging overhead. Rolling Martin over, Diego drags him across the floor as hot cinders timber fall all around them. The scent of burning hair fills the air and at any moment a burning plank of wood will end it all.

Arriving at the edge of the doomed shed, he hears Mauricio over his shoulder. "Are you crazy Diego! Here let me help."

They pull all two hundred and fifty pounds of Marty's unconscious body toward the Firechicken. By the time Mauricio and Diego get him into the car the roof collapses and all that's left are ten burning polls reaching into the air. With glowing sheet metal and timber in the middle, it looks like the emaciated hands of a cancer patient cupping burning coals.

"Damn Diego, did something hit him in the head?"

"No. The asshole thought Jonathan was here and he wouldn't leave. I had to knock him out." Wouldn't it be perfect though? He dives into the Firechicken grabbing for his cellular phone. He has to redial three times as panic overtakes him.

"Hello"

"Jon is that you?"

"Hey, oh hell! Diego this isn't a good time."

Diego feels relief pour over him. "Sorry to fucking call you but um…well I could actually use your help with Marty's drunk ass."

The phone is silent. "Sorry man, I've…Something's come up. I'll call you tomorrow alright." And the line goes dead.

"Maybe we should take him to the hospital." Mauricio says.

"I've seen him hurt worse. I'll take him to my house tonight. That way tomorrow morning, when he's good and rested, I can kick his ass."

Chapter XXV

Fall of the Wheat Capitol

In 1927 Bodie proclaimed itself the Wheat Capitol of the World. It was nothing less than a miracle for a community left without an identity when the mines dried up five decades earlier. Bodie had stopped existing on most maps, and many who lived around the town didn't call it their home. But once designated world famous by California Department of Agriculture every soul within the town's sphere of influence, and even a few outside it, proudly declared themselves sons and daughters of Bodie.

Bars, restaurants and stores closed for decades, reopened. Old houses, abandoned since the gold strikes, were torn down and new ones rose in their places. Soon everyone forgot that five years earlier Bodie stood on the verge of vanishing. Wells were drilled everywhere to accommodate the new influx of people. The town would never again be taken off the map.

For three years, the people of Bodie held their heads high as kings of grain. Then, as with the mines, the glory time passed as the wheat suddenly died. Some shouted that God sent a plague to punish the people for their sinful ways. "Bodie is cursed! The Lord will not grant us happiness until we repent and devote ourselves to serving His greater glory." The truth of the fall was less divine

As more land was irrigated to grow the wheat, the water table rose, bringing long buried salt with it. The ground, so perfect for the production of grain became a poison. The alkalinity rose, and golden fields of wheat turned black and vineyards, orchards, dairy ranches and subsistence farms quickly replaced them. Some farmers unable to transfer quickly enough went out of business. The sign proclaiming the town world wheat capitol stood for many years, though no grain ever grew on the land again.

Chapter XXVI

When the Land Lets Go

Jonathan brushes drops of beer from his pants before they can soak through.

"That was very good Jon. Very smooth."

"It's not my fault Laura. Diego's distracted me."

Hector's smile flashes with the reflection of sparklers and says, "Don't tease him. He was about to get to the point."

"Jon's always about to get to the point, Hector."

The breeze shifts and they're engulfed in a red cloud from smoke bombs set off on the far side of the yard.

"What did Diego want?"

"I guess Marty's wasted."

"Do you have to go?"

"I'll wait."

"He might need help Jonathan."

"With Diego, you wait till the second call, then you know he's not just panicking." The smoke subsides and Jonathan see's aunt Debra standing in a sea of children wired on home-made peach ice cream, waiting impatiently for her to unwrap another carton of sparklers.

"I gotta change. Be back in a minute."

Walking across the front yard Jonathan slaps hanging branches of Japanese Maple before walking straight into a spider web. Another art learned from years in the field. No sudden movements, don't swipe at it. Just back away slowly until the last thread of sticky silk comes loose. He stands still for a moment until the silver of the web comes into focus and then he inspects it. No damage done.

Ducking down, Jonathan hops the three steps to the back door. The aroma of past meals is accompanied by the memories of arguments, laughter and meandering conversation stretching back a hundred years. It's the family homestead, the place his Dad played as a child, and his home after his parents death. The other house his father built, but this is the Heffron's home, the one constructed at the founding of the farm. It may have been rebuilt after that sinkhole swallowed up half the structure during the winter of '67, but it's still the same. He passes through the kitchen, leaving the ghostly whispers of the past behind.

Even in the dark, Jon finds the closet where some of his clothes remain. He flips through four pairs of jeans, and a pair of slacks until choosing some faded Levi's. God, how embarrassing, but they'll be the most comfortable.

Jonathan pulls the jeans, throwing the dirty pair into the hamper. Passing back through the living room, Jon remembers sleeping on the old leather couch for a month while Ian transformed the garage into a full on home with a sauna. All so his orphaned nephew had a place of his own. At the front door Jon glances over his shoulder.

"Jesus Ian, you scared the hell out of me."

"Come on, harden up."

"Turn on some lights in here man?"

"I just want to be in the dark for a while. Given enough time everything becomes it's opposite. Did I ever tell you that?"

Jonathan nods.

"I used to be afraid of the dark when I was a kid. Your dad used to get mad cus I'd keep the light on all night and he couldn't sleep. Now I find the dark more soothing."

Ian sits in his favorite chair; a recliner covered in worn cloth upholstery. Over his head is a replica model of the long rifle used by American soldiers during the Revolution. Ian's grandfather made it as a reminder of their family's link to the founding of the country. The story goes that a Heffron acted as George Washington's bodyguard in 1781. It isn't true, but they needed a story.

Generations of smokers saturated the pine planks with carcinogenic tar and with each inhale, Ian makes his contribution. The red glow radiating from Ian's cigarette illuminates his library of strange books; a collection that implies his only true interests lie in bizarre stories and forgotten philosophies. In that momentary illumination from the burning tobacco Jonathan sees small tears welling up in the corners of his uncles eyes.

"What are you doing in here," Ian asks while taking a deep drag.

"I had to change my pants."

"Fireworks frightening you?" Ian smiles.

"All you've talked about for weeks is watching the fireworks." Jonathan looks his uncle over more closely. "Debra'll be pissed if she sees you smoking in the house."

"It'll be alright."

"Come outside Ian. You can help me convince Hector that football's a better sport than baseball."

"I'm not in much of a celebrating mood Jonathan."

"Why's that?"

"Do you remember back when we were still doing raisins, and you threatened to fire that crew?" Ian chuckles without joy.

"What?"

"You were seven or so, and we were rollin up the trays. If I remember right we planned on picking um up the next week. They weren't quite ready so we told the crew to roll um loose so they'd dry a little more before we picked up. Me and your dad were on one end of the vineyard, and you walked off to the other side. In the last row you found a couple of guys rolling tighter than we wanted. By the time your old man caught up to you, you'd lined up six workers, and were telling them if they didn't straighten out, you'd fire them. You spent the rest of the day walking up and down the vineyard, checking the quality of peoples work."

"Yeah, and Dad and you spent the rest of the day apologizing to the workers and the labor contractor. Dad was pretty mad when we got home. He gave me a long lecture on how you had to treat a man with respect if you wanted him to work hard for you."

"Gabriel got a kick out of the whole thing. I don't know how many times he told that story and every time he'd be laughing hysterically by the end." Ian chokes taking another drag. "That was a beautiful thing Jon. Bankers don't have those kinds of memories with their sons."

Jon squints his eyes and focuses his sight, trying to cut through the darkness. "Are you smoking dope again Ian?"

"I'm going out of business, Jon."

Jonathan can't remember ever praying. There, in the darkness of the family home, he begs God that he misheard what his uncle said. He pleads for something to materialize and save him, taking him to some other safe place. Anything to make the moment feel different from the one all those years ago in his parents living room. Jonathan remembers his father's face and how badly Gabriel needed a kind word from his son.

"It'll be alright, Ian."

Ian whispers as though surrounded by people that he didn't want to worry with the news. "Yes, it'll be alright. That's the point Jonathan."

"You're not telling me everything."

"Two bad years in a row, and this one doesn't look any better. I've been to the banks, to get an idea of how hard it'll be to get another loan. Each one gave me the run around, but the main point is I won't get a dime unless I show a profit; a big profit. Anything less than ten percent, and the only places that'll give us any money will charge me an arm and a leg in interest. It'll guarantee me going broke next year, and then it'll all go to the bank, and I'll have nothing." Ian pauses long enough to let the sound from a newly lit screamer pass. "There's a developer buying up land all around Bodie. I talked to a friend at the city planner's office. He said that they're looking to expand the city limits out this way within the next ten years. This whole area is going for commercial, so I should get a good price."

"Even if it's just the slimmest of chances, shouldn't you take it? Why are you just going to throw in the towel without a fight? Five generations grew up…"

"I can't sacrifice the future of this family for the memory of past ones. That's never what this farm has been about."

Flashes shine through the windows but no sound penetrates the thin walls. No talking, no fireworks and no noise from the party outside. It's like the farm is telling him to leave, even giving its permission. Jonathan can hear the land speaking, in the voices of every Heffron that died in Bodie, that he needn't worry. It told him to go see Diego. Take Laura, get drunk with his friends, and don't waste time mourning.

A firecracker pops outside and cheers fill the air. The land stops talking, but no words are spoken in Ian's living room. They sit quietly, uncle and nephew, each waiting for the other to speak. The only noises are the laughs and the soft explosions from the last of the fireworks. Soon everyone will be saying goodnight, and some will be coming in. Holiday or not, there're still nectarines to pick in the morning.

"Didn't you always say we're borrowing this land from future generations Ian; that we owe it to them."

"I understand what you're saying, and all things being equal, you'd be right. But all things aren't equal are they. My boys'll be ready for college in a few years, and I'm responsible for their future. Me and Debra, we could never send them to school, and pay off the debts we'd have if we took the chance and failed. Plus, with the farm gone, we'd have nowhere to live. I can't sacrifice their happiness just so I can maintain the faint hope of holding on to mine."

"If Dad had another chance…"

"Your father did. The same chance I have now." There's a deep melancholy in Ian's voice and it still doesn't rise above a whisper. "I explained to Gabriel how we could do it, how we could take out extra loans on my place to cover the loses on his. Gabe wouldn't go for it. He didn't want to risk pulling my place into bankruptcy with his, or to force you to put your dreams on hold. That was six years ago Jon, before the market went to shit. What's best for the family was always at the center of this farm. As hard as it was for Gabe then, and as hard as this is for me now, that has to be remembered. It's the last thing the land'll do for us."

Why'd Dad do that? If he had other options he should have taken them. He should have explained it all. It'd been a long time since Jonathan felt anything toward his parents other than sadness and regret. What right did they have to put this burden on him? He could have carried his fair share of the sacrifice.

211

He imagines, as he has a thousand times before, Gabriel standing outside his bedroom door. It was just after he announced the selling of the farm, accused of quitting by his only son. Jon always wondered what his father was thinking on the other side of the door, now he knows. Jonathan knows that Gabriel was considering whether to explain the real reason he let go of the land. Instead, Gabriel walked with a hanging head to the end of the hall, and went to bed.

"I don't feel good Ian. I'm going back to my apartment."

As he walks out the door the noise quiets again and Ian whispers, "Sometimes there is no such thing as the right choice Jonathan. You just got to pick a path, and hope everything works out in the end."

Chapter XXVII

Abomination Once More

"What the fuck are you doing?" Diego says.

"Something's burning."

Diego tosses the morning paper into Martins' face, but a spinning head makes it impossible to focus. The center picture shows the charred ruins of a pole shed and the caption reads 'Illegal fireworks at unauthorized Independence Day party causes structure fire. Nobody hurt.' He tries to read the story, but as the nausea increases, he tosses the paper over the side of the truck.

Smoke from the wildfires shrouds the sun, and Martin recalls the morning he woke with Kelly Ikeda laying next to him. It had been a hot night, forcing Kelly's glistening body to the top of the blankets. That was good. Then, one Christmas morning, Kayla Dougherty covered her son's legs with presents, and there were all those times he rose from bed dreading school only to remember it was Saturday, making the rest of the day feel better. The last time mom gave dad a chance, that was good too. But waking in the back of his neighbor's pickup with Diego's silhouette above, this is not the way to meet a summer dawn.

"Jon may have missed out on his destiny last night."

The mouthing of Jon's name brings it back. The revelation of the Heffron farm, the redhead with the potbelly, and the burning down of the old pole shed. Suddenly he springs to an upright position sending Diego out of the truck and to the ground. It would have been better to wake in a gutter or found naked at the public pool, anywhere but the parking lot of his apartment complex.

"Stop laughing Velarde?" He brushes off the layer wildfire ash. "What happened after we left?"

"I'm more interested in what happened this morning. I mean your shoe's under the fucking truck."

"Did I fall last night?"

"Why?"

"Back of my head's killing me."

"Oh. Well you started talking shit to this bad ass Mexican. I didn't recognize him."

Marty gets on his hands and knees to retrieve his shoe. "I gotta get to the yard. Can you give me a ride?"

"You've never looked so fucking old Marty."

"What?"

"You woke me up thirty minutes ago asking for a ride, but I'd call in sick if I were you. Fuck man, if you really can't remember having this conversation a half hour ago, you shouldn't be doing anything but sleep this off."

"Did I really talk to you this morning?" Marty asks, trying again to tie his shoe.

"It's not like I give a shit how you slept."

Diego and Marty turn their attention to the car pulling into the parking lot. It comes to a complete stop and out steps Jonathan greeting them with a salute and a scowl.

"What are you doing here?" Jon snaps.

"I crashed here last night. I had to watch over our stupid fucking whiteboy"

"He's the stupid white boy?"

"Yup."

"What's that make me?"

"You're the ugly fucking whiteboy."

Marty tries again to shake the grogginess from his head. "Why are you here Heffron?"

"You called me for a ride to work. You were yelling at me, telling me I never was on time and I needed to hurry. I was so afraid I forgot again, I nearly broke my neck running down the steps of my apartment."

The next five minutes consist of Jonathan asking half-hearted questions concerning the previous night. Jon hadn't heard about the fire, not that it matters. It's July, and there's no world to a Heffron outside the farm.

"So, which of you is going to give me a ride?"

"Not me, with that fucking attitude," Diego says.

"Well I didn't want to get up early for no reason," Jonathan yawns.

"What are talking about? Since when does a farmboy not get up early?" Diego shouts.

"What can I say, Global Warming's a bastard."

Diego bends over and wipes the ash from his shoes. "What the fuck does that mean Jon?"

"I gotta go Heffron," Martin storms past his friends and falls into Jon's Honda with such force that the springs sound ready to buckle.

"Damn Marty, I can smell the alcohol on you. You should take the day off."

"I gotta lot to do."

Jonathan continues to speak, but by the time they cross the freeway, Martin has dozed off.

Ten minutes later Jonathan wakes Marty as they jerk to a halt in one of the parking places in front of Bodie Trucking Company's office.

"You trying to make me sick Heffron?"

"Something's a matter with the breaks."

"Have Velarde look at it."

"Man, I can't afford those prices."

Martin takes a look at the yard. Nothing's getting done. "Thanks for the ride." Walking through the doors of the poorly ventilated trailer, nothing moves except for Eric and Jose going over shipping orders in the offices only shady corner.

"You're late boy," Eric says with venom in his voice.

"Sorry bout that."

"You're gonna have to stay late to make up for it."

"I stay late every day."

"Yeah well, who do you want to pick up these supplies from Langley's. They need to be picked up at V.A.S. and run to Indian Hills Packing?" Eric hands Marty a manifest of materials. "Langley's can't make the delivery for some reason and they asked us to."

"I'll go get it. Saldana's gonna go with me."

"Why do you need Pablo?" Eric asks.

"Don't worry about it." Martin grabs a radio off the table and presses on the trigger. "Saldana, go get the van with the electric lift and bring it up front. We gotta run an errand." He releases the button and looks back at Eric. "Cover the dispatch til I get back."

Eric goes back to his paperwork and snarls, "No problem, Bossman."

Martin quickly inhales a cigarette while he waits for Pablo at the front entrance. "What took so long?"

"I couldn't find the keys. That room's a mess," Pablo says.

"I told those guys to keep that place organized," Marty sighs. "Tomorrow morning, before you do anything else, get that room straightened out. And if you find out who's messing it up, I want to know." He can hear the vein traveling down the center of his forehead throb against an over sensitive nerve. "You'd think they'd care more considering how much time they have to spend here."

Marty crawls into his seat closing his eyes as more of the previous night's memories trickle back. He can smell the faded scent of raisins from the old shed. He can feel the rhythmic thudding from the sound system. The buzzing insects and the dull lights that attracted them begin to appear and he remembers Rene, her unfolding wing tattoos swaying under the rings of reefer spiraling around her. Then there's that smug air as she tells Martin exactly what he already knew.

"Stop the van for sec."

"What you forget?"

"I gotta go talk to Radmonavic."

"About what?"

"Keep the AC running would you Pablo, this heat is killing me."

Martin walks, head down, each step creating small clouds of dust that bellow out from under his boots. To an ant, they might look like large sandstorms sweeping across the terrain. People, cars, tractors, animals, breezes, even falling leaves create little sandstorms all over the Valley. All these little clouds combine and by dusk, Martin will look onto a sky painted with colors of such grandeur one would think it the work of God.

He pushes open the small wooden gate and winces as its rusty hinges squeal. Strolling over the stepping-stones toward the house, Martin feels Leo through the front window.

Quickly scurrying toward the rear of the house, Leo tries to imitate the confident gate of Martin Dougherty, and whispers a curse as he fails. He rounds the corner and starts fiddling with the loose knob on the stove, like it needs fixing at that moment. The front door is flung open and peaking around the corner of the stove, Leo stares at his employee who stands silently, lost in thought.

One whiff, and Martin feels like he grew up playing on the wood floor. It's like old dust trapped inside a barn, then collected in bags and sprinkled throughout the living room. He knows what's about to happen, at least the important parts, at this point it's about going through the motions.

"So, who told you about me and Estelle?" Martin says.

Is this what Estelle saw? She saw Martin and realized that there was nothing that really scared him, and she liked it. He could be flustered or made nervous, but never scared. It's why Leo loved her, because she of all people saw something in him worth marrying, even though she knew that beneath it all he was a coward.

"Don't you say her name you bastard."

"Answer the question Radmonavic."

"You fucked my wife!"

Martin takes a deep breath. "She told you."

"She didn't have to. I saw it on her face the day I told her I was moving you to Madera to take over the new yard. She looked at me with nothing but a twinkle of humor. She asked, with this arrogant little tone, what made me think you'd move all the way to Madera for a job promotion." Leo still feels his knees hurting, when he pathetically begged for another chance. He promised to never lie again, never to cheat; to sell everything he owned and dedicate the remainder of his days to making her happy. It would be like it was at the beginning.

Leo takes another step forward, followed immediately by a half step back. "I told her you'd go and if you refused, I knew how to talk to you. I told her, she wouldn't know how to handle a man like you. Then I looked at her, sitting at the dining room table in that arrogant pose that was there just to remind me where she came from. I knew what that smirk meant. It meant she knew something I didn't."

"And after you found out, what then Leo?"

"I asked, and she told me she was going off with you to God knows where. Then she disappears and you keep showing up like nothing happened. What, were you going to try to get a few more paychecks outta me so you could start a new life with my wife? She left that night, in the car that I bought for her, she left in it to be with you. How long has this been going on and where's Estelle!"

The love of his life searched out his opposite, for better and for worse. When choosing Martin, Estelle must have been willing to take all his flaws so long as they didn't remind her of what she left behind, and when she rose to leave she was turning her back on everything he stood for.

Leo hollers like a child throwing a temper tantrum, but Martin doesn't hear. She never left or ran away, something happened that had nothing to do with the man in front of him. Who else could it be other than Leo? He starts running faces through his mind and tries to make them match the one that could have done something to Estelle. The only thing that stops Martin's thought is the inconvenience of having to fend off an attack from the irate millionaire.

Martin flicks his forearms and Leo travels back across the five feet, landing on his kitchen floor. He bounces and slides another foot into the small round table at the entrance of the kitchen. Leo screams with pain as the leg of the table jabs the center of his fragile back.

"You ungrateful loser. Get out of this house and when I have proof, I'm going to ruin your life. You'll never have anything in Bodie."

"Well then you better get up and go take care of that thing for Langley's yourself."

"She probably thought you were so damn brave. I was just a coward in her eyes. Well fine, but if I'm a coward then so are you."

"Yeah, you may have a point there."

Back out the door, through the squeaking gate and into the yard creating little sandstorms, Martin thinks of the science club in sixth grade. He didn't want to be there, but a Dougherty always takes part. So every Wednesday after school he'd spend hours in Mr. Bernard's class doing experiments and building models so he could spend his Saturday's at some far off school competing for the right to spend another week doing the same thing.

And they kept winning. And with each success the moral slipped deeper as they realized that another of their precious childhood Saturdays was lost. And if Mr. Bernard had just understood, everything would have been fine, but for all his experience, that man didn't understand anything about children. So there he was, excited that they would soon be spending their fourth Saturday in a row at the science club competition.

"Well Marty, we're still alive," Mr. Bernard would say.

"Yeah."

"It's going to get tougher Marty. We're not going to be competing against other local schools, now we'll start taking on big time city schools."

"OK."

Even the man's sigh was condescending. "You know Marty, I wanted you on this team for a reason. It wasn't because you're a brilliant mind, there were several of your classmates that were better students, I picked you for your leadership."

"Leadership?"

"You are a Dougherty after all, and I have to say I've been disappointed with your representation of that family."

It wasn't bad, having to go to another school. It was hard not being in the same class as Jon for three years, but at least Diego was there. In fact, had he not punched that arrogant old teacher, he might not have become friends with Diego Velarde.

Afterwards, came that strange sensation. There was embarrassment when he told mom that he'd attacked a teacher and been thrown out of school, but that was the only bad part. The rest of the time there was nothing but freedom. A Dougherty needed to be a leader; it was the weight he'd carried since he was a child, but not anymore. Sure, they all thought him a punk, and at times with certain people, the disappointment was hard to accept. But for the most part, it was nothing less than liberating.

Martin climbs into the van next to Pablo, now settling into the pulse of his hangover. As he leans back and counts the seconds between throbs in his head he sees Eric scurry across the yard toward the house.

"So what did Leo have to say?" Pablo asks.

"Drop me off at my apartment. I'm taking the rest of the day off."

"You can't take a day off. This is the busiest time of the year."

"Sure I can, I raised efficiency by thirteen percent. Plus, I gotta see the mayor about a job opportunity."

"You're funny guy," Pablo says as he spins the van onto Lac Jac.

Chapter XXVIII

Coffee at Manda's

At the center of town, on Whitney St, across from the large Catholic Church made of red brick, is Manda's Stash. Amanda Weinberger had been a neat, slightly bored homemaker until her husbands' sudden death. He left her enough money to live a comfortable life, but nothing could stymie the fear of finding herself alone in the world. At first people complemented her resolve to carry on unchanged, but once rubble began collecting around the once pristine property, people realized the truth. Shattered, Amanda decided to glue herself together using whatever crossed her path.

Amanda followed her love to the grave, leaving a daughter Alice a pile of junk held up by a decaying house. Alice began sifting through a decade of random objects collected during her mother's madness. When something of value emerged, she cleaned it, placed a price tag on it and put in the front yard, which she had landscaped to attract buyers. In time she even put out some tables and chairs. Against all odds she began making money, and Alice showed her appreciation by providing free coffee and donuts for her customers. It wasn't long before people started showing up at the house across from the brick church asking Alice to help them with their own excess goods, which she agreed to do for a fee.

Her growing reputation soon attracted Martin Dougherty for no other reason than to snag a free coffee before class. When Alice noticed, she told him to help himself so long as he came by once a week to help her move furniture around for free. And so it was, that each morning before heading to work, Martin Dougherty stopped by Amanda's Stash for coffee and a donut.

One morning, as he slowly snapped the lid onto the paper cup, someone spoke to him. "You're the Dougherty boy aren't you?"

Without turning around Martin sighs, "Yeah."

"I've been wanting to meet you for some time. Enrique Ramirez."

Turning slowly, Martin extends his hand. "Pleasure to meet you Mayor."

As smoke from the wildfires spins in the first rays of the morning, Martin thinks of the movie he went to see the night before. The story ended and the credits rolled. Some stayed in their seat quietly, while others quickly left, saving discussion for the drive home. He did the same thing as always, he waited patiently until his row emptied before making his exit. The rituals differ from person to person, but it's the same purpose; to make sure the tale is absorbed completely before moving on. The real world is different. Nothing stops, nothing waits, so Martin knows better than to find comfort in the illusion that it will all be over soon.

"Yes, yes, Martin Dougherty, the man who got Leo Radmonavic to apologize. Impressive."

"I'm not following."

"I heard you told him off before storming out of his business. There's even a story making the rounds saying you threatened him if he tried any kind of retaliation."

"You believe that?"

"Well, working in politics you gain an ear for exaggeration, but I admit to being a little gullible in your case."

"Why?"

"I have friends who work for the school district, and they claim you're not the type to take anything lying down."

It was a line taken from the history books; he read it in Craig Dougherty's "Stories and Myths of the San Joaquin Valley." That local historian said the same thing about Lena and Ulysses. They never took anything lying down.

"Well let me set you straight. Radmonavic said something he shouldn't have. It wasn't anything worth repeating, but I didn't like it. I didn't yell, or threaten him. I quit. We worked it out, he asked me back."

"Well I've never known the man to do that. You must be quiet an employee."

"You'd have to ask him."

"Well, regardless of whatever else I think of the man, he knows a good worker when he sees one. I've always trusted that."

"The way Radmonavic tells it, you've made a career out of poaching his crew."

"Now that is an exaggeration, but like every story in this town, there's a bit of truth behind it."

Chapter XXIX

On Spare Time

Jonathan remembers when the rhythms of early July couldn't be distinguished from the rest of summer, but the workload lightened after Gabriel's went under. Coordinating the planting on the two Heffron farms had been a stroke of genius, but when Gabriel lost his land, gaps opened in the harvest. Ian filled most of these with new orchards, except for the September gaps, intentionally left open because the prices were typically terrible that time of year. The second lull falls at the beginning of July, but once he replaced the more lucrative slots, Ian had no money for more planting.

Parking his car under the shade of the old Black Walnut tree, Jonathan strolls toward the shed as Ian works on the old air compressor. He should've tried harder at the club. Everyone from Fresno State talked about it and, calling it the hottest spot in Fresno County, but Jon didn't get it. It wasn't for him.

It was the first week of school all over again. "Write an essay telling what you did over the summer class." There were things to write about; lots of them. There was sitting on top of the tractor, listening to the crew tell stories in Spanish. Then, on those especially hot days, they would all run down to the ditch and jump in the water fully clothed. Sometimes, when the days got monotonous, a challenge would go out among the cousins. They'd stand at the packing table while Ian stood above monitoring the shed. When Ian turned to attend to this or that, they'd run out, hurling pieces of fruit into the nearby pomegranate orchard. Quickly they'd run back to their stations to argue over who threw the farthest, hoping Ian hadn't noticed. This could all be in an essay, but what was the point; you had to be there to understand the magic of it all.

"Ian, why don't you get rid of some of this stuff when it starts breaking down?"

"That's part of farming Jon, part of life too. Trying to squeeze out one more year, whether it be an air compressor, a block of trees, or the farm itself. I've managed to squeeze one more year for some time. Look at that thing over there."

Jonathan looks at the spray rig that at one time had been red, but now only sports a few patches of original color. The rest of the long cylindrical tank is a muddle of oil stains, rusty patches and bare steel. To find the name of the company that made the rig, one would have to spend an hour scraping a layer of grime off the logo. At its top is a hatch that could double for an entrance into a World War Two submarine. Two huge tires support the machine, and with their faded white rims and mud stained rubber, they look comical, like something drawn for a Saturday morning cartoon. At one end of the cylinder are controls used to connect to the back of the tractor. On the other end, dozens of dull spray nozzles stick up like a perfectly symmetrical wreath of metal thorns.

"I remember me and your father working on that thing for two days straight during your second year of high school. Everyone said it was shot, and we needed to get a new one. We didn't have the money, so we kept working. It took two days, but we got it running. Since then I've probably spent three days a summer working on that thing, trying to squeeze another year. I guess it doesn't matter in the end, but it's important to go down fighting. Not to prove anything to anyone else, because nobody else will really care. You do it to prove something to yourself. To prove that you can take it." With that Ian turns back to his work on the compressor.

"You feeling better this morning?"

"What?" Jonathan replies.

"You said you were sick last night. That's why you left early."

"Oh yeah, I feel a lot better."

"Laura was pretty upset about you leaving without her."

"If it gives you a laugh you should know she's still pissed even though I said I'd make it up to her."

Ian gives Jonathan a short smile. "Aside from abandoning your girlfriend, you also left without saying goodbye to Hector. He'll probably never admit it, but I think the man was hurt."

"I'm sorry I left like that." Jonathan kneels next to his uncle, and begins helping where he can. Jumping around the shop, Jonathan feels the muscles of his heart scream, 'I'm sorry Ian. I just don't know what else to do.' What right does he have to give up, to have accepted defeat so quickly at the night club?

"Hand me a nine-sixteenth socket. The motor's gone." After some pulling, tugging and a half a can of lubricant, they manage to loosen the motor and load it onto the back of Ian's truck. Ian ties it down before heading off while Jonathan engages in another futile battle. Grabbing his favorite broom and starting on the north side near the box scales, Jon begins the daily sweeping of the packing shed. It'll only take a few hours of use, or one good gust of wind, and there'll be no evidence the job has ever been done. Still, the sheds there, so it must be swept.

How long has it been going on? The green roofed packing shed was built in 1953; in fact someone might have died during its construction, and every day since, someone has pushed a broom across that smooth, cool surface. Someone will be the last to sweep the shed. It'll be monumental, like the last person to see an extinct species in the wild.

Three days a year repairing the spray rig. Three days Ian has to fill. What will Jon do with a summer all to himself when every July he fails to fill a week? He should be able to. He wears fashionable clothes and drives a modest, but common car. He lives in a respectable apartment, decorated with ordinary belongings, in a normal town. The music he listens to is garden-variety, so is the food he eats. He drinks when he can, that's pretty standard as far as he can tell. An average white male with a typical sexual appetite, and now he'll have an ordinary heritage. He isn't a farmboy anymore. He can be another middle class working stiff.

Ian returns in the old Dodge Ram that, like everything else on the farm, he's managed to keep running past its prime. Together they work at putting the compressor back together.

"Is that the last belt Jon?"

"Yup."

"They look a little loose."

"They're not."

"You sure?"

"Yes."

Ian pauses, looking at the belt. He bends over and pulls on them, testing the tightness.

Jon frowns. "Why'd you ask?"

"I don't trust you," Ian laughs. The old farmer bends down and begins to lose balance. Without thinking he reaches out and puts his hand on the compressor to steady himself.

The frame shakes, and the tank vibrates as every belt spins into action. Jonathan immediately reaches over and turns off the breaker. Ian jumps to his feet before bending over to clutch his right hand. Blood oozes from between the fingers of his left hand.

"Man, it tore your finger off!"

"Get the truck Jon." In a moment's notice Jon, Ian and the old Dodge pickup tear across country roads toward the small, underfunded doctors' clinic at the center of town.

"Would you watch what you're doing Jon! It'd be an embarrassment to die in a common car accident."

"You'd rather bleed to death from your damn finger!"

"That wouldn't be bad."

All those deaths. Hours spent reciting names, years and connecting them with stories, but he's never actually witnessed the moment. Would he tell the tale different, or would it flow in the same fashion as all the rest?

Coming to a halt with a jerk in front of the clinic, Jon rushes to get his uncle through the front door. Once inside he'll be safe. No Heffron has ever died in the walls of a hospital, and feeling overwhelmed Jonathan nearly tosses his uncle through the front door.

"Jon. I want you to go back to the shed and finish putting the air compressor together."

"I'll wait until Debra gets here."

Ian loosens his grip and blood squirts from between his fingers. "No don't. Things like this always look worse than they actually are. It'll be better to tell her after it's all fixed up."

"She's a nurse! I think she'll be alright with a little blood," Jonathan shouts.

"Jonathan, please. That compressor needs to be up today."

Back on the farm, Jonathan imagines Patricia Heffron sitting atop the corral fence back in the fifties. The corral had been across from shed, but by 1965 the family had abandoned livestock for produce and tore the enclosure down, replacing it with a vineyard. Patricia sat on top near the gate watching the bull charge around as the scent of in season cows filled the air. She wasn't taunting the bull, just watching when the fence post shifted, and she found herself caught upside down with lowered horns flashing towards her.

Jon knows what everyone said at Patricia's funeral. 'This could only happen to a Heffron.' Maybe there was one amongst the mourners thinking, 'Only a Heffron could get themselves into something like this.' This person might never utter such a thought, but as Jon completes the compressor job, he can't help but wonder if this fictitious mourner was not a prophet. Jonathan finishes cleaning the shed, knowing this will impress Ian more than anything, cursing himself for not paying better attention.

Back at the hospital Jon steps up to the receptionist desk without making eye contact. "I'm here to pick up Ian Heffron. He was brought in two hours ago with a torn-up finger."

"He's just gone in with the doctor."

"Has he been sitting here bleeding for two hours!"

"We made sure his situation wasn't critical, and gave him some painkillers. We kept our eyes on him. I assure you he was never in danger."

"Not in danger! He was gushing blood!"

"We have a lot of people who come in here, sir. We got to your uncle as soon as possible, and not a moment later. Please have a seat"

Jonathan calms himself, "I understand all that, but are you telling me a man bleeding profusely isn't a priority?"

"All you have to know is that your uncle is being treated as we speak, and he'll be out shortly. Now please have a seat so others can get through?" Jonathan accepts defeat, seeing no point in continuing, and finds a place to sit. Not moving for what seems like a long time, he falls into a quiet trance when he feels a hand on his shoulder. Jonathan quickly springs to his feet. "I should have called. I'm sorry."

"How long has he been in there?" Debra asks.

"I just got back. Ian sent me back to the farm to finish a few things."

Debra stares at her nephew confused. "It's OK Jon, but do you know how long he's been in there?"

"They just took him in a few minutes ago."

She throws her purse to the floor before sitting down.

"How many times have I told that man never to come here. When there's an emergency it's better to drive to Fresno. He'd be out by now."

After a short pause she says, "I cleaned your pants Jon. Ian was supposed to tell you, but I'm sure he didn't."

Jonathan speaks softly, with his head hanging, "I feel terrible. I shouldn't have plugged in the compressor til Ian finished. I wasn't paying attention."

Debra pats her nephew on the back. "Accidents happen, Jonathan. You know that."

They sat in silence, until Debra noticed Ian at the front desk signing some release forms. "How is it Ian?" Debra asks.

"What a disgrace. All it did was take the flesh off the tip. The doctor says it'll be a bit shorter when it heals, and the finger nail may not look right, but it's nothing serious." Ian lifts a little plastic vile filled with alcohol. "This is the part that got ripped off. You know it was still hanging by a piece of skin."

"Ian what's wrong with you?" Debra says with a frown.

"I want it buried with me."

"I'm really sorry about that, Ian," Jonathan whispers.

Ian rifles through his pockets with his intact hand. "I'll need your help for the next few days, if that's alright. Doctor says I need to keep it clean, and I got concrete work to do."

"I'll be there."

"Let's go home. The medication's making me a little loopy, and I haven't eaten. Jonathan, call Laura and the two of you can come over for dinner. You haven't eaten today, have you?"

Jonathan would have preferred to go straight to his apartment, and spend the night making it right with Laura, but what can be done.

Together, they walk into the parking lot. Debra asks Ian specifics about what the doctors said, and Ian answers enthusiastically, more than happy to talk about his mutilated finger. Another piece of the Heffron legacy. Jonathan says nothing and climbing into his uncle's old truck, he hears Ian hollering from across the lot.

"Jon, pick me up a pack of cigarettes on your way over."

Waving in acknowledgment, he speeds off toward the gas station to pick up a Marlboro soft pack. He and the old Dodge cross the streets of Bodie as the last rays of sunlight filter their way through the smoke of the fires. Trying his best to steer the truck with his knee, Jonathan rolls down the window with one hand, dialing Laura with the other.

Chapter XXX

Chance of a Lifetime

Before his first day on the job, Diego confessed being nervous to Jon. Diego earned his ASE certification, but had only ever worked on Ian's farm. What could he offer the most respected mechanic in the county? He got the job because Mr. Wisneswski vouched for him, an endorsement he scarcely deserved. Jon tried to explain that nobody ever got fired from Bad Man Auto so Diego needn't worry. Diego should have listened, and not been so eager to please.

His second week, he volunteered to fill in for the secretary. Diego remembers wondering if the rest of the crew thought him a suck up, and wanted to tell them he only wanted to prove himself to them as much as the boss. They were legends.

Now, twice a month, Diego finds himself bouncing between his work in the shop, and the office where he answers phones and attends to customers. He'd been overanxious, naïve, and the rest of the crew knew it the day he volunteered. All those head shakes and rolled eyes, because they recognized the rookie mistake, and what could be more entertaining for a veteran shop.

"I'm sorry sir, but we don't have any openings for the next three days." Empathy is key. The best secretaries can sell that they feel the pain of the caller, even if they don't. It's a tone of voice saying the fault lies with far off forces, and we can do nothing except lament the injustice together.

"If I can't get to Los Angeles by this afternoon I'll lose my job. Do you understand what I'm telling you?"

"I wish there was something I could do. I just don't have any openings before Thursday. Have you tried the dealership?"

"I can't afford the dealership!"

"Right. You could rent a car."

"I said I can't afford it. Are you listening?"

"Greyhound runs buses down there cheap."

"Are you trying to make fun of me?"

"Never."

"Well what's all this about taking a bus then?"

This is how it goes, call after call. He hates answering phones. He hates paperwork. He hates customers. So when a man named Eduardo Jalisco walks through the front door, Diego prepares for the worst.

"Good morning."

"Tienes tiempo hoy?"

"I'll go get someone who speaks Spanish." Disgust empties from every pore of Eduardo Jalisco's body. It's the same with his parents when they explain that their only son doesn't speak their native tongue. It's a betrayal of the sacred; unforgivable and worthy of banishment.

"I speak English," Eduardo says.

Diego can tell that when Eduardo asks for a ring job on his car, he's really saying 'Well since you're not going to stand with your people, can you at least fix my car?'

Diego rechecks the schedule and says, "There's no way we can get you in today, especially for a job that big. Even when we get to it, it's going to take time to finish."

Diego watches the man slowly wipe the back of his hand across his left cheek. He can almost hear Eduardo say, 'Oh I see. You look at me as another Mexican you can trick, right?'

Finally, the secretary walks in, apologizing for being late. "Maybe she can help."

Diego nods and grabs a work order without looking at it. He enters the shop, retreating to where all the cars are parked. Diego reads the paper, pocketing the keys attached to it. He searches until he finds the white 1988 Ford Taurus and drives it to his workstation.

Eight hours in a hot shop without air conditioning can easily feel like twelve. 'My god I'm tired. I should have grabbed something more interesting than a fucking tune-up and fuel pump swap.' Diego rubs his eyes, trying to focus on the job and manages to stumble through the task until the call for lunch relieves him. The thought of a lunchtime nap in the Fire-chicken soothes; in fact it's the only thing about his workday that still excites.

So when the clock strikes noon, and he doesn't see his sanctuary it's a brutal blow. Isabelle has it for the day. Forced to lunch in the break room, he'll have to listen as the entire crew waste their hour-long escape from the monotony of their work only to yammer on about the trials of their lives. The idea of using time free from ones' problems to complain makes little sense. Better to sleep in the Firechicken.

"I'm so fucking tired," Diego says sliding into the cramped room and taking a seat. He quickly drops his head into his arms in the hope of stemming off conversation.

"Why you tired?"

"I couldn't sleep last night," Diego says without lifting his head.

Diego tries laughing when he should, and makes eye contact, but it's too much and after ten minutes, Diego takes his leave. He walks out and once in front of Bad Man Auto, he lays down on the small brown lawn decorating the front of the shop.

Exhausted he tries to sleep, but who could get comfortable in the heat. He remains motionless on the suffering lawn, trying to think of nothing at all.

"Hello Diego."

"Jesus. How's the coolest fucking second grader in town?"

"OK. My cousin has a new pellet gun," Jesus says with pride.

"Oh, so that's where you've been hiding the last couple days." Diego puts his head back down and closes his eyes. "Did your cousin let you shoot it?" he asks.

"He didn't want me too. He said I was too small. But when he wasn't looking I went over and shot at a few cans." Sporting the mischievous little smile he had the first time they met, Diego takes note of the fresh bruises on his left arm.

"You get caught?"

"Well, not at first. Then I tried to do it one more time, and he saw me. Then he hit me a couple of times."

"That fucking sucks."

"It wasn't too bad. Then he went out and told my mom. She beat me pretty bad." Jesus stops smiling. "He's a jerk! He didn't need to tell my mom. I wasn't going to do it again."

"Was it worth it?"

"Yeah, it was worth it."

Diego looks at his watch. "I gotta get back to work Jesus. Don't go playing with guns anymore. I've never fired a shot worth a fucking beating."

"My older brother Antonio says his car is worth taking beating for."

Diego laughs, "Is your brother the one always working on the El Camino in your driveway."

"Yeah."

"Well it'd have to be a real nice car."

"He said it yesterday when my dad threatened to throw him out if he didn't get it running soon."

The Firechicken sat in front of his parents' house, broken down, for months before he got it running. Every time mom had a bad day at work to see the car in the same spot, she'd go on a tirade for hours. She continued hating it after it was running, but at least it wasn't a broke down heap.

"Your old man won't throw Antonio out. He's probably trying to motivate him to get the thing running. It's an old parenting trick."

"Nah, my dad doesn't use tricks. He's a real man, and he says all the time that a real man always means what he says." Across the street, a car pulls into Jesus's driveway. "That's my mom with lunch. I'll see ya later Diego."

"Alright." Diego watches Jesus run. "Hey, pay attention when you cross the goddamn street."

Jesus looks over his shoulder and laughs.

Diego spends the rest his day changing oil, and replacing spark plugs. From there he checks the tightness of belts and does diagnostics on electrical systems. When Alex goes on break, it falls on him to explain to a little old lady that driving a car with a leaky radiator is a bad idea, even if she keeps an eye on it. The only real excitement comes when a middle-aged man brings in his car complaining that the engine is making funny noises, and thirty seconds later the car bursts into flames. These things are bound to happen. When it comes to an end, Diego quickly cleans up his station and stands outside waiting for Isabelle. He looks up and down the street, listening for the sound of the Firechicken.

"What are you doing out here?"

Diego knows who it is before he even looks. "Stop sneaking up on me?"

Rene smiles perversely and says, "Maybe I'm stalking you."

Diego laughs. "You got car trouble."

"No, I need an escort."

"What?"

"I'm out of weed. Usually I have this other guy come with me, but he couldn't make it."

"This is where you get that stinking shit?"

"These guys got the best herb in Bodie." Rene pulls out a pocket watch and checks the time.

"So?"

"So?"

"You gonna come with?"

"Why me?"

"You're here."

He tries not to care. "Fine, but let's make it quick."

"Don't worry, I'm a fast shopper."

It's a quant ranch style home with a big front yard and rail fence allowing anyone to look into the back. The yard itself is simple, but well kept. It's mostly lawn with scattered shrubs and flowering planter boxes, accented by a magnolia tree shading the back of the house. The paint is faded, and in spots beginning to chip.

There's something about the way the light hits the house, like the angles aren't right. The shadows stretch too far in spots while not traveling far enough in others. Single pane windows resembling those of a funhouse; transforming every ordinary image to something surreal. The tints of the white siding and green trim shift depending on the direction one looks from.

Even little Jesus takes on a more roguish posture as he trots playfully across the front yard.

Only Antonio, who stands next to his broken-down El Camino, is unaffected by the surroundings. It's not a glow, but some kind of barrier keeps the unnatural aura of the place from touching the gawky teenager.

Jesus turns to Diego and speaks. "Hi Diego, what are you doing here?"

Diego watches as Rene gently pats Jesus on the head, which the boy accepts as normal. "Oh I'm just walking with Rene. She's come by to see your parents."

Jesus looks up at Rene and smiles. "I'll take you in to see them." He looks back at Diego. "Me and Rene are good buddies."

"Why don't you go over and help Antonio on his car Diego, I'll only be a minute," Rene says.

Frowning slightly Diego flails his arms as he shouts, "I thought you wanted…"

"It's good. Go help Antonio out." She walks up the stairs, her angel wings in full view as Jesus leads on.

Diego smiles as he lays his eyes on the 1965 El Camino. "This was the best year for the El Camino. After this they got too square, and lost that organic feel." Diego walks around the car as Antonio looks on, wiping the oil from his hands. "My names Diego, I work across the street."

"Antonio."

"So, what's the problem with this thing Antonio?"

"I don't know. I get it running and then a few days later it's dead again. I've replaced the starter and the battery twice. I can't figure it out. I bought this book on the car yesterday, but it's not helping." Antonio lifts a Clifton technical book on the

Skyler Nielsen

1965 El Camino. Diego reaches out and grabs it. He immediately starts flipping through the book.

"You don't know a lot about this car?" Antonio asks.

"Off the top of my head I know more than the average fuck about any car you put in front of me, but I don't know everything. Even the best mechanics turn to these things from time to time. Mr. Wisnewski always said you shouldn't waste time memorizing details that can be looked up. You ever met Mr. Wisnewski?"

"No." Antonio answers.

Diego looks at Antonio. "I go and talk to Mr. Wisnewski regularly. You know who he is right?"

"Everyone knows Alistair Wisnewski."

"Well, maybe I can get him to help you out. That man'll teach you more in an hour than I could in a year."

"Could you really do that?"

Diego lies down on the ground and pulls himself under the car. "Well, I could try anyway. Past that I won't make promises. He's kind of pissed at me right now."

"Why's that?"

"I borrowed some shit from him, and forgot to give it back. Maybe I didn't have permission, I don't know, but he's pissed."

"Man, I'd give anything to be taught by that guy. He's a legend."

"I'd give anything to see it happen. Maybe I can set up a meeting."

Diego starts fidgeting with some wires running along the undercarriage. "Some of these are pretty beat up Antonio. It'll be a pain in the ass, but I think you need to start replacing these fucking wires. I got a hunch that you have a short somewhere." Diego climbs out of the dirt. "There's no more a shit job in a mechanics life than electrical problems. Do you know how to use an ohmmeter?"

"Um…I've never used one before."

Diego pulls a small object out of his back pocket with wires coming out of it. "You can use 'em to isolate shorts in the electrical lines. It keeps you from having to check each wire manually."

Diego feels that presence behind him again before he hears her voice. "Maybe you should start making house calls Diego."

"Did you make your purchase?"

"I'm telling you this stuff from NorCal is the best."

"I guess I haven't kept up on these things."

Rene frowns at his comment. "How are you Antonio?"

"I'm doin alright. Diego's helping me out."

"I was talking to your Dad about it. I told him he should lay off. Even so, if you get this thing running Diego, the old man'll probably give you a lifetime discount."

"I don't need a discount. I'm just looking to give back to the community." Diego smiles and says, "Like in San Francisco."

Rene smiles, probably the first time she's smiled at Diego. "Good for you. You see, now you're teaching a man to fish."

"What are talking about?"

"You know, give the man a fish he can…"

"Oh yeah, yeah, yeah." Diego turns to Antonio. "Work on what I said and I'll come back tomorrow after I get off. Oh, and come by the shop, I'll give you an ohmmeter to use." Diego walks past Rene and says, "Hopefully you have a little more respect for the charitable nature of the people of Bodie."

"Well I am a little more impressed with you." Rene swings her head around and the smell of reefer bombards Diego's senses. He imagines days when women smelled like women.

It might have been better that way, but who remembers things like that. He looks over his shoulder to say goodbye, but she's already gone.

"I guess you want to get started on that thing. Go get me a piece of cardboard so I don't have to lie on the ground."

"Right now?"

"Get over here and I'll show you how to use this thing." A quick lesson and Antonio goes to work checking the wires with Diego watching intently. At the same time, he looks over every other aspect of the car, answering Jesus's questions as the young boy bounces around the work site. Occasionally Antonio's anxious head pops out from under the car.

"Take your time Antonio. Getting something done fast isn't as important as getting it done right."

Antonio takes a breath and Diego tells about the time he put headers on the Firechicken with Jon, but in his hurried excitement, he put on the wrong kind. It cost him two days and hundreds of dollars.

"I think I got it!" Diego climbs down and there it is, a burned wire running along the frame. "I guess I got the touch," says Antonio.

"Don't get too happy. I guarantee it'll happen again." This'll give a bad impression of what working on an old car is really like. "I'll go see Mr. Wisnewski tomorrow. Come by the shop later in the week, and I'll give you his message."

Rene reappears back on the porch, now sporting bloodshot eyes and a vacant expression. "Diego Vellllardeeee!"

"What are you still doing here? I thought you left."

"I just couldn't help it. I had to come back and give myself to you." Diego watches as Antonio quickly gathers his tools and takes them back to his father's garage.

"What are you talking about!" Diego asks.

Rene shakes her head slowly. "You're an idiot."

Diego feels his face redden. "Ya, well you're becoming a pain in the ass."

"How'd everything turn out for Antonio? Were you able to get the car running?"

"He lit that fucker up himself. I gave him a few pointers and he took it from there. From what I saw he's going to spend a lot of time working on that cars electrics, but if he gets the chance he could be pretty good mechanic."

"Why wouldn't he get that chance, because of what his parents do?"

"I'm not judging, so don't give me any shit. They may be doing what they have to, or maybe they have no good reason for the life they've chosen. As far as Antonio goes, that's not the fucking point. He's going to have to face things you and I don't know anything about. It'll make it harder for him Rene, even with talent."

"You work in the field, you have connections. There may be a lot in Antonio's way, but you could improve his chances."

"I'll do what I can, and I'd like to do more, but..."

"You have a responsibility. Go get him started on his training. You've got friends all over Bodie, and maybe some of the other towns around here. You could get him a job, something that would give him some skills and get him out of this house. Show him that there's more out there than what he's grown up seeing." Rene gives a slight pause for effect. "You have to do it Diego, you owe it to everyone who's ever given you a chance."

"There's some things I could do, but that doesn't mean it'll be enough."

"Giving someone the chance is all anyone can ask. After that it'll be up to him to make the most of your help."

"Rene: the great philosopher."

"Blow me Diego! I'm not going to stand here and let you kill my buzz." With this she again pushes past him and disappears.

Like approaching thunder, Diego hears the Firechicken getting closer. Diego turns and calls out, "Remember to come see me later in the week, Antonio"

Chapter XXXI

An End To Isolation

Hailing from a small town once meant living off the beaten path. As popular music, fashion, and literature changed in the cities, they would stay largely the same in the small towns of America. The blues that played for generations in small hamlets dotting the banks of the Mississippi River was not pushed aside by the bluegrass of Tennessee or the advent of Texas swing. When it changed, it did so organically. It became a distinct style called Delta Blues. Each town had its own flavor, maybe a little bland compared to the spice of the city, but it was distinct. It was special.

The days of the truly isolated small town has come to an end in the San Joaquin. In the world of twenty-four hour news, Internet and wireless telephones, isolation is not only unnecessary, it's practically impossible. It's not all bad. People previously thought of as backward inhabitants of the boondocks suddenly find themselves as hip to trends as any living in Manhattan and a man who a generation ago may have been uneducated to the greater movements of the world can be more aware than an identical twin living in downtown Los Angeles.

Yet all things have a price, and the people of the villages of America must pay theirs. They are no longer free to play their own music, and dress their own way. The lenses that once allowed these unheralded corners of the country to see things in a distorted view have been taken and smashed, leaving only the clear vision of who they are, and what the world is. The small town may no longer be backward and isolated, but it is no longer free.

Chapter XXXII

Notes And Numbers

The secretary of Bodie Trucking Company moves the stack of receipts until the shadow again covers her keyboard. Her first day on the job she went home with sunburns on the top of her hands. It would be easy to close the blinds, or ask someone to move her desk to the back of the office where it's always shady, but the daily dance with the sun is satisfying. By the end of the day her sun shield will be teetering on the right edge of the desk. First thing in the morning she'll move the stack all the way to the left, and begin again.

"You alright Marty?" she asks.

Light pierces Martins thin collared shirt. It's not sunburn, but the town holding its magnifying glass over him; burning with every second he lets pass without making a move. He re-reads Leo note, trying to find a hidden message from the sixteen words.

I've been seeing irregularities in the paperwork Eric's been bringing me. Keep an eye on him.

"I need the account books. Leo wants me to go over some things, and I don't want to be bothered."

"Use Eric's desk, nobody'll disturb you darlin."

"No, the guys will be asking me questions about this and that, and I'm no good at accounts as it is. I'll be back in a couple of hours, but I'm taking one of the vans with me."

Slowly Martin creeps across the yard, looking at the books to appear occupied. Once he gets into the shop he hurries to the cabinet and with his index finger hooks a pair of keys at random. He jumps in the van and goes racing down the road with loud music and hot air. Small specks of ash slam into the window, forcing him to turn on the wipers, and they screech across the dry glass. With his right hand Martin reaches over and by feel finds The Wild Hare on the radio dial. Like a cool breeze, the pent up frustration of Pearl Jam's *Nothingman* pours through the speakers. He turns up the volume until it drowns out the windshield wipers and when he gets to My Friend's House he drives around the block twice until his favorite Alice in Chains song ends.

The music is over and a commercial for a local tire dealership comes on. Marty parks the van and head for the indoor refuge of the air-conditioned bar and grill. Cold air rushing against the sweat drenched back of his shirt refreshes, and for a moment the weight of the summer lifts. The room is empty but for a single waitress behind the register, and a solitary man sitting near the television. He's indistinguishable from any Bodie farmer and Martin might not have noticed were it not the middle of the day during the harvest.

As the old farmer turns the half empty beer in front of him, Martin imagines him trying to discover the exact speed needed to create a whirlpool in the ale. His worn jeans, neat shirt and beaten work boots are all traditional earmarks that do little to identify him. Next to the twirling beer mug lays a crumpled, sweat stained San Francisco Giants hat.

A heavy bandage that engulfs his right hand and as Martin slowly strolls, he strains his eyes and turns his head to every conceivable angle. He even crouches, looking at the man from a different height. No matter what he does, Martin can't recognize Ian Heffron.

"Mr. Heffron?"

"What the hell are you doing here Martin? You're supposed to be at work."

"So are you."

"I had to come into town to pick up some lumber. I thought I'd drop by for a drink," Ian says while returning to his twirling mug.

"You hate this place. The only person in Bodie that hates it."

"I never said I hated it."

"You called it a hall of decadence promoting a drug culture."

Ian looks around the café, taking it in for the first time. "Actually, it's kind of nice when it's empty. Aren't those buttresses black walnut?"

Before he can answer Martin feels the soft hand of the waitress land on his shoulder. "Hey Marty. You want anything?"

"Bring me a beer. You want another one?"

Ian Heffron has returned to his examination of the spinning glass. He seems to have found the perfect speed. The moment of normality has passed, and Martin again doesn't recognize the man.

"Bring him another, and put it on my tab."

Having seemingly accomplished his goal, Ian wakes from his dream. "No. I've gotta go."

"The beers already coming Mr. Heffron. It's been a stretch since we shared drink."

"It was Easter two years ago, wasn't it?"

"Yeah."

"I remember. Everyone else was in the back. We sat on the front deck. What the hell were we talking about?"

Martin thinks back to that cool spring evening on that endless deck. "My potential."

"That's right, and you weren't listening to a word I said."

The beers arrive and Martin downs half his glass with one swig as Ian returns to twirling his glass; studying whether this fresh beer will react the same as the previous one.

"That's because you weren't saying anything I hadn't heard a million times before," Martin says.

"I know what this town has put on your family Marty, and I've never thought it fair. I watched what it did to your father; the way they all blamed him for not living up to their bastardized version of what your family has meant to this community. It destroyed your old man, and he was as much a Dougherty as Ulysses. People have never understood what makes your family special, and important to this town. It's not that you've always followed the rules, but that you've known when to ignore them.

"I know how that sounds Marty, but it's true. Your family has respected law so long as they believed the law was correct. Their actions have lined up with the rules, and that's why the Dougherty name has a reputation. The great trap you guys have found yourself in is that when you don't align with the expectations, the people in this stupid town immediately think of you as failures. They call you sell outs, but that's only because they never really understood the myths they helped write. Strange."

Ian reaches into his pocket for a cigarette. He pulls out his pack, and throws it on the table without lighting one. "I'm sure you know the story of your great aunt Lena, but I wonder if you know the real one."

"She helped lead the charge against the whore houses and speakeasy's back in the thirties."

"She was the charge." Ian looks down at his pack again deciding such conversation requires the aroma of tobacco. "Whenever the story is told, people pretend the citizens were fed up with the ugliness of it all and were merely waiting for someone to save them, and then Lena appeared. The truth is, she was hated for what she did, and it was years before Bodie forgave her.

"Can't say I blame them, it was the depression; people were suffering. All over the Valley livelihoods where lost. Drink and prostitution were the only things bringing solid income to town. Everyone was getting a piece, one way or another. They weren't all taking cash, but these businesses where building stuff, donating money to the school, putting on fairs and festivals. It was their way of keeping everyone quiet, and it worked. Even by the forties when the depression was subsiding in other parts of the country, Bodie still struggled and the people of this town kept doing what they felt they needed to survive.

"The Dougherty's accepted this to a point. They never liked it, but they understood. They couldn't ask people to let their children starve because of their own moral qualms? So, they enforced the law as much as they felt they should, just to make sure the town didn't go back to the way things were in the mining days. But Lena never liked that; it didn't sit right with her. From her point of view, she'd rather starve, and watch the town turn to dust then sell its soul."

"When World War II hit, things started getting better, but not in Bodie. Lena believed it was because making money off vice had become an addiction. It was easier than scratching out an honest living. She hated it; my mother told me how it used to bring Lena to tears talking about it. Finally, she had enough and took action. She probably would've tried something earlier, but had to wait until her husband and the rest of the men of Bodie were spread across Europe and the Pacific."

"She did her best to raise support, but she didn't get much. The majority of the town thought she was a loud mouth trying to gain a place in the Dougherty legend. People wanted her to shut up and go away. Those few that did support her were afraid to say so publicly. They'd go to her meetings, and complain along with her, but when the time came to act they shirked. Lena got so frustrated she decided to take matters into her own hands. The next part of the tale you know, and it was true."

Martin puts down his beer. "She walked into the biggest brothel in Bodie with her husbands shotgun and killed Mathew Clay. Then she hid on the Heffron farm until the war ended, and continued to lead her fight in secret. I guess it was after that first killing when the rest of the town jumped on the bandwagon."

Ian takes another long drag. "There was never a bandwagon Martin. They called her a vigilante who dreamed of being famous. They locked her up."

"Lena went to prison?"

"She was charged with murder, and there was talk of a death sentence. Then those Heffrons and Dougherty's that weren't over seas went to the mayor and told him if Lena wasn't let go and the charges dropped they were going to burn the town down. The mayor, who'd been taking kickbacks from the murdered pimp for years, didn't think much of the threat. Two days later a brothel burned down on the west side. The next day it was a dead opium dealer behind a little general store on the north end. Lena was released, but it was years before she became immortalized."

"What's the tie in with my potential?"

"If you'd stop worrying about Bodie, and do what you think is right, you could do some good things in this town."

"If I knew you were going to call me a pussy I'd have left you to your glass."

"I'm not saying you're a pussy."

"I don't follow the rules Mr. Heffron. I go out of my way to break them."

"That's no difference. Your decisions are based on policies, written and unwritten. You look at what the town wants from you, what your family wants from you and what society wants from you, then you purposely do the opposite. Your life is still dictated by others. Follow your heart, and if people love you for it, great, if they don't, who gives a shit."

"Shocking language. I think I'll give this conversation a C minus." The young Dougherty waves at the waitress behind the bar who immediately starts running toward them. "So you never answered my question. Why are you in this place in the middle of the day?"

"I had to pick up some lumber..."

"No lumber sold at My Friend's House."

Ian sinks lower and becomes less recognizable. "I've gotta build something with the lumber and I'm avoiding it."

The waitress walks up and Martin orders some cheese sticks before turning back to Ian. "If you need help I can come over after work."

"No, it's not hard." The glass stops spinning. "I'm building a For Sale sign."

The air goes out of the room, and Martin suddenly finds himself unable to breath. He looks up at the pretty waitress behind the bar, and can tell she feels it to. Not the details, but she knows that at the table in front of the big screen television something unspeakable has happened. The room darkens, and the music wafting down the hall goes quiet. They sit together and without ever asking, the young waitress brings them more beers when they're needed.

Finally Ian looks up. "What's all that there?"

"The boss has been in seclusion since Estelle vanished. He's asked me to go over the books. Masterson's been doing it, and Radmonavic thinks he hasn't been keeping good enough track of the money." The trivial nature of it all brings a rush of blood to Martin's neck. No matter how he arranges it, he can't help but come to the conclusion that the bankruptcy of the Heffron farm is a far greater tragedy than physically losing the woman he loves.

Estelle's disappearance is a loss for two men. What's happening with the Heffrons is something grander, more like a catastrophe than a tragedy. Ian and Debra are not the only ones who will lose, they all will. Every Heffron from this day forward will have lost something. Guilt creeps into Martin's heart when he thinks that he enjoyed that land when future generations will not.

"Well, I'll let you get to it, Martin."

"See ya, Mr. Heffron."

"By the way, I'm having a barbeque in a few days at my place. I want you and Diego to come."

"We'll be there."

Ian turns and walks away, and as much as he would like to say something, Martin Dougherty remains quiet. He can only stare down at the table, spinning his beer.

Chapter XXXIII

Stealing Fruit at Midnight

A fourteen year old boy walked along Nebraska Ave turning off irrigation valves, not thinking of anything in particular. He paused to watch a pair of Jays run off a Red-tailed hawk flying too close to their nest. The peaches ripened faster than Dad expected, and they would have to pick a day early. Most of the water would be gone by morning, but the crew would have to slog through mud to cover the two-acre orchard. Hearing the crunching sound of gravel behind him, Jonathan waved politely as a middle-aged woman stepped out of a minivan.

"Excuse me, is this your farm?"

"It's my Dad's."

"We're driving through from LA to Sacramento. We're moving up there."

Jon waited for a moment, but when the woman said nothing more he replied, "Permission granted." The back of his throat goes dry. There's never a need to say things like that.

"Would it be OK if I grabbed a few pieces of fruit for my kids. They've been in the car for three hours, and they're getting restless."

Jonathan looked in the van and watched as the sister and brother push and pull at each other. "You better let me get 'em. We just finished watering."

"Oh, if it's too much trouble don't worry."

"No worries, but if my dad comes by, tell him you're a big-time fruit broker searching for future suppliers." Jonathan started rummaging through the tree, and before long he returned with an armful of fruit. "They can eat the softer ones now. The firmer peaches will be ready in a day or so."

"You didn't have to do that."

"It's fine. Have a nice trip." It felt good giving away the fruit like that. Not that it was saintly, but giving food to children had to count for something.

Eight years later, on a similar roadside, he turns off the ignition to watch dim lights move around in the far off plum orchard.

"They're in the Casselmans. We're gonna pick them in a few days."

"Jon, let's just go tell Ian."

"You don't have to whisper Laura. We're hundreds of yards away, inside a car, they can't hear us."

"Fine, but I still think we should go tell Ian so he can call the sheriff."

"I'll bet anything it's Quinn Ohrnberger."

"There was never any proof that he…"

"That guy's been stealing for years. He takes peoples livelihoods to stock his fruit stand in Fresno. God, it makes me sick to think how his yuppie customers all complement him on the quality of 'HIS' produce while the farmers he stole from spend sleepless nights wondering how they're gonna hold on for another year."

"Jon, it's just as likely a bunch of teenagers messing around out there. It doesn't matter either way. We need to go to your uncles and CALL THE SHERIFF!"

"They could have asked first."

Jon remembers his father teaching him how to lay out an orchard on that very corner of land. It had been the last bit of Ian's farm that supported vineyard. The summer before Gabriel's death, they tore out the vines, and that October burned the giant piles. Ian spent days on the old Massey Ferguson, driving back and forth, tilling the field to get it ready for planting. Jonathan watched his uncle and father adjust the width of the irrigation valves to fit the wider rows needed for the orchard. When that was finished, Gabriel pulled out the long-knotted cord he used to mark where each tree would stand. At each knot Jonathan dropped a baby tree bought from Jim Hanson Nursery. Behind him, Gabriel dug a hole and then Ian followed, carefully planting a tree." It took several days but now, years later, an orchard stands.

Jonathan climbs out the car, quietly closing the door behind him. "Walk back to Ian's and call the cops. Then tell Marty and Diego to come, and to be quiet when they do."

"Jonathan stop it! What are you going to do? Just come with me to your uncles."

It's one of those dusty nights, creating glowing rings around the lights of the thieves' trucks. It's hard to breath, and he can feel a buildup of dirt sticking to his skin. He used to go out on nights like this, and when he'd get home there'd be lines of dirt along his shirt and across his brow, marking where the sweat stopped.

It'll be gone soon; the house, the orchards everything that makes the land Heffron. A quarter mile away is Ian's glowing deck, where thirty people enjoy what he calls the first in a long line of goodbyes. Quinn must hear the laughter. Whenever the breeze shifts they must smell the barbeque.

Jon crouches as he moves over the rough terrain, doing his best to stay behind the trees. If only they hadn't plowed six days earlier; the tall weeds would have made for good cover. His eyes adjust to the darkness and shadows cast by the ivory moon take shape. Jonathan hears voices, and he's only a hundred yards away now. He doesn't understand what they're saying, but they're not teenagers looking for fun. He reaches down and grabs a handful of wet soil and smells it. It's a sterile scent, but in smelling it Jon feels he's showing appreciation for all the land has done.

Jon moves slowly, bouncing from one irrigation ditch to the next. After each leap he looks over the furrow and around the tree trying to identify the robbers. Each row is eighteen feet wide, he remembers that much. Eighty yards away and with each jump to the next ditch Jon does a quick calculation in his head.

At forty-two yards butterflies flutter in the pit of his stomach. Jon always felt that nervous joy when he played on the land at night as a kid. It was that safe-fear of running in the darkness while knowing in his heart that nothing bad could happen. He'd climb trees and pounce on his unsuspecting friends as they searched for him. Hours spent lying in wait behind piles of brush to shoot rats coming out from the barn. Then he and his cousins would take their places behind forts they spent all day building so they could spend the night attacking each other with rotten fruit and cheap water guns.

They're all wearing headlamps, like the ones cave explorers use. At thirty-six yards Jon sees Louis Aguilar, who worked on Gabriel's farm in the last two years before his death. Loading boxes of fruit into the truck is Rey Tatupu, and next to him is Charlie Fitzpatrick who played football with Martin until he was kicked off the team for failing too many classes. These people all know him. They know his family.

The Heffron farm's a dying animal, but before it goes the jackals will get their fill. At twenty-four yards Jonathan hears a truck door open. The faint sound of a classic country song comes through, and when the door shuts it goes quiet. Around the corner of the truck, the heavyset shape of Quinn Ohrnberger appears. He calls out to his pack, "Well I gotta say, these Heffrons grow a hell of a piece of fruit." The jackals all snarl with pleasure.

Eighteen yards and Jonathan looks behind him. The giddiness has now become a violent shake. In the distance he can see Ian's deck. Laura has made it there by now, and soon the sheriffs will be on their way. Before that, Martin and Diego will arrive and Jonathan wonders what will happen from there. For Martin there will only be one course of action. Diego will shrug his shoulder and say, "Whatever you fucks want, I'm in."

Lying down as flat as he as one approaches, Jonathan remembers the sensation of playing hide and seek in the old barn. The best parts were always those moments right before being found.

"Com'on Eddie we got to get outta here."

"Hold up, I gotta take a leak."

Jon hears the voice and recognizes it. It's been years, and there's a little more bass to it, but Jon knows Eddie Messi. Jon tried to talk to him at Mauricio's wedding, maybe even apologize for losing his temper all those years ago. It wasn't really because he felt bad, but Ian always says there's nothing wrong with admitting a mistake. Eddie wasn't having any of it. Every time Jon approached, his former teammate would walk away. When Eddie did stand around and talk, he tried to hide the small scar from the busted lip Jon gave him by the cold waters of the Dead Man.

Quinn's throaty voice calls through the Valley night. "Damnit Eddie, pinch it off and get over her before Ian comes down and shoots us all."

"Fuck that broken down old man. There's not one Heffron that frightens me." The sound of urine splattering against the freshly plowed soil is clear, and Jon knows Eddie is no more than five feet away. "Hell, one of you can go tell them what we're doing, I'll take care of 'em one by one. I'll leave that bastard Jon for last."

There's a loud pop of Eddie's nose breaking that brings everyone's attention to Jon Heffron who's materialized out of the darkness. Eddie falls back, unconscious with his cock out. Covered in wet dirt, Jon appears like a ghost of some long dead Heffron in the thin light and falling ash.

"Nobody here is taking anything from me, not without a fight."

Oblivious to the absurdity of it all, Jonathan runs toward the thieves. He almost gets to Quinn when he's pushed from behind, and slammed onto the hard dirt road where the cars are parked. Sharp pain shoots through his elbows, and the air is chased from his lungs. Half from his own effort and half from that of the assailant, Jon is spun round until he's on his back looking up at a silhouette on top of him. In the second before his head bounces off the ground from the force of a falling fist Jonathan recognizes Nick Amado. He feels several more punches before the weight is lifted from his chest.

There's a scream of spinning tires, and Jon knows it's over even as Martin shouts, "I saw you Oherberger you bastard! You better turn yourself in before I can find you!"

Jonathan tries to raise himself, but is immediately pushed down. "Lay the fuck down Jon."

"I'm alright Diego. Just help me up." Pulling himself upright, Jonathan sees two other men have followed his friends, probably from the party. Jon tries to focus on their faces, but decides it doesn't matter.

"Let's get back to the house," Jon says.

Martin grabs Jon's shoulder and says, "Hold up Heffron. Your uncle's gonna be here with the truck any moment."

"I feel like walking." Jon passes the two other men with an ear-to-ear grin on his face. "Besides, it'll give you time to help me come up with a story explaining this to Laura, and it needs to be a good one."

Diego looks around at the three unconscious bodies still lying on the ground; Eddie and the two Martin took care of. "Shouldn't we stay here until the fucking cops show? If these three wake up they're gonna walk away."

Jon laughs again. "I don't care if these guys steal all our fruit. We're going outta business."

Martin watches as Jon stumbles back into the darkness. He begins to follow then looks at Diego who's still taking in the scene. He takes a step toward his friend, leaning down until his lips are almost touching Diego's and whispers.

"Why is there a gun hanging out your back pocket."

"I got it out my car. That's what took me so fucking long."

"Do I have to ask?"

"I took it from Mr. Wisnewski's house, right before he went up to Fresno. I don't know why, I saw it sitting on his damn table and grabbed it. I was holding on to it until I thought it was safe to give back."

Martin stares at the handle of the gun then back at the tag-along's who are still looking over the aftermath of the fight. "Give it to me Velarde."

"What the fuck for?"

"You can't give it back Mr. Wisnewski, and the fact that you'd bring it to a fight proves you're too stupid to have it. Now give it to me."

"I wasn't going to use it asshole, but if Jon was in trouble…"

"Diego, you're my friend, but don't argue with me on this. Give me the gun."

Diego reaches behind him and quickly hands the gun to Marty who takes it and tucks it under his shirt. "I'll give it to the next truck driver who's going on a long haul, and have them pawn it out of state. When I get the money I'll give it to you, and then we'll never talk about this again." Martin takes out a cigarette and lights it. "Better catch up to Heffron. He's liable to pass out from that beating."

After Jon, Diego and Martin get far enough away, one of the men who followed the excursion into the darkness turns to his companion and asks, "What was that kid smiling, he just got his butt handed to him?"

"Yeah, but he'll get the last laugh."

"Why's that?"

"He's one of the Heffron's, and there are two undeniable truths about that family. They all die bad, and if anyone picks a fight with a Heffron, they also pick a fight with the Dougherty's. In the case of Jon, that means dealing with Martin."

"How'd that arrangement come about?"

"I don't know, but somewhere along the line the Dougherty's decided the Heffron's were worth looking after."

Chapter XXXIV

Reprieve

Laura running her fingers along his swollen side has become unbearable, but the routine makes her feel better. She wouldn't cut it as a farmer's wife. As soon as she became accustomed to seeing him home at five o'clock, the harvest would start, then she'd be alone in the house until dark. One summer might see him working sixty hours a week, the next eighty. The routine of the farm is simple, everything constantly changes, and adapting to the land's needs is the only order.

They lay together uncovered on Jon's old mattress, but the heat of the day with the labor of breathing soot filled air leaves them coated with a thin layer sweat. Jonathan has blocked the windows and covered every seam so no sunlight enters, dropping the temperature a few degrees. He doesn't need to see the sky; August always looks the same. It's no less hot, only darker.

He takes a deep breath and the three-inch gash on his scull pulls at the stitches. Jonathan thinks about how he yelled at Ian for sending him home that morning.

"I can still work, Ian."

Ian shook his head slowly and smiled, "Jon, tell me what's the point in suffering needlessly for a dying farm?"

Unable to think of an answer, Jon got into his little car, and left to enjoy a day off with Laura.

"Maybe we should look into buying a little piece of land," Laura whispers as she gives him a quick, affectionate squeeze.

Jonathan holds back a yelp. "You want to be a farmer?"

"I just said we should get a farm. Nothing big, just five or ten acres to live on. You're always saying it's the best way for children to grow up."

Jonathan sighs and his head begins to throb. "We can't make a living on ten acres Laura. Hell, my uncle couldn't make a living on ninety, and he's the best farmer in the county."

"What if I took that job in Fresno?"

"You said you didn't want to do that kind of work."

"With that salary, and what you'll be making from teaching, we might support a place in the country."

Jonathan gingerly rolls out of bed. "It's not the same."

"It wouldn't be for you, or even us. It'd be for the kids."

Jonathan limps slowly toward the kitchen to get some water and says, "You've always said you wanted a place in town."

Silence fills the small apartment as each lover waits for the other to speak. Jonathan imagines Laura living in a small, well-kept farmhouse near the Sierra's. He pictures her battling unending waves of dust that coats their furniture. He thinks of her eating dinner alone because he and the kids had to fix broken irrigation lines for the third time in as many weeks. He sees the disappointment on her face when he tells her that another summer will pass without a family vacation. In the dark silence of the hot apartment Jonathan imagines their life on a small farm, and can't picture her happy.

"Are you pregnant?"

"God no Jonathan!"

"Then why are you so worried about kids we aren't having yet?"

"I don't know. My mind was wandering." The noise of sheets ruffling fills the room as Laura lies down, remembering their first time together. They'd been dating for a year and at fifteen, they were the first in their circle of friends to lose their virginity. Jonathan immediately acted more serious in everything he did. Somehow, he thought it made them more sophisticated, even as it made part of her feel ashamed. The only comfort came later when he reverted to his obnoxious self; it helped her feel like it really didn't change anything in the end.

There wasn't anything sophisticated about it anyway. Two bumbling teenagers in the passenger side of Gabriel Heffron's truck parked under the canopy of Ian's Eucalyptus grove. It was quick, awkward, and for the most part unpleasant. Laughing to herself, Laura considers letting Jon in on the joke, but he wouldn't understand. He wouldn't see the beauty that sprouted from the awkwardness. Laura remembers her mother saying once she gave herself to a man all they'd want to do is leave. That first night she held on to him and wouldn't let go, but Jon never so much as moved. Even when Ian tapped on the window at daybreak, he did little else than turn his head and acknowledge they were caught. It still reassures her knowing that when their relationship gets rocky, these moments keep them together.

She hears him sidle up to the bed, and place a glass of water on the nightstand for her. "You don't have to make any sacrifices for me, Laura."

"I wasn't planning to sacrifice anything, but it might be nice to hold on to a piece of your past."

"This isn't something you can have just a piece of. This is different. This is like being excommunicated from your church or exiled from your country. It's nothing that can be held onto halfway. This is one of those things you have, or you don't. A small cottage in the country won't replace it Laura. We're losing our identity, and we'll never get it back." Jon climbs into bed and puts his arm around her before quickly rolling onto his back when breathing becomes too painful.

"I don't want our kids growing up like this."

"Like what?"

"Trapped in the past, unable to connect with the present."

When his parents were killed his relationship with Laura didn't change, it was transformed. Before the accident, they were high school sweethearts many around town felt spent too much time together. Suddenly they were expected to spend time together. For weeks, she'd come home only to be chastised by her parents. "He needs you right now Laura, what are you doing here?"

"I think he wants some time alone, Mom."

"Laura you're his girlfriend, and he lost both his parents. It's your responsibility to help him get through this."

Now it's changing again, and they'll have to start over. Will this new person love her, and will she love him. Maybe they won't even recognize each other, and will anyone understand if suddenly they weren't right for each other.

Laura jumps from the bed and in doing so jabs him in his damaged ribs. Before he can find out what's happening he's blinded as the whole apartment explodes with light. When the pain stops and his eyes adjust there's Laura lying next to him, staring with the slightest smile on her face.

"Laura, what the hell are you doing?"

"I'm sick of being in the dark."

"It's a hundred and three degrees today. Close the window."

"No. I want to look at you."

Jon looks out the window into the dusty Bodie afternoon. "So let's close the window and turn on a lamp."

"Stop being a baby, Jon."

Jon looks at his girlfriend and sees her eyes shaking frantically. "What's the matter with you Laura? Did you take mushrooms while I was in the kitchen?"

Then she feels something coming that she doesn't expect. As an explosion of tears overtakes her she shouts, "You're scaring me Jon!"

"What happened? What'd I do!"

"You're acting like nothing will ever be right, and I don't know what I'm supposed to do. I've always been able to help you."

"You help me everyday." Jonathan moves closer to her and holds her. She squeezes until his ribs move in his chest. It doesn't matter though, he feels frantic to stop her. "You're the only part of my life that any good right now. Hell, it's been like that for a long time."

"I want to help."

"I know you do."

Jon lays there as Laura sobs lightly in his arms as the temperature of the already hot apartment rises. The sheets of the mattress begin to soak up sweat, and her body becomes slick but he holds on. He wants to be angry with her. It should be about him not her. What does she have to fear; what is she losing? Still he loves her more than ever because she'd gladly abandon her happiness to share his pain. It's the most beautiful thing anyone could do.

"I'm sorry Laura, but you have to know that anything that happens, we'll be together. We have to because there's nothing in Bodie that's left for me but you. You're all I want." Jonathan gets quiet again. Laura is still crying but is less animated than before. "Besides I made Marty promise that if anything ever happens between us, he'll marry you."

Again she jabs her boyfriend in the ribs, this time intentionally. "Can't you pretend to take something serious for once?"

Jonathan feels relieved to hear her laugh. "You're right. Let's talk about our little farm. The most important thing is that we own some ducks."

"Jon."

"I don't want to live on a farm part time, and there is no way to do it full time. It's something I have to leave behind. It'll be alright." Maybe things will be alright, but he doesn't believe it. In fact Jon believes the opposite, that things will never be alright again.

"I think I'll take that job anyway."

"I don't need a little farm."

"Well if you don't want a little farm, I want a big house in Bodie."

"Well if you want a big house in Bodie, make sure it has a wading pool in the back yard."

"No way. You'll get drunk with your idiot friends and I'll find you drowned."

Jonathan imagines another future. He thinks of a roomy house in the new neighborhood on the south side of Bodie, no more than a mile from schools, parks and My Friend's House. With eyes closed, Jonathan sees Laura and himself strolling down Main Street on a cool Saturday morning window-shopping on their way to a late brunch. He pretends to work in his front yard while children play. Occasionally a neighbor will come over, and they strike up conversation. Laura's inside preparing for a Friday night get together with friends, which isn't difficult as the house is always neat and tidy. Jon imagines Laura is happy, but can't see himself feeling anything.

Jon then imagines himself dying in a common pool drowning, and this simply wouldn't do. "I don't need a full size pool then, just something big enough to stand in with a beer. If I pass out, then it'll be too skinny for me to drown in."

"That sounds like an attractive thing to look out at. When people come over I can tell them to look at our custom made drunk pool."

Stiffening for more pain, Jon rolls toward Laura again. "If you get your big house, I get a drunk pool."

Chapter XXXV

They Came to a Green Desert

They came from far and wide; from every corner of the world to build something. They dug canals and drained marshes. They carved roads into the sides of foothills and across the great flat of the Valley floor they laid steel rail for the iron horse. They cut down trees for building fences and barns, then dug up mud to cook bricks for their homes. They came from Oklahoma to escape the dust bowl in the hope of sewing new crops in fertile soil. They came from Mexico and Central America wanting to give their children a better future, even if it meant sacrificing their own to the harsh nature of California agriculture. They escaped from under the sword of the Armenian genocide to a place where they could live and worship in peace. From the Far East they traveled on cramped boats to San Francisco before arriving in the San Joaquin to harvest oranges and build railroads. Some abandoned their homes in the south for the hope of a world without Jim Crow. Others fled the cities of the eastern seaboard for the last of the wide-open spaces. They followed the oil, they followed the gold, and they followed the promise of open land. The Mexicans called it the Green Desert, and they all came to build something out of it.

Chapter XXXVI

A Road Never Traveled

At Augusts end, as vineyard owners entered their thirty day wait for the sun to transform their plump, green grapes into shriveled, purple raisins, the air is made thick with the smell of dust and sugar. It's a reminder that everything fails, and this truth dims the world of the San Joaquin Valley. Even as Diego heads home in the dead of night, the evening seems blacker. The streetlights turn faint and the road signs become dull. It's not sinister, it's a world grown tired.

Diego reaches over to the radio dial and start flipping channels, hoping for one good song before he gets to Isabelle's. The Firechicken hits the massive pothole in the center of Lacy Ave and Main Street and Diego's finger slips, and the local news channel comes on.

"To recap, Leo Radmonovic, husband of Estelle Radmonavic, who disappeared on July 1st, has gone missing himself. The police are looking for him in connection with his wife's disappearance and are now saying he is the prime suspect. This is leading some to question why, if he is a suspect, has the connection not been made at any time for the last seven weeks. We will keep you informed as this story develops. This is Rosaline

Sanchez with 90.2 KZON, your source for news in the Central Valley.

"Holy Shit."

Coming up on a small street connecting Main to Logan Ave, Diego spins the steering wheel to the left and toward Martin's apartment. The street runs between the small soup and sandwich shop owned by the Torres family, and a postal supply store. By most accounts the narrow street is nothing more than an alley, but according to every town map it's a street.

He slams on the brakes in time to avoid driving over two people standing in the shadows of the poorly lit street.

Todd Flynn spins around and walks to the driver side door of the Firechicken. "We got him Diego!"

"What are you doing you two-first-name-having motherfucker, I almost killed you!"

"We got the kid who's been vandalizing Bodie."

"What are you talking about?"

"We organized town patrols to drive around Bodie at night looking for the tagger, and one of them caught him."

Diego stomps on the high beams, brightening the small street as Todd marches on. Quickly he turns the lights back off; finding the illuminated alley less accurate. The old brick walls have the events they've witnessed written in each chip and stain sprayed across their facade. Randomly placed patches of white plaster dot the brick and appear to change size and shape as shadows roll across them. It's like the night and plaster spar playfully for dominance over the alleyway. All the light in the narrow road comes from a single lamp unlike any in Bodie. Across town the streetlights are made of black aluminum or gray granite. Here the lamppost is copper, stained green by years of battering weather, and the bulb pulsates with a yellow glow.

High above, stars peek through long black fingers of smoke from the slowly fading fires, like children hoping to steal a look at something taboo. The streetlamp occasionally dims in the ally and then pauses, leaving the crowd to wonder if they should leave. Each time it darkens, everything stops and waits for the alleyway to brighten again. The thin passage of asphalt and sidewalk smells like fresh paint at first, but this passes and a sterile odor takes over.

It's this odor, or lack thereof, that slows Diego. He thinks of all the other smells that dominate the town at that moment and how none of them are present on the street. He can't smell the fires that have become a trademark of Bodie in the last eight weeks. The ever present dust is nowhere in the air and Diego tries to imagine the town without the dirt of the Valley and it frightens him. Then there's the missing decay of the grapes.

Diego feels drawn to the crowd, like when the waves wash over your feet at the beach. There's a tattered cardboard box full of spray cans with an wood orchard ladder pushed against the brick wall. He looks over the heads of the mob, and sees the half finished mural.

It's the image of a man constructed of art supplies; on his knees asking forgiveness of someone for something. Diego steps forward, wanting to distinguish the half-finished shape hanging over the prostrate man. He feels something crunch beneath his feet and looks down to see a puncture vine growing through a crack in the asphalt. Ash covers the pavement, but there are no markings to hide. He looks at the defaced wall, and in the darkness of August, the half-finished painting shines bright. It's hard to tell if the man in the painting reaches toward what will be the sun, or if the circle is meant to outline some unfinished image. Then down in the corner, in crimson red, is the signature of Bolivar.

"You son of a bitch city-boy," yells one of the crusaders.

Another shouts, "Let me guess, a juvenile delinquent who got kicked out of every school in Fresno, and now you've been dumped on the decent people of Bodie."

In the voice of Jonathan Heffron, the overlapping plots of every story from Bodie's past floods Diego's mind. He remembers the shoot-outs and liquor runs. He imagines the whorehouses and the time when unwritten segregation still existed in California. He remembers all the stories and wonders how anyone can call the people of Bodie, past or present, decent.

The man standing in front of Diego is tall and wears too much cologne for an evening out with a lynch mob. Diego steps around him. He gets to the front in time to see someone make a thunderclap against Bolivar's face, dropping the young criminal. Hearing a helplessly whimper, Diego feels ashamed to be part of the affair.

"He's not some random juvenile delinquent Bill, he's from that family of drug dealers across the street from Alex's place. It's in his blood; drug dealing and vandalism."

Diego looks closer and though darkness shrouds much of the boy's features Diego can tell he knows Bolivar.

Antonio tries to climb to his feet only to slip and fall back to the pavement. His paint stained hands transition from trying to steady himself to a position of readiness for another attack.

"What should we do to this damn outsider, boys?"

Some in the crowd snort suggestions, others laugh in a menacing tone that makes Diego shiver. It's hard to see Antonio as a criminal. They worked on that El Camino together, and he never appeared interested in anything but escaping to anywhere else. He thinks about Antonio's little brother Jesus, and what he revealed about their father, and how threatened to throw Antonio to the streets.

A hard bump from behind forces Diego to lunge forward. Slowly, he turns to see where the push came from, when his vision turns white, and a sharp pain shoots across the side of his head. For a moment Diego loses all sense of where he is until the cool feel of concrete brings him slowly back to reality. There's a ringing in his ears, but above it he can hear, in little more than a mumble, the sound of Todd's voice.

"You hit Diego!"

"Who threw that! Which one of you threw that can of paint!

Diego doesn't recognize the voice, but it sounds penitent. "I didn't mean to. I was aiming for the kid, you know, to scare him a little bit."

Diego feels the hands of some of the bystanders trying to help him up. Becoming aware of what happened he says, "Let me ask you this you fucking cunt! You think it would have been alright if you hit a kid with a paint can instead of me?" The warm trickle of blood mixed with the cooling summer night air sends another chill down Diego's spine, but this one is laced with anger rather than disgust.

"We were trying to…teach him a lesson."

"What right do you have to teach anyone, you asshole! You're the biggest drunk in this town Juan. And Danny; yeah I see you trying to sneak away! Are you going to stand there and tell me you have the right to judge when you spent three months in jail for beating the shit outta your wife?" He looks around at the stunned faces. "I know every filthy fucking thing each one of you has ever done in your meaningless little lives, so I dare you to step forward and tell me painting pictures on a wall is worse than any of your fucking actions."

He looks over his shoulder and sees that Antonio has climbed to his feet, but has kept his back pressed firmly against the wall. "Antonio get your ass home, and don't go out again tonight."

"What a minute Diego, we should at least call the cops. I mean, even if things got a little out of control, he's still a vandal."

"Alright Todd, you douchbag. While they're here they can arrest all of you for attacking a minor and assaulting me." Everyone stands still. "Antonio, get in the car, I'll drive you home myself."

When Diego hears the door to the Firechicken slam shut he turns to leave himself. After a few steps he stops, kneels down and collects Antonio's scattered art supplies carefully putting them back into their cardboard box. The ladder will have to wait until morning. With box in hand, he walks to the Firechicken and climbs in.

"You alright Diego?" Antonio asks.

"I'm fine, but whoever threw that can is in trouble when Marty finds out. He's been looking for fight."

"I owe you one, Diego."

"You mean that?"

"Anything I can ever do, say it, man"

"OK. I want you to paint my car."

Chapter XXXVII

Of Reflexes and Consequences

"Why didn't you just let it fall Diego? Now we have to study fractions after recess."

"Yeah, why do always have to be such a teachers pet?"

The sixth grade boy felt his face burn with shame, and he wished above all else that he'd kept staring at Julie. She was wearing her hair in pigtails, and even though they all made fun of her for it, Diego still thought she was pretty. He'd been looking at her most of the morning, barely paying attention to the lesson. Then Julie noticed his staring and gave him the slightest of smiles. Embarrassed, he looked toward the projector. Suddenly Mrs. Swanson made a quick movement toward her desk to grab another dry-erase pen, and caught her foot on the overheads extension cord pulling the whole projector off the table.

Still it wasn't like he wanted to save the thing. He hated it. Somehow learning off the chalkboard felt better. The projector fell, and like swatting at a fly buzzing around his head, Diego reached out and grabbed it. He didn't catch it all the way, but he did enough to keep it from shattering against the ground.

Diego sighed and stepped back against the wall. "Look, I didn't mean to, it was an accident."

"Stop lying, you're always doing stuff like that Diego."

They had Diego up against the wall of the boy's bathroom when the biggest sixth grader any of them ever saw suddenly appeared around the corner. The giant stopped and looked at the group, and though he'd only been at the school a few days, Martin Dougherty knew what was going on and what he needed to do.

"Leave him alone," Martin said.

"Stay out of it new kid."

"Wait a minute guys. That's Martin Dougherty."

"So what?"

"He came here because he got kicked out of his other school for punching a teacher."

Martin blushed before saying, "Yeah that's right. So what do you thinks gonna to stop me from punching any of you."

It took a few moments, but soon Martin and Diego were standing alone against the bathroom wall as the three bullies ran off toward the swing sets.

"What's your name?"

"Diego Velarde."

"Marty."

"Did you really punch a teacher at your other school?"

"Yeah."

"Did they deserve it?"

"Guess so."

Diego looked at Martin and even though he knew almost nothing about him, save for his last name, he could tell he was ashamed.

"Well," Diego said, "Screw him then."

Marty and Diego stood together watching the rest of their classmates run around the schoolyard. There was a bounce to everything they did, as though gravity struggled to keep them attached to the ground. Martin and Diego stood aside, watching with envy and frustration. They both knew how to fake it, and it would be easy to go over and play along, but they couldn't hide the weight; one carrying the heavy load of the past, the other trapped by chance.

"Why'd you catch the projector, Velarde?"

"I don't know. I do things without thinking sometimes."

"Next time, don't get involved."

Chapter XXXVIII

Revelations

Laid out on his couch, Martin recalls Bolivar's mural at Riverbend Cold Storage. Thick strokes of frantically placed paint creating a young woman in flowing white fabric that reflected the sun's rays. If not for the dimming effect of the waning wildfires, it might have been impossible to look at the mural directly. The ribbed metal siding along with shadows cast from passing drifts of smoke created the illusion of motion in the woman's robes. The mantle of glowing white hides any semblance of a body, but with her flawless dark complexion and black hair against the white, there's no doubt that those wrappings covered the most perfect woman."

Like a sinister halo, shaded shapes of men and wolves grip and tear at the fabric. These beasts were empty of everything but fear hidden under a shroud of anger. They wanted those delicate fibers of life, which set this angelic woman apart. The white barrier held them back, but the bloody slobber of the wolves' and clawed fingernails of the men proved their resolve would never waiver. Never.

The stupid futility of those late-night trips to dive bars and seedy apartment complexes asking about Estelle. She couldn't be protected, not by him. So, Martin watches the second press conference in as many days with only passing interest. There were details that may count on some level, but what mattered most was on the metal wall of that Cold Storage, painted by the teenage son of drug dealers.

Martin hears the Firechicken groan to a stop outside. The hinges of the car door whine as they slowly open, and a few moments of silence pass before there's a knock on the door.

"Yeah."

Diego enters and sees Marty on his couch facing the television with the sound off. "What's the latest?" Diego asks while taking a seat at the graffiti ridden dining room table, turning to hide the swelling on the side of his head.

"Nothing new," Martin mumbles, "The Chief went over the same stuff. Leo is being charged with Estelle's disappearance, which they're calling a kidnapping, but Leo's vanished. The search has gone statewide. They say they have several leads."

"Anything more on her?"

"Nothing, but they have no reason to believe she's…hurt."

"Have they already questioned you?"

Marty lifts himself to an upright position. "They asked me the same things they asked before, except they added new stuff about Leo's behavior, when was the last time I saw him, things like that. It's all senseless. Rene was right, it was obvious." Marty stands to his feet and slides over to his kitchenette. "Want a beer?"

"They questioned everyone?" Diego asks.

"Well except Masterson. He went on a fishing trip for a week. I don't know where he gets off taking the first vacation of his career at a time like this."

"Where's Jon?"

"It's he and Laura's anniversary. They went out. He said he's going to swing by later to pick up his cell phone. He left it here last night."

As Diego looks at Martin hunched over staring blankly at the carpet, he can't help but remember what Jon said all those years ago. The Dougherty's blood is in the town, and they feel the pulse of the community more severely than anyone.

Not knowing what else to say, Diego says, "Marty can I ask you something seriously?"

"What?"

"I want you to tell me the truth. I've noticed that Jon's been acting strange, and I want you to be honest with me, as a friend."

"Alright Velarde."

"Is there even the slightest fucking hope that Jonathan isn't completely whipped?"

Laughter echoes in the small space as the quiet tension melts away. The conversation regresses to the normal discourse of the friendship, though with a different tone. It's like two people who have mourned a loved one for days, and suddenly find themselves laughing, just so they can give their sorrow a rest. Time slows, but the crushing truth is that it's getting late, and work calls in the morning.

Diego groans with shame as he finally rises. "I gotta hit the road Marty."

"Wait til Heffron gets here."

"He won't fucking come, he'll be with Laura all night."

"Not since he found out about Ian's farm. He keeps that phone on him at all times."

Jonathan was always so unafraid; unbothered at the prospect of being alone or different. He moved around Bodie almost like he was walking through a dream, believing with all his heart that none of it was real. It was entertainment, and he watched it, waiting patiently to wake back to the real world of the Heffron farm. The dream has become real and now Jon Heffron, who long proclaimed cell phones the modern day ball and chain, fears being without it.

"Fuck it Marty, I gotta get to bed." Diego hurries, not allowing his friend a chance to protest. He walks out the door but before closing it he shouts, "Tell Jon I'll see him tomorrow." Now comes the guilt, and he stops for a moment. How can his own understanding that Jon has changed forever be so great, yet he won't sacrifice a few hours of sleep to share a laugh or two before retiring?

The small apartment is empty and Marty calls Jonathan on Laura's phone. He has nothing to say, but being alone with his thoughts overcomes him quickly. The phone rings for some time before he hears Jon's voice.

"Yes?"

"Why didn't Laura answer?"

"Why do you think?"

"She's pissed I called."

"I've always been impressed with the innate ability you Dougherty's have to analyze a situation and instantly come to the correct conclusion."

Martin hears the phone get shuffled around. "You busy, Heffron?"

"Actually, I was trying to get busy, then you called."

"I'm going to bed so if you want your cell, come get it."

"I'll be there in a bit."

Martin always considered himself lucky, as comfortable on the floor as a thousand dollar mattress. On this night he wants something more, something that cradles him. Instead, he tosses and turns, hovering in that semi-restful state, better than being awake, but not really asleep. Ideas and memories pop into his head, and he finds himself jumping toward some unwanted recollection of the past.

This quasi-restful state marked with spikes of energy doesn't last and he wakes to a loud knock on the front door. Marty looks at his bedside clock which reads two in the morning.

"Heffron you jerk! At this point you could have waited til morning." Marty gets out of bed and falls toward the door.

Flinging the door open Martin shouts, "What's the matter with you, it's two in the goddamn morning?"

"How ya doin Marty."

"Masterson! I thought you…what are you doing at my apartment?"

"I think it's time me and you settle this little thing between us." The disquieting look that Eric has displayed of late is nothing compared to the strange flashing in his eyes.

"You're a lunatic. Get the hell outta here."

"We got things to talk about."

"It can wait."

"Can I come in?"

"No. You can get off my front porch before I knock your teeth through the back of your head."

"Let's get this over with Marty-boy."

"Look, you can't come in."

Marty closes the door quickly, but before the door shuts Eric sticks out his foot causing it to pop back open. Marty looks down at the mud stained boots then raises his gaze back up, becoming fixated on the pistol in Eric's right hand.

If he'd grown up in Bodie of old, he'd have watched such confrontations unfold every day, and what action to take would be second nature. The town has changed and it no longer breeds the same kind of man, so Martin Dougherty slowly backs up as Eric enters the apartment.

Eric spent three hours preparing the different ways his nemesis might react, but when the young Dougherty does nothing, he can't help but hesitate. Marty has grown more aggressive over the last few months, and in a sudden turn, he appears appears timid. After some uncertainty, Eric finishes his entrance, closing the door quietly behind him. There's no turning back anyway.

"You shouldn't have done it Marty. You didn't have the right."

"Didn't have the right to do what?" Marty says, racing down trails of memory trying to discover something that will help him formulate a plan.

"Estelle was a good woman. Too good for the two of you. She deserved something better than having her heart broke by Leo, and disgraced by you."

"I didn't do anything disrespectful to Estelle. I'm the only one in this worthless town that didn't disrespect her.

"Yes you did! You finished what Leo started. You should have seen her in high school then. She was beautiful and pure and kind. Then she started dating Leo, but not because she loved him. She thought she did, but she didn't even know who Leo was. I watched the whole time and if I told you what he was like, you wouldn't believe he was the same man. He made promises, and painted this picture of a perfect life. It was bullshit, all of it, and now you've taken her self-respect, the only thing of hers that Leo hadn't already taken. He didn't know how lucky he was. None of you realized. I would have given anything to have what you had, and I wouldn't have wasted it."

"I didn't take her self-respect. Neither did Leo."

"She was beautiful; a way of smiling with her eyes that just…and now I'd watch her walk around her front yard like a zombie. Every day I could tell that a little more of her died and she wanted peace."

"What do you mean?"

"She was tired Marty, didn't you see that. Of course you didn't, because all you cared about was kissing Leo's ass and fucking his wife."

Just then the door flies open and the silhouette of a short man who can only be Jonathan stumbles in. "Get up you lazy dog!"

Before even grasping what's happening, Eric turns and lights up the small apartment with a flash of a gun.

Marty doesn't see his friend fall back into the door and drop to the ground. Martin listens, hoping to hear a moan to indicate that Jon Heffron is still alive.

Regaining his sight, Marty flies into a rage. Tackling Eric and taking hold of his wrist Marty squeezes with such force that Eric struggles to keep hold of the gun. Anyone else probably would have let go of the weapon, but Eric doesn't. Using his free hand Eric fends off many of the punches, but each one that lands sends vibrations of pain through his body. Finally Eric gets his legs in position to push Marty away but before he falls back, the gun is knocked from his hand and slides under his couch.

Eric turns to see where the gun fell, but not finding it, he jumps at Marty, and begins strangling him. Marty continues to punch Eric who refuses to loosen his grip. With a mix of desperation and blind rage Marty grabs Eric by the waist, lifts and slams his head into the coffee table. Springing to his feet and gasping for air, Martin pins Eric to the ground with his knee. Marty uses what strength he still has to pummel Eric with a borage of fists.

Marty catches his breath and dives over to his bed. Reaching under the mattress he feels around until he grasps the pistol he took off Diego the night of Jon's beating, and in a moment has it pressed against Eric's forehead.

"What happened to Estelle you motherfucker!"

"She's where she needed to go."

Marty pistol-whips Eric across the face with all his strength before placing the gun barrel back on Eric's forehead. "I'm asking for the last time Masterson. What have you done to Estelle?"

Eric looks at him and says with a resolve that sends a chill down Marty's spine, "He ruined my life and the life of the women I loved. What was worse, he saved me. He gave me a job and that forced me to watch him live what could have been mine. I was the one who wanted to own a trucking business, and I was in love with Estelle when he was out smoking dope and fucking anything that walked." Eric pauses as if he expects Marty to say something, but there's no reply. "He got what he deserved!"

Marty goes instantaneously from the white-hot rage into a cold sweat. It takes all his concentration to keep his hands from shaking.

"No more bullshit. Where's Estelle."

"They're dead."

Marty presses the gun to Eric's head until thin ribbons of blood from the barrel, then he cocks the hammer. He thinks of Lena Dougherty facing off with those drug runners during prohibition and wonders what she'd do. He thinks of Ulysses charging into the Bad Man's camp instead of heading for those mountains. Tears run down the side of his cheeks as he admits that any other Dougherty would have

saved the woman they loved. He glances at his friends' motionless body while out of the corner of his eyes the flashing
lights of the Bodie PD fill the room. Twenty seconds before
they come crashing through the front door. What would a
Dougherty do?

Chapter XXXIX

Dust

At the center of a cloud of dust, fog and smoke, one man stands, another stares down the barrel of a twelve-gauge shotgun while kneeling in the dirt. The standing man, with his sheriffs' tin shining in the morning glare, wants to pull the trigger; he knows it's the right thing to do; the just thing to do. Still he can't, not with the kneeling man looking into his eyes.

There's no fear or anger from the kneeling man. There's only sorrow and shame. He's sorry for what he has done. Not his crimes, he does not apologize for them, he's sorry only for the pain he's causing his brother.

"Nobody'll blame you Ulysses, in fact they'll probably make you the bloody mayor."

"No time to joke Seth."

"You don't owe me anything brother."

Ulysses lifts his gaze to the West and sees the charging Federal Calvary riding toward them. It was supposed to be coordinated. His posse struck from the foothills in the East while at the same time the Federal Calvary charged from Bodie in the West. The cavalry is on time; he led the posse early. Now all thirteen men of his troop, including three of his deputies, are dead, and he doesn't have much time.

"I figured you for the Bad Man two months ago when you hit that bank down near Bakersfield. The paper said you dropped something."

"Fathers stripes. The ones he earned at Shiloh."

"I knew it was you then, and I said nothing. Now I'm going to cover for you again." Ulysses slings his gun back over his shoulder and walks toward his horse grazing on a small patch of Indian Paintbrush growing along the outskirts of the battlefield. It's a beautiful bay mare that still needs seasoning, but it's the best he's ever owned. He reaches into the saddlebag and pulls out a bundle and carries it back to his brother, who hasn't risen from his position in the dirt. "Change into these and put your clothes on one of your gang."

"Then what?"

Ulysses sighs, "Then you leave forever, and you never come back. I told you a long time ago Seth, I can't be that person anymore. If you can't stop, you have to go. We can't be brothers."

Seth still stares at the ground.

"You've already made your decision, no point in wasting more time. Change into the clothes and pick who you want to be the Bad Man because tonight, one way or another, all of California is going to celebrate his death."

Quickly, and in silence the two brothers make the final arrangements. When all is done, Ulysses looks to the West. The cavalry is only a few minutes away now. The only thing concealing what's happening is the gun smoke and dust, which refuses to settle. "You have to leave Seth."

"I'm sorry brother…"

"Don't ever come back."

Seth rides towards the foothills, but he'll turn South before the ground starts to rise into the Sierra's while Ulysses watches the only family member he has left ride away. He would like to see his brother ride as long as possible, but the dust covers his figure after a few hundred yards.

Chapter XL

Aftermath

"No comment at this time."

The Chief makes no eye contact with the reporters buzzing around the grove like flies to a rotting carcass. It's only when he hears that practiced tone of authority that he looks up.

"Chief, it's really bad in…"

"Quiet. I don't want these reporters having anything we don't choose to give them."

The Fresno County Sheriff's office may be running the show under the eucalyptus grove, but the information that led to the discovery was by Bodie PD while investigating an apartment shooting. The Chief knew Leo and Estelle Radmonovic were dead the moment the call came in. If they were alive he would have been contacted by a secretary, not the Sheriff.

He imagines what it might have been like to tell the Sheriff, 'You didn't want to work with us when I suggested we make Estelle's disappearance a joint investigation. I said this was bad, and you laughed me off as paranoid. You told me this was Bodie, not Los Angeles, and things like that don't happen here. Now you can go out alone and explain to the world how these people were being held prisoner in your jurisdiction and are dead because you were half-ass looking for a runaway housewife?'

Still, despite everything else, he has to see it for himself.

"Just go through and you'll find the clearing. Sherriff's waiting for you."

"Have they moved the bodies out?"

"I think they were waiting for you."

"Why does it always have to be in places like this?"

"What was that Chief?"

"Nothing."

In the center of the clearing is a large hole surrounded by deputy sheriffs and Fresno County forensics. Standing near the edge of the crime scene, the Chief compares it to all the others. The ones with children were the worst. Something about the eyes, as if in their last moments, they wondered what they'd done wrong. That's what made it so hard, knowing they blamed themselves right up until the end. Then there was that suicide he investigated in the hills above Malibu, what did that smartass forensics officer call it? Darwin suicide. The man dug a hole, doused himself in paint thinner, lit a match and jumped in. The narrowness of the pit snuffed out the fire, and he got stuck. It took two days to die of thirst with a body covered in second-degree burns.

"Glad you could make it Chief."

"Sheriff."

Slowly the Chief strolls across the thick mat of fallen eucalyptus leaves and dead weeds to see the conclusion. He can only hope that in this final moment he'll find an explanation for why he moved to this small Valley town wanting to escape the madness only to find himself trapped in something fouler than anything he saw in L.A. He witnessed violent acts, but they didn't feel like this. This is something old, something that has been coming for decades that he's been caught up in.

"I thought there were more victims."

"There are. One was Eric's son. We haven't had time to make sure, but he looks like he was about nine or so. Then there's Eric's ex-wife, and Estelle Radmonovic. They were buried about fifteen yards from here in a smaller hole. They were buried deep, but not enough to keep the coyotes from catching hold of the smell. Damn things were trying to dig up the bodies, but they never got to them. We haven't locked down the time of death, but by the looks of it, they've been dead three or four days."

"So that's Leo Radmonovic."

"Yeah. He was killed sometime yesterday. My guess is Eric killed Leo, brought the body out here to bury, and then decided to go see the boy, what the hell was his name?"

"Martin Dougherty."

"Good thing your guys didn't kill him when they shot him. How's the other one."

"Diego Velarde. He's in a coma. Eric shot him in the top part of the skull. The doctors say there's a chance he'll make it, but they're not optimistic. And for the record, my guys didn't shoot Martin on purpose."

"That so?"

"They walked in the room as Martin blew Eric's head off with a gun that was reported stolen a few weeks back. After Martin shot Eric he realized my men had entered the room. He jumped to his feet in a panic still holding the gun in his hand. My men couldn't take the chance. They shot him in the shoulder to immobilize him, not to kill him."

"Well, these things happen."

"Anything else?"

"There's quite a bit of drug paraphernalia around this groove. Mostly methamphetamines and crack cocaine, but there's a little bit of everything. Then there's the beer bottles that you probably noticed as you entered. The farms owner said people come out here all the time to do this kind of stuff so we can't be sure any of it's Eric's, but we suspect that at least some of it is."

"Why's that?"

"Sent a couple of my guys to check out his house over by the Deadman, and apparently, there's evidence of similar drug use all over his place. I haven't been over there myself. We've ordered a toxicology on Eric, and I wouldn't be surprised if it comes back with high levels of narcotics even by the standards of addicts. Chances are he hadn't slept in several days."

"What condition were these people in before they were killed?"

"The ex-wife and kid don't look bad, that is, they were killed quickly by a .45 caliber pistol to the back of the head. Executed. Estelle had bruises around her neck. But she looked like she'd been fed and kept during her captivity, if that's any consolation. He obviously looked after her, and then in some kind of rage, killed her before bringing her and the others out here to bury."

"As for Leo Radmonovic, he wasn't so lucky. He got the crap kicked out of him. He's got a broken jaw, nose and several busted ribs. It looks like Eric had been putting cigarettes out on the back of his neck. I'd say Estelle got killed, buried, then he tortured Leo for a few days before heading over to...what's that kids name again?"

"Martin."

"Wait a minute, is he one of the Dougherty's?"

"Yeah."

"I've heard he's kind of a fuck up."

"Wouldn't know."

"Is he going to be charged?"

"Not with murder, it was clearly self-defense. He's probably going to get charged with position of an unlicensed firearm, but I doubt it'll stick."

"Why wouldn't it stick?"

"I just gotta a hunch it won't."

"Have you questioned him?"

"Preliminary questioning only. He's being released from the hospital this morning. He's at the station as we speak. In fact, I've gotta get over there to see what's going on."

"Wait, you're leaving? I need to talk to you."

But in a flash, the Chief is walking away. He makes a quick survey of the hole where Estelle and Eric's family were buried. While there, he manages to chase off some reporters trying to get a picture by sneaking through the backside of the grove, then lectures the deputies about the importance of crime scene security. Walking back to the squad car, the Chief decides that before going to the station, he'll swing by the house to get a hug from his daughter.

Chapter XLI

Embracing the Madness

"It was a beautiful service Mrs. Velarde," Laura says.

"Thank you for coming." For several days the stricken mother could barely answer yes and no questions between her fits, but now she's mastered speaking in an even tone while sobbing. "There's food and drinks in the back yard. Jonathan, make sure and eat something."

"Thank you, Mrs. Velarde."

"You haven't been eating Jonathan. Go have some food."

With arms locked, Laura pulls Jonathan around the side of the Velarde's home. Rounding the corner into the backyard, Martins' red head towers above the crowd even while seated at a picnic table.

"Get a seat next to Marty, and I'll get you a plate of food," Laura says.

Jon maneuvers through the crowd, making sure to accept nods of condolences from the people he passes. He takes a seat across from Martin, leaving room at the end of the bench for Laura.

Martin looks at the throngs packing the Velarde back yard. Leaning toward Jonathan he asks, "When was the last time this many showed up to a Bodie funeral?"

"Probably not since Ulysses Dougherty died."

He feels Laura tap his shoulder. "I haven't seen the Inez family since they left Bodie." She places a plate of enchiladas and a cold beer in front of Jonathan, and slides another beer toward Marty.

Jonathan looks over at the family that left Bodie for Sacramento seven years earlier. "That goes back a ways. Diego accidently found out who'd been stealing their newspapers every morning. After that, old man Inez had a soft spot for him."

"Hey Heffron."

"What?"

"How many people you think are here?"

"Over two hundred."

Occasionally one of them tries to start a conversation about Diego, and the good times they had with him, but it never feels right. So they sit together quietly as faceless people walk by, giving quick sympathies before heading on to the main table where the rest of the Velarde family sits.

A chair drops beside the table and Father Lopez sits down. He performed the service, his first as the new priest of Bodie's Catholic congregation.

"You're Martin Dougherty and Jonathan Heffron, aren't you?"

Martin nods yes, but Jonathan says nothing.

"Mrs. Velarde says you were both very close to Diego."

Neither moves.

"At times like this, it's hard to accept God's plan, especially when it includes the loss of someone as profoundly good as Diego. Diego was here for a purpose, one he served. The one thing everyone seems to say about him is that he was always there."

"Yeah, he certainly was wasn't he," Jon snorts. He looks up and catches a disappointed glare from the priest, which only makes Jonathan smile.

"He's sorry bout that Father. Please go on, we know you're trying to help," Martin says.

"It was too short, but brief as it was, Diego Velarde made a positive mark on the lives around him, and we should all take solace in the fact that he's receiving his rewards at the feet of our Father in heaven."

Jonathan bites his tongue until he tastes blood mixing with saliva in his mouth. He can feel himself mouthing words behind his grinding teeth. The man's trying to help, just doing his job. It's like being angry with a plumber for changing a faucet, or a carpenter for hanging a door. Plus, he's not a true local so how could he understand. Jonathan puts his fork down on his plate of uneaten food and slowly rises.

"Will you excuse me for a moment, Father?"

Father Lopez looks up, doing nothing to hide his disappointment. "Of course."

Jon imagines being that animal at the end of its evolutionary journey, having watched others close in to fill the niches it once occupied. Those lost species made this choice without thinking. They marched towards oblivion, knowing their only hope rested in finding a new purpose in some far off place. His destination is in the distance, but he senses no need to run to meet it. Just amble in the right direction at an even pace. If there's still a place in this world for him, it'll be there regardless of how fast he goes.

Jonathan circles the corner of the house, which is littered with mourners, and notices a young man walking, toward him. He's only seen Antonio one other time, when Diego pointed him out at My Friends House weeks earlier. Jon never gave the boy much thought until the town learned that he was Bolivar.

Antonio stops next to the window looking into Diego's room. "We never met, but I knew Diego. My name is..."

"He talked about you, Antonio."

"I was going to give this to Mrs. Velarde but…I don't know if it's right."

Jonathan extends his hand and takes a folded, wrinkled piece of drawing paper. He opens it and looks at the sketch of a 1968 Firebird with a dark green paintjob. Running down the cars side and across the hood are black and gray flames colored in a flat tone that contrasts perfectly with the bright shin of green. The bumpers and emblems are chrome, as are the elaborate rims supporting low profile tires.

"After he got me out of that jam, he asked me to come up with a paintjob for him. He wanted something with flames, but nothing that's been seen before. I was going to do it for him, he just needed to pay for the paint." Jon waits as Antonio takes a moment to control himself. "I was going to offer to do it for the Velardes anyway, but I don't know."

"I'll make sure they get the message."

Carefully sliding the drawing into his pocket, Jonathan watches Antonio turn and leave. Jon continues through the front yard when the squeaking hinges of the wooden gate draw his attention. He looks up and sees a clean shaven and well dressed Mr. Wisnewski walking toward him.

The town and countryside have changed, and with the ash from the hills still covering the ground it seems years since things have looked normal. There was a time when he would walk down the streets of Bodie and knew everyone as well as their family history. Now he recognizes only half the people, and knows little about where they hailed from. So, it's comforting to see Mr. Wisnewski walking with purpose, lacking the drunk stagger that became his hallmark after the death of his program.

The old teacher stops a few steps from Jonathan and looks up. Before either person can say a word Mr. Wisnewski pulls Jon into his chest with such force that it almost breaks his nose.

"I'm so sorry Jon."

"It's alright Mr. Wisnewski."

"No matter how hard I tried to make him, that boy never gave up on me. Everyone else in this town did, but not Diego."

"I don't think Diego ever gave up on anyone. I don't think he knew how."

Mr. Wisnewski releases his hold, but doesn't lift his eyes from the ground. "I wish there was something I could have done before the end, something to let him know that it was all worth it," he blubbers. "He stopped by the other day, talking about some kid. He thought I could mentor him. I can't believe there was someone who still thought me capable of mentoring anyone. I yelled at Diego, told him to leave me alone, and that I didn't care. He just said he'd see me next week."

Jonathan looks back and see's Antonio talking to Rene. "That's the boy over there Mr. Wisnewski."

The old teacher follows Jon's finger until he makes Antonio out. "I'm not sure what to say?"

"Just offer to help." That'll be enough."

The old teacher wipes his eyes and straightens the first tie he's worn since his teaching days. "Where can I find his parents?"

"They're in the back. Mrs. Velarde's running all over the place, but Mr. Velarde's sitting at the head table near the stage."

Mr. Wisnewski walks past, and Jonathan watches as Rene introduces the man to Antonio and the two shake hands. For a moment they hold each other's grip exchanging sympathies. Without saying a word Rene turns and walks out of sight, her wing tattoos peeking from under her mourning shale.

Laura catches up with him at the edge of the front yard, just after crossing the threshold of the gate. "Jonathan, would you please wait a minute?"

"How'd Diego end up in that apartment Laura?"

"It was bad luck Jon, nothing else."

Jon's eyes turn red and he shakes with frustration. "Nobody see's it."

"What is it, Jon?"

"I should have been the one in that apartment."

"Another five minutes, and you would have been."

"That would have made sense though."

"For God's sake, you have no reason to feel guilty."

"It has nothing to do with guilt Laura. I mean Diego just happens, for no apparent reason, to go back to that apartment in the middle of the night and walk in as Marty's fighting with a…psychotic…serial killer who's randomly targeted him? That shouldn't have happened to Diego. It shouldn't have happened to Marty either. It should have happened to me or Ian or any other Heffron, but not them. It's like the priest said, Diego was always there at the right time. Well Heffrons are supposed to be there at the wrong time."

Laura feels that familiar rush of panic, and does her best to hide it but what could she say, even after all these years she still doesn't understand the fascination with the 'legacy'.

"That's not what the priest said, I don't think."

"What'd the priest say then?"

"He saved Martin, one of his closest friends like he saved that boy who was painting all those walls. Maybe he was even saving you, Jon."

"There is no way Martin Dougherty gets taken by a drug addict. That priest moves here a few months ago and thinks he knows what the duties of the people of Bodie are. Fuck him and this town; I'm leaving!"

"Just wait a minute Jon. Let me get my purse and I'll come with you."

"I want you to come with me, but I don't think you will."

"Of course I will, don't be stupid."

"Even to Iowa?"

"Iowa?!"

"How bout Louisiana? I'll let you choose as long as it's not somewhere in California."

"Jon, shut up right now, you hear me?"

"Come with me. I'm not staying, but I don't want to leave you."

"You don't want to leave me, but you will because of some stupid, perverse obsession with death! And in the middle of one of your best friends' funeral!"

"Laura you have to understand…" Jon thinks about explaining everything to her, really trying to hear how it sounds. It's not the legacy, it's everything together. What word choice would best convey that the land being gone, and the town changing are what really hurts and Diego's death is nothing more than the final pin dropping. How to prove he loves her more than anything, but he still can't stay? That staying would mean to become something else, and he can't do that.

"I have to leave Laura. There's nothing left for me here."

"There's me! There's Ian and Marty!"

"I don't know if that's enough."

"I was there for you when your parents died and I helped out on Ian's farm whenever your family needed me. Now you don't need me and you're going to leave unless I turn my back on my home and everything I love to run away with you to Nebraska!"

"I'm sorry."

"You're not sorry, you're selfish! You used the farm, and me, and now we don't serve any purpose so you're going to leave to find something else you can hide behind."

He watches her pull her arm back. She's earned it, and without moving Jonathan lets the love of his life slap him across the face and he feels one of the stitches on the back of his head open. Laura storms off, almost knocking him over, but refusing to show that she feels anything toward him.

"What the hell was that about Heffron?"

Jonathan turns to see Martin standing where Laura stood a moment earlier. "What's going on back there?"

"People are telling stories about Velarde. I think they expected me to speak, but I don't know what I would say. I came out here to see what you're doing."

Jonathan hears Laura's Jeep start behind him. He considers running after her, begging her to come with him, promising that if she does this one last thing, he'll spend the rest of her life doing anything to make her happy.

"Heffron, where's Laura going?"

"It's over."

"I can't handle cryptic, half sarcastic crap Heffron. What happened?"

"I gotta go Marty. I'll see ya around." Jon sticks out his hand and waits for Martin to extend his. After a few moments, Jon raises his hand to his forehead and gives a stiff salute.

Jonathan walks toward his little Honda, fishing in his pocket for the keys.

Martin watches his friend walk away, making sure to catalogue each movement.

"I'm sorry it all turned out this way Jon."

Turning around and walking toward the service, Marty wants to ask where he'll go and what he'll do when he gets there, but doesn't have the courage.

Falling into his car, Jon waits until Martin disappears behind the Velarde house. He can hear singing, but he doesn't recognize the tune. Glancing to his right, he sees the Firechicken parked in front of the fence like a monument. Everything about it is familiar save for the small FOR SALE sign in the back window.

Chapter XLII

First Time Around

It was a cool fall morning when Gabriel and Yvonne Heffron drove into the foothills. The stories differ, but one way or another they came across an abandoned gold mine with a stock of hidden explosives. The national media ran with the story, and all over the country, people speculated about how the buried dynamite got lit. The theories ranged from bad luck to murder/ suicide, but the one that never caught traction nationally was the most popular around Bodie. They were Heffrons, so there was really no other way for them to die.

Jonathan rushed to his uncles' house as soon as he heard. Nobody called him, they didn't need to. He knew the balance of probability, and one member of the family had to be involved. At the time, he was closer to his uncle's farm than his father's, so he went there, finding Laura Theroux crying on the deck.

Laura stood sheepishly in front of him as Jonathan quickly climbed the steps.

"What happened Laura?"

"There was a…"

"I know about the explosion Laura! I want to know who it happened to!"

"It was your parents Jonathan…they were up there… and somehow they came across an abandoned mine and…" Laura jumped at Jon, hugging him before he could fall.

"I'm sorry I yelled Laura."

"It's OK."

There was something in the way Jon held her that she didn't recognize. "Oh god Jon, what are you going to do?"

"Something stupid, but I have to do it." Jonathan held her tighter still, hoping somehow it might make her understand. "I gotta leave Laura."

"I can make this better for you Jon, just give me the chance."

She kissed him deeply.

"Don't I deserve the chance?"

"Yes, you do."

Chapter XLIII

Pajaro, Argentina

There are no tall buildings covered with neon. The asphalt streets with faded lines and potholes are gone, as are the dim streetlights. Wood planks and an occasional old man smoking a cigar replace the cracked cement sidewalks packed with drunk American tourists. Hand carved signs identify each building and everything is in Spanish rather than the bilingual signs of Tijuana. The pungent odors of the city are replaced by the endless sea of grass that makes up Las Pampas. The street is dark dirt and the sun reflects off simple wood buildings stained by the harsh weather of Northern Argentina.

From the moment he climbed off the crowded bus carrying him from Buenos Ares to the small town of Pajaro, Martin has felt the sun draw energy from him like a syringe. Before he left, he checked the weather and was happy to find the numbers compared to those of central California. People warned him that this meant little since California had a 'dry heat'. Marty ignored these cautions; "Hot is hot, I don't care about dampness."

He stands in the center of the street watching waves of heat dance off the buildings. One day he'll expand to all sorts of livestock, then build a meat packing plant. Leo talked about it from time to time; about one day going from shipping food to producing it. "Marty-boy, true wealth lies in controlling the means of production." Martin knew there would be unforeseen problems in such a venture, but hadn't expected finding a labor force would be one of them.

Hadn't America been the birthplace of the cowboy; the place where the reality and myth were forged? The idea that there would be nobody in his country qualified to do the work angered him. So, he's in Argentina looking for *Gauchos*. Hector said he could find them in a town called Pajaro. "It's not really a town, more a supply station that they come to before returning their herds and huts. They can be hard to find, but they're the best in the world, if you can convince them to come." Martin Dougherty walks down the single street that makes up Pajaro looking for cantinas.

The first thing that catches his eye is not a building, but a dark green 1968 Firebird with black and gray flames parked in front of the building at the end of the street. He'd seen many over the years, more than he thought possible, like he's haunted by the memories of his dead friend, and the other friend who's now a wanted car thief.

The sight of the old Pontiac draws him toward the building. It's a hundred yard walk, and in the heat he feels trickles of sweat running down his back as his drenched shirt can absorb no more. When he gets there, he walks around examining every inch of the car. Its body and interior are in better shape than Diego's, but surely it's no match for the Firechicken.

There's a loud clatter as three small children emerge laughing from the side of the building. The oldest carries a bucket of water with rags slung over his shoulder. Marty knows a little Spanish and can tell the other two are teasing the one carrying the bucket.

When the oldest notices the giant foreigner he quickly steps in front of his two little brothers and barks, "Que Queries."

"Neccesito una cantina, por favor."

"Aqui," the oldest says while pointing to the front door. The boys walk around Marty and begin washing the car, each taking to their specific task with ease and confidence. They move around each other in an almost chaotic frenzy, but never once does one get in the way of the other.

Marty goes to the front door and the sign swinging overhead reads *El Casa de Mi Amigo*. Marty looks back at the kids and his eyes meet those of the oldest brother. They stare at each other for a moment, then the boy smiles and flicks a salute.

Martin opens the door to the cantina and steps inside. Wood planks make up the floor and ceiling while creaking fans spin overhead. The large windows make the room well lit, but Martin imagines it's quite dark at night. The stucco-covered walls are painted with murals, most are scenes of farmers working in fields and women cooking. Then there's one above the bar of a small farmhouse with a large porch covered in lights, surrounded by *Acer palmatum* and *Gingko biloba*.

Martin Dougherty is smiling when he looks at the black marble bar that's strangely out of place in the otherwise modest structure. Behind the bar is one unlabeled beer tap and thirty bottles of Fernet Branca. Standing behind the bar is Jonathan Heffron. His hair has thinned in the last fifteen years, and it's much longer. It hangs around his head and along with the thick beard it's almost impossible to see his face. Martin walks toward the bar and Jonathan doesn't notice, as he's engrossed in reading something.

"If I'd known you were really going through with it, I probably would have said more before you left," Marty says slaming his hands down on the bar.

"Is that right?"

"Yeah, and if I knew you were going to steal the Firechicken, I'd have stopped you."

Jon looks up calmly, and for the first time in a long time he cracks an ear to ear grin.

"So how did you end up here Jon?"

"This was where the Firechicken broke down on me." Jon pulls an unlabeled bottle of liquor out from under the bar and grabs two glasses from the end of the counter.

"It isn't easy finding a good mechanic down here."

The room is quiet but for the squeaking sounds of fans. Martin and Jonathan remain still because once they start talking it'll really be over. They'll enjoy meandering conversation about the past, accompanied by and occasional space of silence that would have been filled with words from the lost. The shadows will move, the light will dim, and memories will feel more alive than when they forged. They stay silent a bit longer, not wanting to accept it as said and done.

About the Author

Growing up in California's San Joaquin Valley, Skyler began writing fiction after the farm went under in 2003. He moved to the Santa Cruz, CA in 2005 before relocating to Southern California to work at his alma mater as landscape supervisor. He graduated from the University of California Riverside with a BA in History in 2003 and his work has appeared in Adelaide Literary Magazine, Main Street Rag, the Literary Nest, Crack the Spine and Oddball Magazine. His first novel One Left Inside the Well will appear with Adelaide Books in the Spring of 2019.